Keith Geddes qualified as a barrister, worked as an oil broker and was part owner of a pub before eventually choosing teaching as his career. He has taught in Argentina, the UK and Kenya. He was Head of four prep schools in London, Kenya, Derbyshire and Cheshire over a period of fourteen years and has now retired to live with his wife, two daughters and dogs (called Banda and Kora) in Spain. There he runs Twiga Art, a website for artists (to be found at *www.twigaart.com*), plays golf and cricket and tends the almond, orange and lemon trees in his garden.

Visit his website: www.keithgeddes.com

The right of Keith Geddes to be identified as the Author of this
Work has been asserted by him in accordance with the Copyright, Designs and
Patents Act 1998

Copyright © Keith Geddes 2007

All characters in this publication are fictitious and resemblance to real persons,
living or dead, is purely coincidental.

All rights reserved. No part of this publication may be reproduced, stored in a
retrieval system, or transmitted, in any form or by any means without the prior
written permission of the publisher, nor be otherwise circulated in any form of
binding or cover other than that in which it is published and without a similar
condition being imposed on the subsequent purchaser. Any person who does so may
be liable to criminal prosecution and civil claims for damages.

ISBN: 1-905988-09-5   978-1-905988-09-9

Cover Art by Peter Thaines

Published by Libros International

www.librosinternational.com

Acknowledgements

Very many thanks to Chrissie Carriere, Julia Phillips and Sue Cohen for all their help and especially to Patricia McManus of Libros International who has been a wonderful editor!

Edward
I hope you enjoy this!

'Please Sir, there's a snake in the art room'

The Memoirs of a Headmaster in London and Nairobi

Keith Geddes

Keith Geddes.

Illustrations by Chrissie Carriere

Libros International

This book is dedicated to my family, Helen, Robyn and Tamsin who have been very long suffering during my efforts at writing.

Introduction

'Those who can, do, those who can't, teach' was what my father said to me as, coming up to the end of my time at university, I wondered how I was to keep myself. I had read a combination of natural science and law at Cambridge; having enjoyed the latter I set out on the route to qualify as a solicitor by becoming an articled clerk to a London firm of shipping solicitors. After a year I decided that it would be more interesting to change direction slightly and began a correspondence course to prepare myself for the Bar exams. Whilst beavering away at this in the evenings, I took a job in a country prep school teaching maths, science and games. I enjoyed it immensely. I got quite a kick out of explaining how to solve simple equations to boys who hadn't previously 'got it' - it was good to hear 'Oh, I get it now, Sir.' And how pleasant it was to be paid for teaching games to keen young players and making small explosions in the science lab in the pursuit of education.

I did take the Bar exams, passed and became a pupil to a Birmingham barrister - but it wasn't easy in those days to find a permanent place in chambers so I moved off to work for my old man in London in the family business - oil broking. I didn't take to the city commuter life at all so decided to go back to the job I had previously enjoyed - teaching in a prep school.

After a time I began to apply somewhat optimistically for headships. Several failed attempts later I was appointed as Head of a London day school - and very soon discovered that the job was not by any means the easiest way of making a living. I somehow survived my first turbulent year and gradually began to get the measure of things - pushy London parents took a lot of handling and could behave in the most extraordinary way whilst defending their young. Along the way I was fortunate enough to work with many splendid colleagues - some a touch eccentric perhaps - and also some great children and parents.

I was very much in two minds when, after six years in London, I was offered the job as Head of a large Kenyan prep school on the outskirts of Nairobi - a school I had taught at some years earlier. I took the plunge; here there were very different problems to be dealt with - the parents seemed to be rather more laid-back and the predators to watch out for were more often animals than humans! Tom Thorne's experiences in this book are very loosely based on situations I came across.

Chapter One

'Mr Thorne, I think you should look out of your office window.'

Barbara Stevens, Tom's newly acquired secretary, pointed through the window to a parent rummaging around in the dustbin Tom had put outside his gate earlier. Barbara had been Headmaster's Secretary at Shaftesbury Prep for years and thought she had seen everything.

'This I haven't seen before!'

Tom had moved into the Headmaster's house, which was situated right next to the main school building, only a fortnight previously. The local dustmen had informed him curtly that residents put their own dustbins out each week. He had complied that morning.

Tom wondered what on earth the parent was doing. Apparently, Barbara informed him, the parents were so keen to know what this new youngish bachelor Headmaster was like that he should not be surprised if they went through his rubbish to find out what they could. What did they expect?

Bad luck, you nosey woman, he thought, - only the remains of last night's takeaway curry this time!

Barbara grinned widely. 'Well, you must expect them to be inquisitive. Mr Black was incredibly secretive and used to hide from the parents if he thought he could get away with it. I saw him climb out of his study window once to avoid a complaining parent - and he had been

Head for years. You are fair game! I'll do my best to keep them at bay though.'

It was Tom's first full day at the Headmaster's desk - and if this was typical of the scrutiny Heads of London day prep schools had to contend with from their customers Tom wondered how he would measure up. He looked across the room to his 'seen it all before' secretary.

Barbara was a slight, grey-haired woman of about fifty; she looked rather a gentle person but Tom suspected could be quite a steely character if required and he was mightily glad to have someone with her experience and common sense in charge of the office. He was certainly not going to be too proud to ask her advice.

Shaftesbury Preparatory School, to give it its full title, was a day prep school for about 300 boys and girls between the ages of 4 and 13. The original building had been a solid Victorian town house with three storeys, built of red brick with large sash windows. The rooms were spacious with high ceilings. When it became a school, some thirty years earlier, a large gym and Assembly Hall had been added along with a single storey classroom block built at the back around a large grassed area. There was also space for two hard surface playgrounds, both of which could be used for netball and tennis. A few years previously, the school had bought the next-door property, which became the Headmaster's house. The street outside was normally quiet, its leafy tranquillity only disturbed at the beginning and end of each school day by hordes of parents arriving to deliver or collect their offspring.

It was day one of the new school year. As Tom stood in front of curious pupils and staff at Assembly he was well aware of the importance of making a good first impression. The 300 or so children plus their teachers sang the hymn, listened to the new Head's talk reasonably quietly and clapped in the right places when the names of the head boy and head girl were announced - no surprises there, Tom had just followed his Deputy, Mike Dawson's advice. Everything seemed to go smoothly and Mike nodded in approval as Tom finished. Public speaking was not his forte and he was glad to have survived this little test.

Mike had been teaching at the school for eight years, the last three as Deputy Head. Originally from Australia, he had come over to the UK for a year's experience and stayed ever since. He was tall and athletic having played Australian Rules football in his younger days. He now confined his exercise to golf, managing to maintain a very respectable handicap of ten. He seemed extremely good at his job - he was an excellent administrator - but would often say, 'I don't want to be the front man - I don't want a Headship - I enjoy what I do right now. No, you can keep the hassle!'

Barbara had warned Tom that his first appointment was with the notorious Mrs Bland. This lady had been a thorn in the side of Tom's predecessor, constantly complaining. Barbara, who always asked parents who rang for appointments with the Headmaster, 'What was it in connection with?' warned him that Mrs Bland was certain her son, James, was exceptionally bright and wanted him moved up a year so that he would, in his last year at the age of thirteen, sit a scholarship to his senior school. The problem was his teachers thought James to be a good average student but not a real high-flier and that he would be better off staying in his present class.

Mrs Bland turned out to be a large and effusive lady. She clasped Tom warmly by the hand and wished him great success in his new job. Once settled comfortably in the chair on the other side of the desk she gave the impression she would not easily be budged.

'We need a bit of new blood here with more progressive ideas,' she said. 'One does need to be flexible, don't you think?'

Tom was wary. 'Quite. What can I do for you?'

Twenty minutes later Tom was fully briefed on James's so far brilliant school career and on the dangers of holding back such a capable pupil. When she paused, waiting expectantly for his agreement to her request for James's immediate promotion to Year Four, Tom gently suggested it was early days in the new school year and perhaps it would be better to wait and see how James got on in his present form. He promised to have a talk to his teachers in due course and then they could speak again. Mrs Bland went off only mildly put out - Tom thought he had done well by way of his first encounter with a parent.

Tom had always been pretty keen on sport and for many eleven-year-olds it can be the most important part of school life - lessons become just about bearable if you know you can play rugby or netball in the afternoon. So, a couple of days into the term as Tom trotted out onto the games field to help Simon Bragg, the master in charge of sport, Tom needed to show he knew his way around the rugby pitch or credibility would be lost with the boys. Mrs Williams, a fanatical supporter of school teams (especially if her son, Tim, was captain which, owing to massive parental lobbying with the rather naive but well meaning sports master, he apparently often was) had already accosted Tom with fluttering eyelashes, saying, 'We hear you're a Cambridge rugby blue - aren't the boys lucky - my son, Tim, is very keen and wants to go to Cambridge.' Tom had hastily denied such sporting prowess admitting that he had performed in a rather lowly college team but had been engaged in quite a bit of coaching. This seemed to satisfy this rather frightening lady and Tom wondered what problems would arise if son, Tim, wasn't appointed captain or worse if he wasn't picked by young Simon for the first match.

Simon had been on the staff for four years and was well liked by the pupils. With curly, sandy coloured hair and a boyish face he looked barely out of his teens but was ambitious to succeed in his job. He had been a very promising soccer player at school, being taken on as a trainee by Chelsea at the age of sixteen. Unfortunately he hadn't quite made the grade and decided to train as a PE teacher; Mr Black had recruited him straight from college. Clearly football rather than rugby was his game.

As they ran out onto the playing fields, it struck Tom as odd that the games session seemed to be run not by Simon but by a large, loud man he had not seen before.

'Who is that chap?' Tom spoke to Simon as they jogged

round the field warming up.

'Oh, that's Gareth Williams. He's Tim Williams's father. He has some job in the City and often takes the afternoon off to help with the coaching - he's a member of Rosslyn Park - he's a good chap.'

Good if you want to make sure your son gets into the team, thought Tom, but said nothing except 'Hmm.'

The first match was imminent and Mr Williams and Simon organised a very good training session followed by a game - and then sat down to discuss team selection and positions. Tom trotted about encouraging everyone in a rather low-key way.

Later that day Tom had a meeting with the Chairman of the Board of Governors, a cheerful, red-faced, thickset man called Ted Whittaker. Mr Whittaker was a banker and a pretty successful one by all accounts. His two children had been at Shaftesbury Prep a year or two earlier and both had moved on to well-known boarding schools; Mr Whittaker appeared to be fairly traditional but was prepared to listen to new ideas. Tom had been invited to his club in the City to have dinner and report on 'his first impressions'. No doubt there would be some probing questions for him too!

As they sat consuming an excellent bottle of claret and with Tom tucking into a steak, Mr Whittaker listened quietly as Tom reported that he thought the first few days had been OK. The staff couldn't be persuaded to say much at the first staff meeting - it seemed that under the previous regime they were not expected to have opinions on how the school might be better run - they simply carried out orders from on high. Mr Whittaker nodded. Tom suspected that he hadn't really approved of the somewhat dictatorial manner in which his predecessor had ruled the staff, but he wasn't going to be critical of him; perhaps he would approve of a more democratic regime.

'Want to get rid of anyone?' he asked. 'What about that fellow Alastair Begg - we have had some complaints about him.'

Poor guy, Tom thought; he had seemed inoffensive enough so far. A bit eccentric maybe but you don't want schools to be dull.

Mike Dawson had previously regaled Tom with the story of how Mr Black had been showing some parents around and they'd gone into Alastair's classroom during a Latin lesson. Alastair had seated himself on the top of a large cupboard behind the door and was asking questions round the class, holding up a bunch of bananas and tossing them to anyone who answered a particularly difficult one. Quite a good way of keeping his pupils attention, really. He was hidden from view by the door as Mr Black brought his visitors in.

Mr Black glanced around the room. 'Where's Mr Begg?'

With aplomb, a boy in the front row replied, 'Sir, he's just popped out for a moment to get a book.'

'Ah,' said Mr Black, 'Then we'll move on to the next classroom and see what they're up to. Thank you, Harry.'

The visiting party departed leaving a grateful and undiscovered Mr Begg who gave Harry a banana and the class a short lecture on 'using your initiative'.

These are the sort of teachers we need, Tom thought.

'And what about that art teacher, Mrs Eales?' the Chairman continued. 'She's always off sick and I don't think she's that good anyway. You might also like to keep an eye on Paul White - I'm doubtful about him. How are you getting on with Mike Dawson? He's a good man - use him as much as you like - I'm sure you will work well together.'

Tom reassured him on this point and after further discussions on the merits or otherwise of the staff room they parted, Mr Whittaker assuring Tom that he could call him anytime at all if he needed his support or advice. He gave Tom various private phone numbers and they arranged to meet again in a month's time.

Friday morning was quiet (was he going to make it safely through the first week, Tom wondered) and he was sitting at his desk pretending to look at some papers when Barbara knocked at the door and brought through a coffee and some biscuits.

'There's an American lady outside who says she and her husband are moving to London and they have a very bright son. Do we have a place in Year Five? Have you a moment to see her?' Tom was looking for things to occupy himself this early on in the job so of course he asked Barbara to show the lady in. He knew there wasn't officially any place in that year but maybe another body could be squeezed in.

Mrs Hector Barnley was some lady - exceptionally pretty, with neat blond hair and very smartly dressed in a grey suit. Her expensive perfume preceded her into the study. Tom introduced himself and ushered her to a chair

- he was going to enjoy this interview.

'So you are moving to London - whereabouts will you be living?' enquired Tom.

She said that her husband worked in the hotel business and his company was taking over several hotels in West London.

'Our son, Martin, is a really bright kid - he's had Grade A's all through his schooling so far in California. We want him to go to a British boarding school when he's old enough - either Eton or Harrods.'

Tom digested this information and smiled to himself, wondering whether Mr Al Fayed would take him! He then gently explained the intricacies of Common Entrance and how children were prepared for this exam; we could have Martin in for the day and see how he got on. Would she like to see round the school?

It was a good feeling taking an attractive prospective mother around the school - for the men on the staff a good-looking mum asking them about their lesson and allowing them to show off a bit brightened up their day considerably. The women tended to eye the visitor up and down, initially hoping to be able to criticise their clothes but usually warming to them if their class showed how polite and intelligent they could be. Tom was relieved that all the children did behave perfectly on this occasion. Mrs Barnley was suitably impressed and they arranged a day the following week for young Martin to spend a morning at the school. He would join a suitable class so he could see what it was like and at some point during the morning Tom would extract him for a chat and an informal test in maths and English.

The week ended without any further incidents. As Tom

stood at the school gate watching the busy throng of children escaping for the weekend an angel-faced boy of eleven smiled at him and asked gravely, 'Enjoy being a Headmaster, Sir?'

'It's all right so far, thanks.'

The boy nodded and said 'good' before wandering off to join what looked like his twin brother. The two of them disappeared into the back seat of a large four-wheel drive vehicle - essential for the wild areas of Twickenham, no doubt.

Monday came round soon enough.

'Here's your mail today, Tom.' Although Barbara wouldn't have dreamt of calling Mr Black by his Christian name they had already progressed onto more familiar terms. 'There are quite a few applications for jobs - you'll like that one on the top!' and she plonked a motley pile of correspondence onto the desk.

The school year had only just begun and despite a supposed teacher shortage there still seemed to be plenty of people looking for a teaching post. Most were probably fairly clueless although perhaps there might be the odd one or two returning from abroad a bit too late to apply who in normal circumstances could be excellent. The top letter turned out to be a bit of a classic - it was from an Irish lady who claimed to have lots of qualifications, hadn't stayed in any job for longer than a couple of terms and wrote:

'I am keen to broaden my experience by taking sabbaticals'.

Not from a job with us she won't, thought Tom as he skimmed through the other speculative applications and handed them back to Barbara; she had a standard polite 'no' reply.

The school's everyday finance was run by Liz Freeland, the Bursar - she also acted as Secretary to the Board of Governors. Tom had met Liz at his interviews and at first sight found her to be a rather formidable lady. She was in her mid-fifties and had been quite a high-powered civil servant working in the centre of London. She had decided now her children had left home it was time to slow down a bit and had taken on the four-day a week job at Shaftesbury Prep. Perhaps to her surprise she found herself extremely busy - and she was already wondering if she would have to go full-time to deal with all the problems that seemed to land on her desk. Although Tom had initially found Liz rather intimidating, he had tried a little humour and she had softened. She herself had a sharp sense of humour and increasingly allowed it to escape.

Tom went to see her about some books, which had been ordered but not yet arrived, and found her grumbling about Alastair Begg. She looked over the top of her steel-rimmed spectacles at Tom, her grey eyes glancing up to the ceiling. 'Alastair really is the limit! He has no idea about keeping accounts. Did you know he organised a school trip to Greece last summer? He told me all the bills had been paid and now he says he forgot the bus costs to the airport. The bus people are complaining we haven't paid them. I'll have to take it out of the classics allocation for this year otherwise we'll run his trip at a loss.'

'I agree he is a pain in the neck at times. But he is a good teacher - Latin is very popular, you know - and the parents like him.'

Alastair was certainly a bit eccentric and increasingly there seemed to be less tolerance around for people like him. Not many could get away with calling his pupils 'silly old buffoons' when they got something wrong - or indeed giving them the option of twenty press-ups instead of re-doing poor homework. He also kept a three-foot long panga (a fearsome looking knife he said he had used in the Burma jungle when in the army) behind his desk. This he used to throw down into the wooden floor when in the mood. It would stick in, oscillating gently. Alastair insisted that this ensured pupils paid attention to the 'point' of grammar he was trying to make. The Health and Safety people, had they known about this, would probably have had a point of their own to make!

Tom sorted out the book problem with Liz; she really had been very helpful since he arrived, going through the accounts and explaining how the school managed its irregular income (it came at the beginning of each term and amounted to just over a million pounds each year). At times there were large amounts on deposit; these gradually diminished as the term wore on. Tom promised to ring up recalcitrant parents and chase fees not paid on time - there were apparently always the same few hard-core ones who needed to be shamed into paying!

Tom had always admired old Jim Whitty - he had been Headmaster of a prep school Tom had worked at for a time in the West Country. Jim used to keep a private filing system on parents - strictly for his eyes only. He entered all manner of information which shouldn't really be written down but which might prove useful for future reference. As well as things like 'Mr Beattie - works for

Dunlop in PR - has two sons 6 and 8 - been at school in Malaysia - wants places for Jan', Jim would also add 'dad ugly looking fellow, large nose - pleasant though, knows Beales - keen on cricket - younger boy could be thick - plenty of money.' Tom had started his own system - kept in a locked drawer in his desk. The entry for Mrs Barnley read:

Mrs Barnley 10th Sept Pretty American woman with son Martin aged 9. Did not see boy - she says he is bright - at school in California so probably behind - Mrs shown round - impressed with quietness of classes and them saying good morning - will test for Year 5 next week. Husband in hotel business. Martin will come in on 18th Sept for morning.

Mrs Barnley and Martin arrived promptly, as arranged, at 8.45 am. Martin turned out to be a rather long-haired but charming boy trendily kitted out in a leather jacket, jeans and the latest trainers; rather different to the Shaftsbury lot in plum-coloured blazers and short trousers. Two boys from Mrs Jones's form were waiting outside the office ready to take Martin off to their class where he would spend the morning and then try out the school lunch. After introductions, the three of them trotted off happily chattering. Mrs Barnley agreed to return after lunch to collect her son - no doubt having spent the morning shopping. Tom wondered if she would try Harrods.

Halfway through the morning Tom went upstairs to collect Martin. Mrs Jones was in full flow on the properties of quadrilaterals. Martin sitting next to his minders looked rather bemused.

'Excuse me, Mrs Jones, may I remove Martin for a bit?'

'Of course, Mr Thorne,' she replied, somewhat relieved - she did not like her class disrupted or in fact any routine being changed - not always possible especially when there were away sports fixtures or a school play being rehearsed; her world was her classroom and nothing should be allowed to intrude. Still, she was a very sound teacher, the parents liked her and she needed to be kept happy!

Tom sat Martin down in the study and set him some standardised tests in maths, spelling and reading. Not entirely surprisingly, he did well in reading and spelling with a reading age two years older than his chronological age - which would normally be expected for prep school pupils. However, there were quite a few gaps in his maths test. He had not covered as much ground as Mrs Jones's Year Five class. Surprisingly though, when Tom explained some of the methods to him he quickly picked things up - a bright chap, thought Tom, we'll take him!

Just before lunch Tom took Martin back to Mrs Jones, wondering how he'd enjoy Alastair's Latin lesson.

After eating, Martin appeared outside the office accompanied by William and Scott, by now firm friends. He said lunch was 'OK' and could he stay on for the rest of the day.

'Mom,' he said, turning to his mother, 'I've been learning Latin – now that we didn't do in LA – it's fun!'

Mrs Barnley was delighted when Tom said he'd be very happy for him to join Year Five as soon as she liked though not quite so pleased when told he would have a bit of catching up to do in maths. She signed up on the spot - one more on the roll - Mr Whittaker will be pleased, Tom thought. Mrs Jones may not be though - Tom would have to try and sweet-talk her into taking on another in her already bulging class.

Liz Freeland and Tom regularly toured the school. Being a former civil servant, Liz liked to be sure of a set routine and was all for establishing a 'system'. Although they would often meet during the day to sort out this or that problem, they also agreed to meet once a week in her quiet office for her to brief Tom on financial matters and to let him know 'off the record' of any bits of information she felt he should know about; it was amazing how she managed to keep her finger on the pulse of what was going on, even though she made only brief visits to the staff room to replenish her supply of coffee.

One morning, on one of their tours, Liz and Tom had inspected all the classrooms and were deciding on an order for the rolling programme of painting classrooms - this would be done in the holidays by the caretaker-cum-handyman, George Millar. George was by trade a painter but he enjoyed his much more varied job at Shaftesbury Prep where he could be 'in charge' of the cleaners, boss the children about a bit when they stepped out of line and also disappear into his 'office' (actually more like a cubby-hole) when he needed a break. Sometimes computers would need replacing, teachers would want their blackboards replaced by 'whiteboards' or the gym equipment would need to be serviced yet again. All these mundane tasks would be carefully recorded in Liz's notebook.

They arrived at a rather scruffy area in the building,

which was used as a sort of common room for the older children.

'Liz,' Tom began, 'I wonder if we could use this area more profitably - I'd like somewhere to start teaching design technology - a sort of practical workshop with workbenches and space to store tools, materials etc.'

'Ah yes, my son really enjoyed doing that sort of thing at St Paul's. Lots of prep schools are getting into practical technology these days. It takes a bit of thought and funding though. Still, I think we should look into it. Let's have a look and see whether we can extend this area a bit. You could broach the subject at the Governors' Meeting in November.'

'I'm glad you approve of the idea. I think this is certainly one of the ways we could move the school forward; I'll definitely raise it with the Governors.'

Tom went off feeling very well disposed towards former civil servants who didn't mind new ideas.

Tom remembered something Ted Whittaker had said to him when he rang after his final interview to offer him the job at Shaftesbury Prep. Ted had told him there had been several strong candidates for the job, but what had influenced the Governors in his favour was Tom's casual remark that 'school should be fun'. The introduction of design technology would certainly be 'fun' for the pupils. Tom was also keen to improve the range and standard of sports available – and that would also fall into the 'fun' category. He was well aware that whilst these were admirable aims, he would have to, at the very least, maintain academic standards – for some parents that was all that mattered. It was not going to be easy to please everyone.

Each morning before school started, Mike Dawson would come in to brief Tom on what was to take place that day.

'Mike, I just want to thank you for your support during my first few weeks – I really appreciate it. You've kept me out of trouble and let me know what is going on in the staff room - most important!'

'No worries, Tom. I'm enjoying this term. Just ask if there's anything you need to know.'

'How about coming next door for a beer when you've finished this evening?' Tom knew Mike seldom left before six in the evening.

Later, Mike was sitting on the terrace, cradling a can of Fosters and giving Tom the low-down on teachers and parents.

'Why Mr Black ever employed Paul White I'll never know. I suppose we were desperate at the time to find a French teacher but he really is a bit of a disaster; he's always late for his lessons and even when he's there he's too laid-back by far. Most of the time he just sits, reads the paper and plays French tapes or videos to the class. He also claims to be a member of the MCC and wears their tie. We asked him to run the under elevens cricket team last term and it was obvious he knows nothing about the game. Quite a few parents complained. Is there some way we can get rid of him?'

'Not so easy, I fear, but keep your eye on him and we'll record any problems as we go along.' Actually Tom had quite liked Paul when they first met; a tall man in his mid thirties, he was an easy-going, affable fellow to talk to. The children quite liked him though Tom suspected it was because they could get away with being cheeky at times. The fact that he wore a rather obvious hairpiece to supplement his prematurely thinning hair did not help.

He spent a fair bit of time down at the local pub where he had acquired an eclectic group of friends including Pierre, the pub's French cook. Paul had gained the reputation as a peacemaker after an incident involving Pierre. The two of them were sitting quietly in the corner of the crowded bar when suddenly Pierre, who had consumed several glasses of claret, slammed his fist down on the table and shouted, 'I have never been so insulted!' The bar went quiet. Paul asked him what on earth was wrong.

'Those people are talking about Waterloo - they are insulting my country!' Pierre was standing up and looking aggressively across at the next group of drinkers. Paul also had heard the neighbouring conversation and, leaning across to his friend, calmly explained that it was only the train times to London that were being discussed and that his beloved France was much respected. Pierre sat down slowly and peace was restored.

'Any other problem members of staff?' asked Tom.

Mike took a long gulp of Fosters before continuing. 'Well, there's Harriet Morse. She's one of Eileen Trammer's classroom assistants; you need to be careful what you say to her - she's a terrible gossip. She has lots of friends among the parents and is liable to let slip confidential school matters. Be careful what you tell her!'

'What about Eileen - she's seems well in charge down there?' Eileen was the teacher in charge of the pre-prep.

'Yes, she's great - she's extremely loyal and handles the staff very well. She's not too confident dealing with awkward parents though and you may have to give her a bit of support now and again.'

Mike had obviously made it his business to know the quirks of all the staff and this would clearly be invaluable to the Head. Tom fetched him another can of Fosters. 'Are there any staff who have discipline problems?'

'Hmm.' Mike scratched his head as he thought long and hard.

'Jane Lussac isn't brilliant - she's not that well organised for a science teacher, especially as she's Head of Department, and the children take advantage of her. You should make a point of going into her lessons unannounced and you'll see for yourself what I mean. Otherwise I don't think there are any problems - though young Robin Bartlett can't really be left alone with large groups of children - he's very willing but extremely green!' Robin was a Gap Year student who was working at the school before going up to Durham University the following October.

'You also need to know that some people have it in for Alastair Begg. He's not conventional enough for some and they think he shouldn't be allowed to get away with some of the things he says. But most accept that he's a good teacher and take him with a pinch of salt. He's certainly a good motivator in the classroom - and on the games field; wait till you see him coaching his second eleven soccer team!'

Mike was now in full flow.

'Marion Wilshaw never sees the joke and takes life too seriously; Elizabeth Wade, has a heart of gold but doesn't accept that anything else of importance apart from music takes place at the school. Young Alison Hitchcock has made a good start, I think.' Here Mike allowed himself a slow grin - it was obvious that he already had a soft spot for her. He had spent a disproportionate amount of time explaining the school routine, timetable and duties to her at the beginning of term. Alison had just arrived to take over responsibility for girls' games as well as teaching a Year Four class.

The two of them went on to talk about parents - both supportive and awkward - and after a couple of hours and several more cans of Fosters, Mike got up, saying he just had a few more things to do before going home. Mike's wife was also a teacher who worked at the nearby primary school; he usually didn't hurry home partly to give the impression of how hard he worked to his wife, but also to avoid having to start cooking the supper!

Chapter Two

Tom was discovering that one of the best things about running a school was the tremendous variety of different activities one became involved in - along with the expectation that you would at least be competent at all of them and understand what was going on. So, as well as a grasp of the methods of the teaching of all subjects including music and rounders, you had to appear to be able to follow the intricacies of the school's finance and planning as explained by the Bursar, you had to run meetings as if you were the chairman of a company, you had to deal with all types of awkward and difficult parents and staff and quite often you had to unblock the boys' lavatories if the caretaker was in hiding. There was no training whatsoever for this - you just had to learn on the hoof!

One such duty was the attendance of the Headmaster at each committee meeting of the Parents' Association. Tom had been warned about these by Mike who, as Deputy, also had to attend along with one other member of staff in rotation. The remainder of the PA committee consisted of about a dozen keen parents who had 'volunteered' or rather been 'persuaded' to join after some arm twisting by the Chairperson, a forceful lady called Valerie Hudson. Valerie had three children at the school, was a local magistrate and was obviously not one to argue with, though Tom had found her charming so far. The PA met about once a month in the library at 7.00 pm.

Mrs Hudson welcomed Tom to his first meeting and then, having disposed of the minutes of the last meeting, went on to ask for suggestions for a 'theme' for the Parents' Christmas Party – the previous year they had organised an '`Allo `Allo' party with Mr Black dressed up as Rene. Tom sank deeper into his chair and glanced around the table. To his left was a keen-looking young woman in glasses taking notes; she worked for the local council in the planning department and had two very clever daughters who were always top of their respective classes. Next to her was Mrs Trammer, undertaking her stint as representative of the staff room. Eileen Trammer had been teaching at the school for fifteen years and was a gem. She was motherly with the children, a very capable, rather traditional teacher and stood no nonsense from the younger members of staff in her department. Tom rated her quite highly and expected to rely on her judgement a good deal in the future.

Further round the table was Mr Bane - a genial car salesman who had a son due to take Common Entrance the following June. He seemed a good chap but Tom wasn't looking forward to explaining to him that the staff felt his boy should be aiming at a less academic place than St Paul's.

'Mr Thorne - what do you think?' Tom was jerked back from his private observations to the meeting.

'Good idea.' He agreed enthusiastically to the proposal for a Sixties Disco. 'That's my era anyway - before your time I'm sure, though,' said Tom, looking across at the PA secretary, Anita Wolff.

'Good, that's agreed then,' said the Chairperson, moving onto the next item.

Anita Wolff, mother of eleven year-old twins Ben and Charlie, was a lively and amusing member of the Committee; she had actually offered to take on the job of secretary to the PA despite being pretty busy running her own Employment Agency just around the corner. She had split up from her husband a couple of years previously but she didn't appear to have let it affect her too much, though Tom felt the boys must be missing playing football with their dad. Anita was slim, brown-haired and pretty - fathers picking up their children after school were always attempting to chat her up. Tom could see why.

The others around the table were solid and supportive parents who were happy to come along and agree with what Mrs Hudson suggested; the men at least were looking forward to moving on to the pub for a quiet pint before sloping off home. Most of the committee did go for a quick drink after the meeting ended and Tom thought Mike had been a bit harsh when he said how boring these evenings were. Particularly when there was an attractive mum as secretary!

Dealing with pupil problems was something Tom did know about from previous experiences at other schools - and there were inevitably plenty of those. One morning Jean Lussac, who was experienced and knew her subject but, as Mike had intimated, was not so good on the discipline front, collared Tom before Assembly.

'I'm fed up with David Allport. I've told him time and time again not to run around the Science lab but he won't listen. He's in my tutor group and he's already had quite a bit of extra work from me but it doesn't seem to make much difference. Please would you have a word with him?'

'Certainly I will,' replied Tom, 'I think he'd better go onto a "Behaviour Report Card". I'll see him after Assembly.' Mrs Lussac retreated, somewhat mollified.

David was a perfectly normal ten-year-old, lively and quite bright. He was good at sport and quite a handful, especially for some of the women teachers. They generally preferred the well-behaved girls who competed fiercely for 'stars' in their lessons, always wrote tidily and offered to carry the teacher's books.

Tom saw David and, when asked what he'd been up to, he immediately admitted he'd been chasing a friend who had taken the batteries he had been using for his electricity experiment. Tom told him gravely how dangerous it could be to run in Science labs and said that Mrs Lussac had informed him this wasn't the first time he had been in trouble with her. David reluctantly agreed. Tom handed him a 'Behaviour Report Card' and told him that it had to be signed after each lesson by the teacher and that, at the end of each day, had to be checked by his tutor - Mrs Lussac.

'If there are any "not satisfactorys" on your card you'll be back to see me again when we will have to deal with the matter more firmly.'

'Yes, Sir,' said David and retreated out of the study.

As David left, Mike was waiting outside the study; he wanted a word. It seemed that three boys, during break-time, had nipped down to Mr Patel's sweet and newsagent's shop on the corner and had not only bought some sweets but also, according to Mr Patel, pinched a copy of Playboy which had not been on a high enough shelf to be beyond the reach of twelve-year-old fingers.

'Sorry, Tom, you'll have to deal with this one. Mr Patel's being very good about it all. His daughter's in Year Two and he is a great supporter of the school. He's quite sure the boys did take the Playboy out of the shop and he says it must be at the school or hidden somewhere else for collection later!'

'Okay, thanks, Mike, I'll talk to them.'

Mike went out to the corridor where three sorry-looking boys were waiting. He wheeled them in.

James, Benedict and Lucas were all in their last year - twelve-year-olds coming to the point when they would be too old for prep school rules and regulations. However, buying sweets was one thing, stealing quite another.

'So, what's this all about then?' Tom asked the three of them as they stood in front of him looking at the floor. No one said anything.

'Come on, Lucas, you tell me what's been going on.' Lucas was the youngest and least likely to have been the instigator.

'Well, Sir,' mumbled Lucas, 'we did go down to Mr Patel's and I bought some Rolos, Sir, but I didn't take anything without paying.'

'Who gave you permission to go out of the school grounds?' Tom looked at the three of them.

'No one, Sir.' It was James who replied this time. There was a silence.

'Did any of you take a Playboy magazine?' The boys shifted uneasily from foot to foot but no one replied.

'What about you, Ben?'

'No, Sir.'

'You, James?' No reply.

It took half an hour of questioning but eventually the

story came out. Ben had picked up the magazine and was showing the others pictures their mothers would definitely not have approved of. As they were leaving the shop James slipped the magazine under his jumper. On the way back to school they decided this had not been such a good idea and hid the evidence in a thick hedge in a neighbour of the school's front garden. Sure enough,

Mike found it after a brief search.

It was decided that the boys would write letters of apology to Mr Patel and deliver them personally. Mr Patel had very decently refused to accept any payment for the magazine and was happy to accept the boys' apologies, not wishing to take the matter any further. Thank goodness, thought Tom

Telling parents that their child has been involved in stealing from a shop was another matter. Tom rang the three sets of parents and asked them to come in at the end of school - fortunately they all could. He gently explained to them separately what had been discovered. What a difference in reactions!

Lucas's mother couldn't have been nicer. She was most apologetic about her son's behaviour, grateful for the way the matter was being handled and very supportive.

Ben's parents were very angry and at first told Tom they would cancel a holiday for the family they had arranged at half term; he would be sent to bed early for a week and generally be given a very hard time. Tom said that this sort of thing did happen now and again at this age and that maybe a good talking to would be sufficient. Basically Ben was a good chap and Tom did not think he would ever do such a thing again. With some reluctance they finally agreed and departed.

James's mother was a different kettle of fish however. When Tom went through what had happened, she refused to believe that a son of hers could have done such a thing. It would be impossible for him with his upbringing to steal anything - it must have been one of the other boys who was really responsible. Tom explained that James himself had admitted that he was the one who actually took the magazine and suggested that she asked him herself what had happened. She eventually accepted this but went away in a thunderous mood.

It was not a good day.

One of the advantages of being the Head of a school is that you can choose, within reason, what teaching you do. Of course, some Heads don't do any. This at times may be unavoidable but it doesn't go down too well with parents who think that a Head who teaches a fair bit is more likely to know what is going on in the classrooms generally. They like a 'hands-on' Head, especially if he or she is adept at games as well - the important thing is to give parents the impression that you know each child personally, although in practice this may be impossible in a large school. The problem can be how to fit it all in.

Tom's subjects being maths and science, he had arranged to take the top set in Year Eight for maths - it was just a small group of pupils (usually boys because the girls tended to move on at the age of eleven) who instead of taking the normal Common Entrance to their next schools were strong enough to sit a scholarship exam. These exams varied between just a bit more difficult than Common Entrance to a standard that was equivalent to the old 'O' levels taken at the age of 16. All very testing for twelve-to thirteen-year-olds. These pupils would be attempting the scholarship exams for, amongst others, St Paul's, King's, Wimbledon and Charterhouse early in the following summer term. All of these were very prestigious schools.

This lot absorbed new topics very quickly and certainly kept one on one's toes. They usually worked fast and needed lots of stimulation. Tom had arrived at the introduction to Pythagoras's Theorem - which involved right-angled triangles and the square drawn on the hypotenuse (longest side) being the sum of the squares on the other two sides. So he told them the story of the hunter, which went something like this:

'There was once an Indian Chief who had three wives. He was naturally very fond of his wives and wanted to give them each just what they wanted for their birthdays. So when the first wife's birthday was getting near, he asked her what she would like. "A moose hide," she said promptly. So off went the Chief into the forest and after a few days hunting he came back with the moose hide. His first wife was very pleased. Then the Chief asked the second wife what she would like. "A reindeer hide," she said. This was a bit inconvenient but, being keen to please his wife, off went the Chief up to the North and a week later he came back with the reindeer hide. "Lovely," said the second wife. The third wife proved more of a problem. When it came round to her birthday, she was asked what she wanted. "A hippopotamus hide," she replied.

So off went the Chief - this time all the way to Africa on a Hippo Hunt. Eventually he returned, carrying a hippopotamus hide over his shoulder. So all three wives were very pleased - they all had just what they wanted to sleep on.

Some time later the Chief was rewarded - the first wife produced for him a bouncing baby boy and then so did the second. But the third wife excelled herself and presented him with twin baby boys.

All this goes to show that the squaw on the hippopotamus hide is equal to the sum of the squaws on the other two hides.'

This was the type of silly story that went down well especially if you drew a picture on the blackboard as you told the story which Tom did, not very well. The boys asked if they could draw a picture of a hippo in their books before getting down to work. But of course!

Some parents may be awkward and bad for the stress levels but in the main they tend to be charming and most supportive; Anita Wolff came into the latter category. Halfway through the morning Barbara tapped on the door and shimmered in carrying a cup of coffee and some chocolate biscuits, which she had quickly discovered Tom particularly liked. What a splendid secretary!

'Here you are - oh, and Mrs Wolff wonders if you could spare a moment - she's outside; I don't think there is a problem with Ben or Charlie. You met her at the PA meeting the other day - she's the secretary.' Tom remembered only too well.

'OK - let me just have a gulp of coffee and then I'm ready.'

A couple of minutes later Anita was sitting opposite Tom, smiling demurely.

'I wonder if I could ask you a favour?' He speculated as to what it could be.

'It's just that we're flying to Washington at half term so the twins can see their dad and we can't get a flight back until the Tuesday - would it be OK for the boys to miss a couple of days of school and come back on the Wednesday?'

'Of course, no problem, I quite understand. Most people don't even bother to ask, so thank you for coming to see me.'

As she got up she shook Tom's hand and asked how he was enjoying the job. 'Ben gave you a good report at theend of your first week! He spoke to you as he left to go home!'

'Ah, yes, I remember!' Tom grinned and said that his job was certainly keeping him busy. Anita departed leaving behind a pleasant perfumed aroma.

Tom was well aware that shortly after a new Head arrived in his or her new school it was the policy for that particular school to be inspected. Sure enough, a letter from the IAPS (Incorporated Association of Preparatory Schools) soon arrived with the information that Shaftesbury School was to be inspected during the following Spring Term and would Tom like to confirm that week commencing Monday, March 10th would be a convenient time. Though not particularly looking forward to the experience, Tom knew that, if they found some poor teaching or other problems, he personally could probably escape being blamed as he would still be pretty new in the job.

There was a great load of bumph which came with the letter - forms requiring information about pupil numbers over the last five years, academic results, sizes of classes, qualifications and ages of teaching staff, health and safety (Tom made a quick mental note – hide the panga!) and numerous other school policies. It would take weeks to assemble all this stuff but it had to be done. Tom showed Barbara the large wad of forms, which would certainly give her a lot of extra work.

'I think,' she said, 'it would be a good time to take a sabbatical next term!'

Tom sincerely hoped she was joking.

Every Tuesday at 4.00 pm there was a staff meeting. Tom informed everyone that an inspection was due the following term. A collective sigh escaped the staff. Some were perched on the arms of chairs sipping tea, a row of three younger teachers sat on the frayed sofa and the PE staff were propping up the wall by the biscuit tins. The more experienced people, who seemed to be pretty confident, would do the paperwork and not mind too much when some Head of another school sat in on their lessons. The younger ones were, understandably, a bit nervous and needed a bit of reassurance.

Tom tried to sound confident.

'Don't worry, I'm sure we'll get a splendid report. It could be very useful. If we can make a case to the Inspectors for any improvements or developments we want and they make the right recommendations in their report, the Governors will probably go along with them.'

'Will they be inspecting the sport?' asked Simon. 'I've heard from a friend of mine who's just been inspected at another school that they aren't interested in games.'

'I'm quite sure they will take a keen interest in every activity that goes on in the school. I do know we must be sure that all exercise books have been properly corrected, up to date and, where appropriate, a constructive comment made. Everyone will have to produce lesson plans not only for that week but from now onwards. They may want to see them.'

A stifled groan escaped from Alastair, who probably hadn't ever used such a thing as a lesson plan in his life. What would the inspection team make of him, Tom wondered?

During one of Tom's several interviews for the job, Ted Whittaker had warned him that the school was due for an inspection. He had assured him that the Governors would be keen to implement all their recommendations, financial considerations permitting; he had made it clear that Tom should be ready to put his own ideas forward to the Inspectors. Ted's readiness to adapt and desire to improve what the school had to offer was one of the reasons Tom had been particularly keen to take on the job. It was obviously crucial to the success of any school for the Chairman and the Head to develop a sound working relationship and Tom felt they had made a good start. Ted left him to run the place on a day-to-day basis whilst being available for advice when needed. He was not the interfering type; on the other hand Tom knew that in the background he kept a wary eye on what was going on and would step in if he thought mistakes were being made. It was a fact of school life that there was always someone looking over your shoulder!

Ted came in to have a chat with Tom to see how things were going in his first term and find out what thoughts he had about future development. Tom knew he was also there to sample the atmosphere in the staff room. The two of them sat in the study drinking coffee, while Tom brought him up to date with some fairly trivial details as well as the news about the impending inspection. Once again, Ted wondered whether Alastair Begg would prove to be a problem.

'Have you had any complaints about Alastair recently?' enquired Tom.

'No, nothing lately. But I did hear there was a problem with some boys in Sandeep Patel's shop. I met James Webber's parents at a party the other day. What happened?'

Tom described how the three boys had stolen a Playboy after going down to the shop without permission. He explained how he and Mike had dealt with the situation.

'Are you sure that it was James who actually stole the magazine? His mother was pretty adamant it couldn't have been him.'

'Yes, I'm sure. He admitted it in front of his two friends - eventually. I don't think he was lying - I do think however that he is pretty scared of his parents.'

'Mary Webber can be a bit difficult, I know,' said Ted. 'She unfortunately seems to know quite a few parents and is liable to gossip; I asked her to come and see you again if she wished.'

'Fine.' Tom smiled, but was inwardly thinking he would like to drop that unreasonable woman down a very deep hole. 'Of course I'll see her and try to keep her happy or at least happier.'

'Good. Now, moving on; how are things in the staff room - is everyone pulling their weight, do you think?'

'Yes, on the whole I think so; it's coming up to break time now - shall we have a walk around the school and you can have a chat with a few of the staff?'

They set off on their tour, passing groups of girls on their way to the gym for a netball team meeting and quantities of other children pouring out of their classrooms into the autumn sunshine. They entered the staff room to a gale of laughter from the occupants. Apparently Marion Wilshaw, one of the older teachers, who was generally thought to be a bit short on humour, had been sitting in for an absent teacher's lesson. Rather surprisingly for her, Marion was telling the staff room about Tim Jeffries - a very amusing but cheeky boy in the class she had been looking after.

Tim had a bit of a cold and was sniffing.

'Do stop sniffing, Jeffries,' Mrs Wilshaw had asked him repeatedly, to no avail. Eventually she barked at him, 'Jeffries, have you got a handkerchief?'

Quick as a flash Tim had replied, 'Oh yes, Mrs Wilshaw, but I make it a rule never to lend it to teachers!'

The listening staff roared with laughter. The Chairman was reassured to see such a relaxed staff room. They continued on their circuit of the school.

'Untidy little chaps.' Ted looked with distaste at several piles of sports clothes and trainers left on the boys' changing room floor. Tom agreed, making a mental note to ask Simon to check the place after games in future. Nothing else seemed to catch the Chairman's eye and they parted genially at the school gate.

A couple of days later Barbara warned Tom of the inevitable - Mrs Webber, mother of James, who had been involved in the Playboy incident, wished to see him. Mary Webber was a strong character, used to getting her own way. An ambitious parent, she directed her only son James into activities she considered would hold him in good stead in the future. He was given the best riding lessons and was sent to Zermatt twice a year to perfect his skiing. His mother's varied and high-profile social life allowed James to meet all the right people. James, in his mother's eyes, could do no wrong. She arrived promptly for her ten o'clock appointment.

She began silkily. 'Mr Thorne, I know that James and the other two boys should not have left the school premises, but it seems to me there is considerable doubt about who actually took this magazine.' Here she paused, giving Tom a chance to intervene. Tom thought quickly. All the boys had already written a letter of apology to Mr Patel; nothing further was to be gained from rubbing salt into wounds and insisting that in his opinion James was the main culprit.

'Well, Mrs Webber, as far as I'm concerned the matter is now closed. Hopefully the boys concerned will have learnt a lesson and I certainly will not mention this in any future report I have to write.' This was important since the Head's reports to their next schools would influence their chances of being accepted – and Mrs Webber had high expectations for James. It was to be Eton for him! Mrs Webber relaxed and even managed a wan smile. She half-heartedly thanked Tom for his time, still not happy that her son had been blamed, unfairly in her view, but accepting Tom's assurance of no further repercussions. As she departed, Tom breathed a sigh of relief.

Shaftesbury's main local rival school was St Ansted's and it was quite early in the term that the two schools faced each other on the rugby field - normally a keenly fought battle. Usually Shaftesbury would struggle against this boys' only school as the latter had rather more to choose from in each age group. This season, however, Simon Bragg seemed to think he had a stronger team than usual and he and his unofficial assistant, the rugby-playing parent, Gareth Williams, were quietly confident. Tom had made himself a bit unpopular by asking Gareth to leave Simon to go onto the pitch on his own at half-time to talk to the boys and generally be in charge. Gareth had been taking over too much, doing the half-time chat and generating a bit of jealousy among other, less well connected parents. It was a bit of a tricky conversation but it needed to be done and Gareth took it quite well. Tom rather doubted that he would be invited to any of Gareth's wife's curry soirées, which she organised for selected members of staff - probably in return for the odd favour now and again.

The first team match at under 13 age level was to be played away and the master in charge at St Ansted's, David Lamb, would be refereeing. Simon said it was always worth a good ten points to the opposition when David did the whistle blowing.

The match turned out to be a tense, error-filled game. The two rival sets of parents on the touchline screamed at the players to 'tackle' or 'pass' - the latter especially when their son might get the ball. The referee, who was apparently normally a pleasant enough fellow, gave three penalties to his own side to every one given to the Shaftesbury team and was roundly abused by supporting parents. One father had to be silenced by a hissed restraining request into his left ear by Tom. Shaftesbury were the stronger team and going into the last few minutes, though both sides had scored a few times, Shaftesbury were one try up. St Ansted's attacked furiously and, despite frantic defence, managed to score a try quite near the posts. There was only a minute to go plus injury time. If the St Ansted's kicker converted then they would be one point in front; if not Shaftesbury would still be just in the lead. It was not a difficult kick but the unfortunate boy skewed the ball off to the left and the Shaftesbury supporters breathed again. Simon was standing next to Tom on the touchline.

'I bet David will add on at least five minutes injury time. That'll give them a chance to score again - you watch!'

The game restarted and, encouraged by their last effort, the St Ansted's forwards drove down towards the Shaftsbury line. Full time was up and Simon waited for David to add on enough injury time for his team to gain a winning score. Then, to everyone's amazement, the referee blew his whistle for the end of the game and came towards Simon grinning broadly.

'What an exciting game! Your boys did really well - just pipped at the post - bad luck!'

'Not really, David - your chap missing the last kick left us one point ahead, I think.'

David's smile evaporated as he consulted his notebook where he had been keeping the score and did some quick arithmetic. His face clouded and he scratched the side of his nose with his pencil. Carefully he added up the scores again. Reluctantly he forced a smile.

'Quite right, Simon - well played. You won 25-24.'

Tom was sure David would do his sums more carefully next match. Such is competitive prep school sport!

In fact rugby seemed to be taking up quite a bit of Tom's time - each week he would go down to the games field on Saturday morning to help with coaching. He really enjoyed this, even in the rain, and it was certainly a good way to get to know the pupils.

He'd just got back from rugby training one Saturday when there was a knock at the door. Tom was in his shorts and rugby shirt. He opened the door and there was Anita Wolff.

'Very sorry to bother you, Tom, but I've got your copy of the minutes of the last PA meeting - I thought I'd drop them round.' Suddenly she stopped. 'Oh.'

'That's very civil of you.' Tom paused, slightly embarrassed, remembering his attire.

'I've just been refereeing some rugby,' he explained. 'Forgive the kit!'

She eyed Tom up and down, colouring slightly. 'That's OK – it's very suitable. So this is the Headmaster's house; isn't it a bit big for you, all on your own?'

Tom thought for a moment - debating whether or not he should invite her in. She was wearing some nicely filled out jeans and for a moment they stood, not speaking.

'Come and have a look round - I seem to have enough junk to occupy all the rooms! Would you like a drink?'

She stepped gingerly inside and Tom closed the door.

'Follow me.'

'Oh, very nice, Tom.'

They wandered into the kitchen and Tom poured Anita a soft drink and opened a can of beer for himself. He handed her the glass, and she took it smiling.

'I'll leave the minutes here, shall I?

'I like your garden,' Anita said as they walked through to the back of the house. Although the front looked out onto a busy street, the back was quiet – a lawn and flower beds were surrounded by a high wall covered with climbing plants. They stood quietly, sipping their drinks, surveying the garden. Anita turned towards Tom and asked innocently, 'How many bedrooms have you got?'

'Er, four - I'll show you the rest of the house.' Tom was wondering what she was up to as they climbed up the stairs.

'This overlooks the orchard behind the school.' Tom stood by the window of the spare bedroom his mother had used when she came to stay for the night the previous week. Anita was standing behind him looking over his shoulder.

'Mmm, peaceful, isn't it?' She put her hand on Tom's shoulder and then slowly ran her hand down his back.

'Should you be doing that?' Tom spoke gently, enjoying it all the same.

'Probably not, but then I don't always do what I should do.'

Just then the shrill sound of the front door bell stopped them in their tracks. Tom ground his teeth.

'Who the devil is that?' Tom shot Anita an apologetic smile and reluctantly retreated downstairs to answer the door.

'Very sorry to disturb you, Mr Thorne, but after netball this morning Rachel left her homework books in the Hall

49

and she really needs them this weekend; please could you let me into the school to collect them?'

It was Mrs Cooper - her daughter Rachel was in Year Six and a delightful girl. Tom snapped back to professional mode.

'Of course - I'll just get the key. If you'd like to wait outside the front door of the school, I'll be with you in a moment.' Mrs Cooper nodded her thanks and made her way around to the school's main entrance.

'I think I'd better be getting along now.' Anita had followed Tom down the stairs at a discreet distance, out of sight of the front door. 'Perhaps you could drop by one evening to my house? I would like to ask your advice on where the twins ought to go on to after Shaftesbury.' Tom caught a glimpse of something in her eyes.

'Fine,' he grinned, 'I'll look forward to that!' and Anita tripped off down the path.

Chapter Three

Shaftesbury Prep was a non-profit-making Charitable Trust run by a Board of Governors. To say it was non-profit-making was not exactly the case - the school usually made a large surplus each year, which had to be ploughed back into the school funds. Quite a large chunk of it went as ground rent to the owner of the freehold on which the school was built. The owner was the former headmaster and founder of the school, Mr Black. He had been rather well advised and, when he decided to set the school up as a trust, he sold the business to the Trust but retained the freehold of the land for himself and his family. The rent he was able to obtain in this part of West London was very healthy indeed! Another large chunk of the surplus was fed regularly into a 'building fund'. Demand for places at the school had always been strong and the finances seemed to be in good shape - in no small measure due to the wily Chairman, Ted Whittaker whose banking experience had clearly been of great value to the school. However, Ted made it clear to Tom that, as the new Head, he would be expected to keep the place financially strong by ensuring the school remained full. Though this should not be too difficult, Tom was nevertheless well aware of the pressure this would create.

Liz, the school's splendid Bursar, attended all meetings and acted as secretary to the Board taking the minutes. Before Tom's first meeting she had spent quite some time explaining who was who on the Board and adding some personal comments of her own. Though at first sight Liz appeared a rather mild mannered and retiring person, she had a sharp intellect and held strong views about the merits or otherwise of the members.

The Governors, she told Tom, were a mixed bunch; they generally had little to do with the everyday running of the place. Any problems in this area they were more than happy to leave to the Chairman and the Head to deal with, but they could either be awkward or supportive at meetings. The awkward ones tended to be two former parents. Jane Skeate's two girls were apparently very good musicians - quite bright but not sporty. She disapproved of sport generally, wanting resources to go to the arts or academic areas. Peter Wallis had been on the Board for years - he was a retired architect and did not always follow what was going on. He certainly was not up to date on many modern ideas and Liz felt he should have retired some time ago.

The Headmistress of the nearest girls' secondary independent school where Shaftesbury sent some of its best pupils at the age of eleven was regularly in attendance. At just four foot eleven, Eileen Rosse was always full of energy and packed quite a punch; she had made a point of arriving early for this evening's meeting to have a quiet word with Tom.

'Just you let me know if you need any support.' She spoke in a conspiratorial whisper. 'If you want to introduce anything new just give me a call beforehand. Your Board can be sticky at times and I know what it's like.'

Liz told Tom that both Eileen and Tim Mount, the Deputy Head of the corresponding boys' public school, were likely to be supportive though Tim did miss meetings quite often due to the fact he had too much work to do at his own school. The school accountant, Philip Greene, kept a low profile but a beady eye on the figures. Two other members of the Board were busy Heads of other prep schools outside London and therefore not in competition with Shaftesbury; they came when they could and provided valuable input.

All eight members of the Board actually turned up this time, no doubt curious to hear how the new man was getting on. Tom had previously prepared a written report on the activities and happenings at the school since September and copies had been circulated. Details included the numbers in the school, how new members of staff were doing, what clubs and activities were being run including music, drama and the sports results so far.

'Thank you for your report.' Ted Whittaker spoke as Tom came to the end of his piece.

A variety of agreeing murmurs went round the table. Peter Wallis, who Tom thought had been quietly dozing at the end of the long library table, his grizzled face propped up by a gnarled hand and his elbow solid on the table, chipped in first.

'Well, Tom, what are your first impressions of the place - what do you think needs to be done?'

Tom began slowly. 'It's certainly a very effective school and efficiently run. The teachers seem to be a very committed and professional lot although one or two are a little set in their ways - maybe some new young blood would be beneficial. I think sport could be upgraded - the council games pitches and swimming pool we rent are not good and we have to travel too far to get there. Maybe we could look into renting the local cricket club's ground. We could also consider extending the range of after school activities - other schools provide more than us and we need to compete. The other item I'm quite keen on is design technology.'

Jane Skeate immediately intervened. 'What on earth's that? Shouldn't we be concentrating on the basic core subjects - our reputation is based on sound academic results and that is what our parents want.'

'Well, Mrs Skeate, to answer your question, I believe design technology is an excellent way of teaching children to think constructively as well as learning a number of useful practical skills. Children are set a particular practical problem - for example, to design and make a simple four-wheeled vehicle using cardboard, wooden wheels and so on. They need to think what they are going to do before they start, putting their chosen design on paper. Then they build their model adapting if necessary as they go along. Finally they test and evaluate what they have made. I've seen this subject being taught most successfully at two other schools and I think we should consider introducing it here. Children love and gain a great deal from it. Quite often it's the less academic children who shine.'

Bob Morton, Head of a well-known Oxford prep school and a good friend of the previous Head - hence his appointment as a Governor - backed Tom up.

'I think Tom has a good point. We have recently introduced design technology for Years Five and up and it is proving to be extremely popular with the children. Of course, you need to think about facilities and staffing. Do you have classroom space and who would be doing the teaching?'

Tom had already broached these points with both Liz

Freeland and the Chairman so he had a draft proposal prepared which he produced for the meeting. After quite a bit of discussion Tom was asked to put more details on paper and circulate them to the Board. The principle seemed to be in agreement and the Chairman nodded approvingly as they moved on to the next item on the agenda.

Jane, somewhat outvoted on the technology front, enquired about scholarship candidates; how many were there and what were their chances? She pointed out that the previous year had been a particularly successful one for exam results. Tom, rather cagily, said that he believed the current year's leavers were not as strong but that the teachers would do their best for them.

Philip Greene wanted to know what sort of rent the local cricket club might want for the use of their field - Tom offered to make enquiries.

After a couple of hours Ted brought the meeting to a close and Tom gathered up his papers with a sigh of relief - the next one wouldn't be until the following term.

From the rather weighty matters that had been occupying Tom the night before, the next morning came as a relief to get back to the sort of thing that Heads can enjoy. Halfway through the morning Barbara put her head round the door and with a grin on her face announced that Eileen Trammer, the pre-prep head, needed to have a word.

'She's very embarrassed - it's about a boy who has been rather naughty and she wants you to talk to him. I'll ask her to come in, shall I?'

Eileen was looking a trifle flushed as Tom sat her down and offered her a cup of coffee.

'No, it's all right thanks, I need to get back. But I wondered if you could talk to Jack Hocking in Mrs James's class. He's been showing off a lot recently and his latest idea is to drop his shorts and pants and show his er....willy,' (here she looked down at her smartly polished shoes, not wanting to use such a word), 'to the girls in the class. He's been sitting at the back and Mrs James didn't know about this until the mother of one of the girls complained to her. I've spoken to Jack but I'm not sure that's enough.'

No, it's not, thought Tom, we really can't have that sort of thing going on. Suppressing a grin as he could also see the funny side, Tom spoke gravely. 'Quite right, Eileen, I'll certainly talk to him - silly little boy!'

A few moments later the small figure of Jack stood apprehensively in front of the study desk.

'So what have you been up to, Jack?'

'Sir, I'm sorry, I won't do it again, Sir.'

'No, I certainly hope not. You don't want me to tell your parents about this, do you? I'm sure they would not be pleased.'

Jack went very red in the face.

'No, Sir. Sir, will you tell them?'

'No, Jack - so long as you promise not to do anything like this again. Okay?'

'Yes, Sir. I promise.'

And a relieved small boy retreated back to his classroom.

The following morning a letter in a childish hand arrived on Tom's desk. It had been delivered personally by Jack Hocking, accompanied by a fierce-looking Eileen Trammer.

Dear Mr Thorne,

I am verry sorry to have been so much trouble. I realy won't do it again. Jack

The Tuesday afternoon staff meetings usually went on for about an hour - less if Tom could arrange it. He and Mike would agree an agenda beforehand and this would be posted on the staff noticeboard a day or so before - people would then be free to add any other items they felt required discussion. The first staff meeting back in September had been an awkward affair - no one was keen to say much and it had all been left to Mike and Tom. Mike was able to pad things out quite well on that occasion by carefully going through what was required for 'duties' and several other routine matters. Discussion on educational matters or policy of any kind was minimal. By the end of October, however, things had changed and almost all the teachers were prepared to contribute; in fact some couldn't stop themselves talking! It was really good to bring democracy into the staff room – good, but time-consuming.

On this Tuesday, after the routine matters had been dealt with, the almost insoluble problem of academic versus sporting interests was due to be discussed. On one side was Jane Lussac, the Head of Science, supported by Penny Jones who took a Year Five class. They had added 'away sports fixtures' to the agenda. The ladies had a point - when matches were played away against other schools the children inevitably had to miss some lessons in the afternoon in order to travel. Jane had complained before to Tom that three rather dodgy Common Entrance candidates of hers had already missed two double physics lessons – lessons that were practicals and could not be 'caught up' later by doing extra work. In the other camp was Simon, who would not be too happy to have his scrum half and two front row forwards missing when playing strong opposition.

'I quite see that the children should play sport but can't matches be arranged after school so that they don't clash with lessons? Can't we play closer schools so they don't have to leave until 4 o'clock?'

Simon gave an exasperated sigh. 'Jane, we have to travel for forty-five minutes at least to get to schools that can give us a decent game and we are trying to improve our fixture list. Obviously it would be impossible only to play matches at home.'

Those who taught the younger children were not too bothered about this discussion since their pupils were not yet in teams and rarely missed lessons. Those teaching the last two years split roughly 60/40 in favour of the academic argument. Tom, though he tried to appear neutral, thought sport was such an important aspect of school life for some children that missing a few lessons now and again was a price well worth paying for representing your school in another environment. But he said nothing.

After more discussion on both sides Mike came to the rescue and said he would look at the timetable and see if it could be re-organised so children missed different lessons when they were going to be away, thus spreading the staff irritation and inconvenience. Somewhat grumpily the meeting moved onto the next topic, but Tom knew the problem would be worse when the cricket season came round and matches took several hours.

The following morning Alison Hitchcock came in just before Assembly to give Tom the results of the netball matches played the previous week. The team captains would come out in front of everybody at the end of the religious section and give a short report on their match. Usually it would be along the lines of 'We lost 6-1 but all the team played well and thank you to Miss Hitchcock for umpiring' or similar. Shaftesbury was not too strong on the netball court and perhaps needed a tougher coach!

However, this week the team had managed to achieve two wins along with a draw and three losses. Tom thanked Alison for her information and congratulated her on all her hard work.

He called to her just as she was returning to her class. 'By the way, I've got Mrs Jacques coming in to see me this morning. Barbara tells me it could be about Fiona not being in the netball team. What is she like - should she be playing?'

Fiona was a very diffident but pleasant girl in Year Six - her mother was ambitious for her to do well, of course.

Alison looked a bit flustered. 'Well, she could be OK but the trouble is she can't come to netball practice after school – I think she goes off for extra tuition at home. If I only see her in PE lessons and can't see her playing with the other potential team players after school then it's difficult to pick her.'

'That is a problem. Is she talented, do you think? Would she be playing if she was available for after school practice?'

Alison agreed that this might be the case and departed, Tom having said he'd let her know how he got on with Fiona's pushy mum!

Thus forewarned, Tom sat down opposite Mrs Jacques later that morning.

'You see, Mr Thorne, we know Fiona is not so strong in

the classroom and she isn't musical but she is very keen on sport. She's very keen to play in a school team. It would do her self esteem the world of good to be selected. I'm sure Miss Hitchcock is a very good netball coach but she just doesn't seem to notice Fiona. Can you do anything about it for me?'

Mrs Jacques, a slightly built, nervous woman with a steely glint in her eye, leant forwards towards Tom, smiling hopefully.

'Actually, I was speaking to Miss Hitchcock about Fiona this morning. She was saying that it was a pity that Fiona couldn't come to after-school netball - I'm not sure what evening that is.' He paused.

Mrs Jacques became a bit defensive. 'Mondays it is, but Fiona has extra maths coaching then from a teacher who lives next door to us. Perhaps if I speak to her I can change the days Fiona has her maths lessons.'

'Splendid. Let us know how you get on and tell Fiona to ask Miss Hitchcock if she can come to the practices - she'll have to play well - there's quite a bit of competition for places in the teams!'

Mrs Jacques thanked Tom for his time and retreated beaming. How nice to have satisfied customers occasionally, he thought - as Basil Fawlty says, we should have them stuffed!

Every so often Tom felt that he needed to wander around the building to see what was going on. Random visits to classrooms and activities would keep the profile up and give the impression that he had his finger on the pulse. Tom knew that Jane Lussac was having a difficult class for double chemistry so that might be worth a visit. Also it had been some time since he'd seen the music department at work.

The music room was always a pleasure to visit and as it was on the way to the chemistry lab, Tom decided to call in there first. On the whole the children looked forward to their lessons. The Director of Music, Elizabeth Wade, had been with the school for years. She was a rather dowdy middle-aged spinster and, outside the classroom, kept a low profile. She had her own spot in a corner of the staff room and at break times consumed coffee and biscuits avidly, chatting to Marion Wilshaw. Once in her music room, however, she was a completely different person. Animated and enthusiastic, she communicated her love of music to her pupils in an amazing way. They sang, played various instruments in groups and generally enjoyed themselves.

On this occasion, however, Elizabeth was having a difference of opinion with a lively but rather cheeky little girl called Sadie Brown in Year Five. They were in the corridor outside one of the music practice rooms.

'It's not good enough, Sadie - you really must take your practising seriously if you are going to make progress. This is the third time this term that you have "forgotten" to come.'

'I'm very sorry, Miss Wade, I had to do some extra science for Mrs Lussac before our lesson this afternoon and I didn't have time. I'll make a big effort next week.' Sadie did not look at all sorry.

'You'd better, Sadie, or I really will be most displeased.'

Sadie turned, saw Tom and smiled sweetly.

'Hallo, Sir,' she chirruped happily and disappeared off for her next lesson.

'That girl is very annoying. She has plenty of ability

and won't use it. It's a pity!'

Elizabeth went back into her room. Tom followed and watched her class practising the carols they would be singing at the end of term carol service. They sang beautifully and, when they came to a break, Tom told them they were wonderful and that he loved their singing. Elizabeth was happy.

His journey to the chemistry lab took Tom past Paul White's classroom. He looked in through the window. The children were leaning back in their chairs and, true to form, Paul was playing them a French tape. His feet were propped up on a convenient chair and the Daily Telegraph was folded neatly on his desk - at least it wasn't open at the racing page! There was an air of calm about the room and it looked as though quite a few of his pupils were dozing. Perhaps they could absorb some of the language in their sleep. Something had to be done about Paul, but what or how, Tom couldn't think. He knocked briskly on the door and went in. Paul slowly moved his feet to the floor and smiled pleasantly at Tom. The pupils moved more quickly, sitting up straighter, one or two nudging their slumbering friends. Tom walked around looking over the pupils' shoulders at their empty exercise books. No written work meant no marking! Tom was not surprised. The tape droned on as he made his way outside into the corridor again. Yes, he thought, a change was definitely needed in that department.

Upon arrival at the chemistry lab Tom was met by an excited hum emanating from the room; a pungent smell wafted down the corridor. As Tom opened the door, Jane in her white lab coat was giving instructions from the far end of the room.

'Be very careful with the sulphur - don't touch it when

it's melted - you'll get burnt badly if you are careless.'

This was Year Seven finding out what happens when you heat various substances. Some, like copper sulphate, change colour and give off steam, others like magnesium, burn with a very bright flame and others just melt like ice. It was a fun experiment and the children were certainly getting the most out of it. Tom was relieved to see they were all wearing lab coats and protective goggles. Jane didn't notice he was there for a full five minutes - she had her hands full keeping an eye on what was going on.

Tom patted her on the shoulder. 'Rather you than me.'

She smiled a wan smile and nodded. He wandered on round the benches trying to give a bit of helpful advice here and there. The lesson proceeded pretty well on the whole and he had to agree that it was a good session.

'Well done, Jane.' Tom congratulated her as the pupils trooped out at the end of the lesson. 'I think you've earned your lunch break! By the way, how is David Allport getting on? Did that report card do any good?'

'It certainly did – he's been no trouble recently, in fact he's doing rather well. Thanks for sorting him out.'

Just as the final bell of the day was going and children were noisily tumbling down the stairs on their way home, Barbara put her head round the door.

'Have you a moment to have word with Mrs Wolff? She says it won't take long.'

'Of course.' Tom unconsciously straightened his tie.

Anita bounced in, smartly dressed in her office clothes. 'I just wondered if you could spare some time later - I have to pick up the twins now and I have a couple of appointments still to do this afternoon and early evening.

I was wondering if you'd be able to come round to my house some time after nine? I wanted to find out what you think about where the twins should go for their next school. I have a good supply of coffee and whisky!'

'There's an offer I can't refuse - of course I'll come! Where do you live?'

This was an unnecessary question since he had some time ago looked up her address in the files; it was only five minutes drive away. However, he took down directions and a phone number and then Anita was gone.

Birch Avenue turned out to be a tidy, suburban street with neat expensive-looking four-bedroomed houses set back from the road. Tom could see Anita's blue four-wheel drive Nissan parked in the drive of number twenty-four. He drove another thirty yards further down and parked on the other side of the road, wondering why he was being so cagey. Remembering the dustbin incident at the beginning of term was reason enough to avoid gossip as much as possible and his red BMW would certainly be distinctive.

'Oh, hi, do come in.' Anita, answered the doorbell almost at once. 'The boys are in bed - asleep, I hope.'

Her living room was surprisingly untidy - there were books on the floor and an unfinished jigsaw puzzle on a tray on the sofa. The boys' football boots had been casually thrown into a corner.

'Sorry about the mess. Ben and Charlie are so disorganised with their things. Now what can I get you? Would you like a cup of coffee or maybe something stronger?'

'Coffee, please.'

Tom followed her into the kitchen. Anita had

exchanged her working clothes for a large woolly sweater and a pair of tight-fitting faded jeans. They took their mugs back into the living room.

'Make yourself comfortable on the sofa while I just put on some music.'

The sofa, a rumpled, well-used piece of furniture was now minus the jigsaw puzzle. They settled themselves demurely at each end as the vital subject of the boys' next school was discussed.

'Peter, my ex, wants the boys to go to his old school Oundle, but I don't want them to board. Anyway Oundle is too far away. I'd much rather they went to somewhere like King's, Wimbledon or Hampton. What do you think?'

Tom suddenly felt disappointed, and realised he had hoped for a more personal opening to the conversation. However he put his mind to the question. Despite having been at boarding school himself, Tom wasn't too keen on the idea unless there was a special reason, so he found it easy to agree with Anita and they discussed the merits of her preferred schools. The conversation soon moved onto other things. Tom certainly found Anita easy to talk to. Without quite noticing, they moved closer to each other on the sofa.

'Would you like another coffee?' Anita leant across Tom to reach for his empty mug; her arm brushed against his. Tom's reaction was interrupted by the sound of a door creaking open and the padding of slippered feet on the landing. This was followed by a pleading voice.

'Mummy? I can't sleep. I've had a nightmare. Can you come?'

'Just a minute, darling. I'll be up in a moment.'

Tom hastily stood up. 'It's getting late. Perhaps I'd better be on my way. Good night and thanks for the coffee.'

He made his way towards the door and drove slowly home.

At the end of the autumn term the school organised internal exams for the older classes; obviously useful as you could get a better idea of children's ability in the various subjects. It was amazing how many children managed to con the teachers into thinking they were brilliant at a particular subject by being keen in class and then getting their parents to do their homework. There were, of course, others who didn't bother much but who were capable and tended to do well in exams.

On the last day of the exams Tom went into the hall to help with the invigilation. There being no music lessons during exams, Elizabeth Wade was also invigilating. They were handing out the geography papers and as Elizabeth put the paper on young Sadie Brown's desk, Sadie looked up at her. 'Are there any questions on music practice, Miss Wade?'

Cheeky girl!

In south-west London there were plenty of pushy parents and Mrs Bland fell into this category. She had come to see Tom at the beginning of term wanting her son James to be moved up a year so that when he was thirteen he would be in a better position to take a scholarship. Since that first meeting she had kept away from the office and Tom had rather hoped he would not need to see her again. It was not to be and he smiled as charmingly as he could as he ushered her to a chair on the other side of his desk.

James's teacher, the humourless Mrs Wilshaw, had told Tom on numerous occasions that James was no scholar and that he should stay in his present year group. Tom had noticed however that James had scored quite highly in the more difficult of the two maths papers his year had taken in the recent internal exams. His written work was often a bit untidy which did not endear him to certain teachers. Could he actually be as bright as his ghastly mother thought?

Mrs Bland smiled sweetly but was clearly ready to do battle if she didn't get her own way. 'You seem to be settling in well and thank you for making time to see me - you must be busy at this time of term.'

'Yes, thank you, I am pretty busy but enjoying myself. James seems to be doing fine with Mrs Wilshaw - I was speaking yesterday to her about him.'

'Well, as we discussed, my husband and I would really like him to move up a year - he'll need to if he is to have a chance to go for a scholarship to Hugh's old school, Charterhouse. Have you given this some thought?' Mrs Bland waited expectantly.

Tom was in two minds over this one. To follow the staff's view and keep James where he was would alienate the Blands and would certainly mean that James would have to take Common Entrance and not the Scholarship Exam - and Charterhouse's scholarship papers would certainly be testing. To overrule the staff and promote James would give more work for his teachers, irritating them and also might be too much for James to cope with. Even if he did manage to get through the work required, the chances of him actually winning an award against what would be stiff competition would be minimal. The most important point really was - what was the right thing to do for James himself?

Tom went through the pros and cons of a move with Mrs Bland; she perked up when Tom said he was an able boy who, he thought, would work hard when challenged but she sucked her teeth and hissed quietly when Tom said his confidence might be shaken if he didn't succeed in what would be a very ambitious move. In the end he agreed to give him a chance to prove himself by promising to arrange for him to be given some extra, more challenging work over the next month or so and see how he managed. If he coped well and responded positively then he could move up a year. This postponed a decision and would give Tom time to persuade the staff to go along with it. Mrs Bland agreed that this was a fair temporary solution.

Tom had arranged a meeting with Liz Freeland to investigate how they could adapt the large but rather scruffy common room they had looked at earlier to accommodate design technology. They stood looking at the rather battered furniture, the wooden floor partially covered by several patterned carpets and in the corner a sink and draining board. There was also a large TV set which was used a good deal on wet afternoons.

Tom spoke his thoughts out loud. 'Can we not find somewhere the older children can use instead of here?'

'I've been looking at that. Yes, I think we can use the top floor of the building. At the moment it's not really used, at least only for storage, so we could convert it into a reasonably pleasant area. It would be rather isolated though.' Her thoughts were obviously running along the same lines as his.

'We need two areas here, I think. One with flat surfaces for designing and also possibly with some computers and the other with workbenches for actual construction.'

After they had wandered around taking a few measurements, Liz said that she had spoken to the firm of builders the school usually used and would now arrange for Charles Mason, their very obliging manager, to come and quote for the work needed to be done. 'Have you arranged to look at any other prep schools to see what they are doing?'

'I'm visiting two schools early next term. Bob Morton was supportive at the Governors' meeting so I rang him up. He said by all means come and see what they've done so far. I'm also going to Beecham House in Buckinghamshire where I know the Head, James Telson - I used to work with him years ago. James's school has been doing this sort of thing for a few years now.'

Tom wondered whether the Governors would go along with this unbudgeted extra expenditure. Liz thought they would - especially if the inspection report was in the school's favour. Tom made a mental note to mention this to the inspection team.

For the staff, the Parents' Association Christmas Disco was an event either not to be missed or to be avoided at all costs, depending on one's point of view. Alastair was certainly looking forward to chatting up the attractive mums but some of the more mature ladies on the staff who were not into dressing up would manage to find previous engagements which would prevent them from attending. So far as the Headmaster was concerned there was no choice and it was assumed Tom would be going.

Actually, like Alastair, he was quite looking forward to it.

On the Saturday of the Disco the committee was busy transforming the austere decor of the gym into a Sixties theme and, to gain a few brownie points, Tom wandered along halfway through the morning to offer his services. When he walked into the gym, Valerie Hudson, who was directing operations, spotted him at once. 'Ah, Tom, you're just the person. We need a tall man - can you tie these balloons up to the top of the wall bars? Anita will help you.'

Virtue rewarded, Tom thought as he said a friendly hello to Anita. He hadn't seen her for a few days – not since he'd been round to her house in fact. She looked as good as ever.

'Well, come on - stop daydreaming.' Anita dug him in the ribs. 'Let's get on with it!'

The floor of the gym was littered with bits of material Valerie and her team were using to drape round the walls. A couple of competent-looking dads were setting up some flashing lights and on the stage stood a large trestle table where some battered-looking sound equipment was waiting to be connected and tested. At the other end of the room, nearest to the kitchens, more mothers were laying small tables. A basic meal plus plonk was to be provided, both included in the cost of the tickets.

Tom climbed up to the top of the wall bars while Anita passed him balloon after balloon and small pieces of string. 'So who or what are you dressing up as this evening?'

Tom hated dressing up and had been wondering what he was going to do for some time. He and Mike had been looking through the play cupboard's contents the day before and had found some wigs. 'I thought I might go as Mick Jagger - I've got a wig and an old pair of flares, but I need a suitable flowery shirt. I had thought of knocking on the Jagger front door,' (Mick actually owned a house not far from the school) 'but I don't think he would appreciate it!'

'I'm sure I could find you a shirt to wear - come back to the house when we've finished here and I'll look something out.'

Anita's boys, Ben and Charlie, had been kicking a ball around in the playground while they had been busy in the gym. Valerie looked with satisfaction around the room and said that that was all they could do for the moment and the helpers began to drift away. Anita gathered her twins together, said she'd see Tom in a minute and drove off.

Minutes later Tom was standing outside Anita's front door.

'Come in.'

The twins were playing some sort of card game on the floor and asked Tom if he'd like to play too. He said maybe later and followed Anita upstairs into what seemed to be the spare bedroom. Along one wall was a long cupboard jammed full of all sorts of dresses, tops and assorted shirts and sweaters.

'I see you have quite a collection, Anita!'

She looked at him.

'Huh. It's mainly junk. I should have got rid of most of it years ago. Now let's see what I can find.'

After a good deal of rummaging she held up two shirts, one pink and the other with a flower design. Would Mick Jagger be seen dead in either, Tom wondered. Almost certainly not. More to the point, could he fit into either of these garments?

'Right, off with your shirt and try this one on.'

She sounded just like a prep school matron.

'I doubt I'll be able to fill this as well as you could,' Tom muttered to himself, struggling to get his arms through the sleeves. The first shirt was no good but the other, the pink one, was cut more generously and didn't look too bad - he removed the shirt and folded it up. From downstairs the boys shouted up - were they coming down? Anita just looked at Tom, her lips slightly moist as she shouted back, 'Yes, just coming, boys.'

The four of them spent the rest of the afternoon playing 'one-eyed jack' on the living room carpet. Tom was quite looking forward to the evening.

The Disco turned out to be extremely lively - most of the parents who came were too young to remember the Sixties but they certainly knew their music and entered into the swing of things. Not too many of the staff came even though they had been offered half-price tickets as a staff concession. Some viewed any contact with parents as being 'on duty' and avoided these occasions like the plague. Pity, really, since hardly any parents discussed their children at these functions.

Mike was there, of course. He had found some round dark glasses and was trying to look like John Lennon. Alison Hitchcock was wearing a very short mini skirt and was much in demand from the younger fathers able to slip away from their wives for a quick bop. Alison did have a boyfriend but he was a junior doctor and was on duty at the local hospital that evening. The Head of Maths, Janet Salter and her husband came along - rather surprisingly, Tom thought. Not exactly trendy, Janet was a very sound teacher - a bit dull perhaps but very thorough. She had a friendly round face with glasses, which in class would perch on the end of her nose and she would peer over them at pupils who were not paying attention. She had a tendency to wear the same dark blue skirt for too many days at a time. Her husband was a local government officer - he worked in the local planning department and was sporting a ghastly purple shirt and orange kipper tie. They seemed determined to enjoy themselves. Alastair, who was not one to miss a party, turned up carrying a clarinet and dressed as Akker Bilk.

'Hallo, strangers on the shore.' He made a feeble attempt at humour.

He plonked a bottle of wine down on the table the staff had gravitated to. Mike immediately operated on it with a corkscrew.

The Disco was being run by two stalwart fathers, Jonathan Hudson, husband of the PA chairperson Valerie, and Geoff Bane, another member of the Committee. They had organised a slide projector to show a sequence of Sixties images on a sheet stretched across the back of the stage - where their slides came from was a mystery but they were most effective. The loud music, flashing lights and wafts of smoke from the artificial smoke machine encouraged everyone to relax and get onto the dance floor.

Mike and Tom spent much of the evening doing their duty - dancing with the mothers on the PA Committee and then with those who had other charms. Tom didn't get together with Anita until later. They were dancing – but not too close.

'Well, Tommy,' she whispered in his ear, 'and where have you been all evening?'

'I haven't been called Tommy since I was a little boy.'

Tom attempted a cool rock and roll move and promptly trod on her toes.

They enjoyed a rationed (by Tom's reckoning) five minutes or so on the dance floor. One must spread one's time around the customers at this sort of public do, he felt.

'I'll see you later - duty calls,' and Tom reluctantly disentangled himself from Anita's arms.

As the evening came to an end Tom grabbed the microphone and thanked Valerie and her Committee for a wonderful party. There was a burst of applause and then people started to drift away. Anita's next-door neighbours, also parents, were taking her home. Pity, thought Tom. That was a job he would have enjoyed doing himself!

The last event of the autumn term was the Carol Service. The school used the local parish church as there wasn't enough room for all the parents and children at school. It was a fairly traditional affair with well-known carols and seven lessons read by children and staff alike. Elizabeth Wade and the choir had been practising for weeks and the readers had been chosen by the English teachers. There was Patrick Leary, aged six, from the pre-prep. He was a pretty-looking fair-haired boy with a lilting Irish accent who certainly caused the mums to sigh as they listened to his clear voice. Mary Lomax was a very confident girl from Year Four who could be heard clearly even at the back of the church. Clare Beamish in Year Six was a studious sensible girl. She was a librarian and not too confident - she had had to be persuaded to read the fourth lesson by her class teacher, but she had a clear strong voice. Finally there was Daniel Foster, the Head boy. He also was not keen to do the job but accepted that it was part of his duties and he had practised conscientiously. The other readers were Eileen Trammer, Penny Jones and Tom. The rehearsal the previous day had been a bit of a shambles because the microphone was not working properly and the seating arrangements had taken a long time to organise. Mike was in charge of directing children and staff into their places.

All were looking forward to the end of term, but it was important that this last event went well. The children had been warned of the dire consequences of any poor behaviour, but as it happened it was the parents who needed chastising! Whilst the choir was singing one of their 'choir only' carols a couple of parents stood up and started to take flash photographs. Not only that but during the last lesson, read somewhat nervously by Tom, a father's mobile phone rang and instead of switching it off immediately he spent a couple of minutes instructing his stockbroker on what to buy and sell. This was not appreciated one bit by his neighbours. Tom resolved to include a paragraph on behaviour during the carol service next year in one of his letters to parents.

The end of Tom's first term came not a moment too soon!

Chapter Four

It was January and Tom and Mike were having their usual chat before the start of school.

'I'm afraid you'll have to have a word in Robin Bartlett's ear.' Mike was looking rather worried 'You know he's started some private tuition in maths for a few of the girls in Year Six?'

All the girls in that year were doing various entrance exams for their next schools in a few weeks' time. Some less confident girls were entered for at least five different schools - and each girls' secondary school in this part of London set their own style of exam, which they believed appropriate for the type of girl they wished to attract. This meant that instead of just one common exam (like the Common Entrance used at the ages of eleven and thirteen by almost all schools outside London, plus the boys' schools in London) the girls had to troop off to different schools on various days to try their luck. It was a bit of a cattle market!

This system caused parents huge worries regarding their daughters' capabilities and their chances of being offered a place at the school of their choice. It was said that the local consumption of gin increased markedly during January and February in West London!

Tom had heard that some parents had asked Robin to give their daughters extra maths coaching before the exam season got under way. Robin, being a very presentable good-looking chap, had gone down well with the mothers.

'Well,' continued Mike, 'he's teaching Karen Rowe on Mondays after school and he may be getting a little too familiar with her. I heard them in Karen's classroom as I was walking past last night. First of all the door was shut and then when I went in Robin had his arm on her shoulder. I am quite sure it was perfectly innocent but you know the dangers.'

Tom knew indeed. When he had first started teaching, nobody saw any harm in putting your arm around a pupil to encourage, praise or comfort him or her. It was accepted that teachers would act rather like parents on occasion and parents themselves were very happy with this. Nowadays of course, with the media gleefully publicising as many suspected child abuse cases as they could find and thereby increasing their circulation, teachers had to be extremely careful not to put themselves in any position where they could possibly be accused of any impropriety.

Karen Rowe was in fact the sort of girl who might be at risk; although only just eleven she looked a good deal older. She was a pretty, fair-haired girl, very popular with everyone and always smiling. She was a very promising games player and had been appointed captain of the netball team. In the classroom she was not so strong and Tom knew her parents were very keen for her to gain a place at the very popular local girls only school where competition was stiff - hence Robin's lessons.

'Okay, Mike, thanks for letting me know - I'll certainly have a word.'

Later that morning Tom found Robin - he was tidying up the library after a fairly disorganised lesson by one of the Year Four teachers - and asked him to come and have a word for a moment in the study.

'Robin, I'm very pleased you are doing a bit of maths coaching with some of the girls - how's it going?'

'Fine, I think, though one or two are certainly going to struggle a bit - Karen Rowe has no idea about fractions!'

'Well, keep up the good work, but I just wanted to have a word about the dangers teachers face these days. You never know what children or parents may say. What I mean is, you must never allow anyone the chance to accuse you of getting too close to the children. That means you must not actually touch a child when you are alone with them - it just might be misconstrued. I'm quite sure there is no problem at all in your case but you do need to be careful.'

Robin, who had two younger sisters himself, looked pretty appalled at the necessity of this discussion but took it rather well.

'Yes, of course, I quite understand. I just didn't think.'

The poor fellow's face had turned a little pink but it had to be said. As he left, Tom added, 'One more thing, Robin; if you are doing one to one coaching you must leave the door of the room open so that people walking past can see what's going on - it's an extra safeguard. That's why our music practice rooms have glass windows. By the way, I was watching your football game yesterday with the under tens - it was great - well done!'

'Oh thanks - I enjoyed it! But I'm not sure I want to be a teacher when I qualify!'

Robin departed, still a bit pink but beaming.

Generally speaking, the teachers left the school buildings as soon as possible at the end of the day. Most had wives or husbands to look after so books to be marked would be taken home and dealt with later that evening. Alastair, not being married, wasn't one of these - he would potter around the school getting ready for the following day, doing a bit of marking and sometimes giving one of his pupils a bit of extra tuition.

Tom, doing his lockup duty one night, found Alastair busy in his classroom marking a pile of exercise books.

'Ah, hallo, Tom. As you can see I'm not quite finished here yet.'

Alastair was not one to shirk hard work and his marking was always up to date; that was not to say his lessons were planned in advance because Alastair refused to be tied down by 'red tape', i.e. the syllabus, and he taught what he felt was right on the day. His pupils were seldom bored - they were lucky.

'I thought you might be out for a quiet supper tonight.' Alastair looked at Tom. 'I hope you aren't letting the grass grow under your feet!'

'What do you mean, Alastair?' Tom coloured slightly.

'You know - that Mrs Wolff - she's a charming lady. Don't miss out. You must know she's pretty keen on you!'

'Yes, she's very easy to get on with.' Tom nodded in agreement.

'Well, my advice is - go for it, she's very good news. Anyway, enough of my prattling - I think I'll take the rest of these books home and leave you to lock up.'

Tom wished him goodnight and finished the locking up. Alastair was right, Anita was quite special.

It was nearly halfway through the spring term. How nice it was to escape from school for a day, thought Tom. It was the day he had arranged to visit two other prep schools to see how they were introducing design technology into their curriculum. Bob Morton, one of the Governors, had invited Tom to visit The Wyvern School just outside Oxford in the morning and in the afternoon he was off to Beecham House in Buckinghamshire where his old friend and colleague James Telson was Head.

Tom's red BMW was soon on the M40 and he took the opportunity of putting his foot down. Fortunately there was an absence of flashing blue lights to slow him down and he arrived at his first appointment ten minutes early. He proceeded cautiously through the gates and down the long drive - it was a calm, crisp morning and the bare trees on either side of the driveway were motionless and covered in white frost. In front of the main door of the school was a large parking area. Tom spotted Bob Morton's treasured Alvis, polished and gleaming, with its nose up against the creeper that grew up the old stone wall of the building. This was an old-fashioned looking place; with still quite a few boarders and it was said that Bob ran the place with a rod of iron.

A sign by the door said 'Please ring and enter' so Tom did. He stood in the hall looking around. In front of him was a wide staircase leading, no doubt, to the dormitories. There was a strong smell of floor polish combined with a faint odour of cabbage. It smelt like a school!

The school secretary appeared and showed Tom to a small waiting room amply supplied with copies of The Field and Country Life. Shortly afterwards Bob arrived accompanied by a dapper little man in a brown lab coat.

Bob vigorously shook hands with Tom. 'How very nice to see you, Tom. I hope you'll excuse me not spending too much time with you but I've some parents waiting to see me. This is Steve Barker who runs our design technology department. I'll hand you over to him for the morning and then we can meet up again at lunchtime.'

Steve Barker, it appeared, had been teaching Latin and Greek for many years but was also a keen DIY person. When the chance to set up a new department came he had been quick to volunteer and Bob, knowing he was an adaptable sort of person, had given him carte blanche to set things up. Steve was clearly a great enthusiast and he led Tom eagerly towards his workshop.

In the first session some older pupils were attempting to make a crane capable of lifting a 200 gram weight. The materials allowed were quite limited and included some wheels, cardboard, wood and string. Most pairs (they usually worked in twos or threes, Steve informed him) had completed their design stage and were moving on to the construction. Tom was struck by how quiet everyone was - they were all concentrating on what they were doing and although now and again a pair would ask Steve for some advice they were mostly able to work without help. The ninety-minute session passed very quickly.

Steve offered Tom some sound advice. 'One thing you must plan for is enough space for storage - you can't have enough of it; otherwise things get lost or broken.'

After the morning break Steve had a younger class who were designing shapes on which to fit a battery-operated clock mechanism (these were supplied, working). After many hours of work, the pupils' individually designed clocks would be taken home and occupy pride of place in their owners' bedrooms! Steve went round gently making suggestions where necessary and toning down some of the more extravagant or impractical ideas. Quite quickly these children too moved onto the construction stage.

Tom made a note of what equipment and textbooks Steve used along with the general size and layout of the room. We really must start doing this sort of thing soon, he thought as he thanked Steve warmly for his time.

After a pleasant lunch and a short cross-country drive Tom arrived at James's school, Beecham House. James immediately said he would hand Tom over to a young teacher, Tracy Cupp, who would look after him and show him what they had been doing.

The unfortunately named Tracy turned out to be a quite delightful and pretty young girl. Newly qualified, she was bursting with energy and very keen to show Tom what they did. Apparently they had a parent working in an engineering business nearby who had persuaded his company to sponsor the expansion of their technology department; they had paid for new computers and some equipment for working with plastics. Tom wondered if Shaftesbury could do the same.

He looked with awe at some of the objects Tracy's pupils had made. There were ingenious puzzles made out of plastic, computer-controlled cranes and various other electrical gadgets, all designed and put together by her pupils. Tom plied her with questions.

Later James joined them for tea.

'So, how did you get on, Tom?'

'I've really had a most interesting time.' Tom could certainly say that truthfully. 'I've been very well looked after by Tracy here and have learnt a lot.'

He rather reluctantly said thank you and goodbye and headed off back to London arriving at Shaftesbury Prep just as the children were leaving. He stopped by the gate to watch them go.

'Had a nice day, Mr Thorne?' One harassed mother collecting her children spoke to him as she piled them into their Renault Espace.

'Couldn't be better, thank you, Mrs Tench.' Tom did not mention that he hadn't been at school all day. He headed home to jot down the ideas running through his head and made a mental note to organise a meeting to discuss his findings.

The next morning at 8.30, just as teachers and children were beginning to arrive at school, the phone rang. It was Alastair, who sounded upset.

'I'm terribly sorry but I've been told by my doctor that I have to go into hospital for a series of tests. I've been having these pains in my back recently and, well, Doctor Walker doesn't know what's wrong but he says I must go into The West Middlesex straight away. I'll have to be off school for a few days, maybe more. I know it's a bad time with the scholarship exams coming up soon but it can't be helped.'

'I'm extremely sorry, Alastair. Is there anything we can do? What about getting to hospital? Do you have transport?' Alastair had seemed in very good form recently, so this was a bit of a bombshell.

'No, it's OK. My sister is coming up from Kent to keep an eye on me. I'll let you know as soon as I can what's happened.'

'Good luck, Alastair.' Tom put the phone down thinking hard.

There were six scholarship candidates taking various exams this term and good performances in Latin were often crucial. Alastair's pupils in the past had done well and his absence from the classroom for a week or two would not be good.

He discussed this with Mike later that morning. Mike did know a retired teacher who might help out but she was away on holiday just at the moment. He'd leave a message on her answer phone. Tom also rang up a teaching agency the school sometimes used but they were not very helpful. Latin, they said - we don't get much call for that subject these days.

Mike drafted an ad for the local paper and then started to re-organise Alastair's timetable so that his scholarship lessons were at least covered by another specialist teacher who could do extra maths, science or French.

The dreaded inspection was due to start shortly and would last for three long nerve-wracking days. Barbara, Mike and Tom had already compiled heaps of documents they needed and put the information onto disks ready to be sent off to the inspection leader. There was still some information which hadn't been collected yet - hardly surprisingly this included the Latin schemes of work which Alastair had not yet finished. Tom would have to 'borrow' something suitable to fill the gaps from his old friend Mark who was Head at another prep school in Surrey; Mark had just finished going through an inspection - without enjoying the experience. Time at the next staff meeting would have to be spent briefing everyone on what to expect and a few days later all were ready and waiting in the staff room at 4.15.

'Firstly I'd like to thank you all for producing schemes of work and the various policies we have been asked for. There are one or two things I still require, but I'll see those people separately. I can now tell you that we have a team of five Inspectors gracing us with their presence. They will be here from Monday March 10th for three days. The leader is a full time Inspector of Schools called Peter Withey. I don't know much about him – he'll be coming to the school for a preliminary visit on his own on Wednesday 19th February. The others are all current prep school Heads. There's Margaret Hale - she's the Head of a girls' prep school in Oxford and will look at the pre-prep and also music. John Wallis is the Head of Grange Hall in Norfolk - he's a good chap, I know him and he'll be looking at maths and science. Henry Beer is a well-known prep school Head. His school is Boscombe House in Hampshire - he will look at our English, history, geography and RE. Lastly there is Felicity Grune (not groan!) Head of a school in Wiltshire. She will inspect our French, art and PE and games.'

Here there was a groan from Simon who was not impressed with the idea of his sport being inspected by a woman!

Tom continued. 'I'm sure they will all be charming and helpful. Try to remember they will be here to help us and not to try and catch us out.'

This did not convince the staff who were clearly not looking forward to having someone sitting in with their classes.

'We must have all programmes of study up to date and in the file in the staff room and, for that week at least, we will have to have lesson plans for each lesson ready to show them.'

If Alastair had been there, he would certainly have asked what on earth they were! Tom wondered if he would be back at school in time to be inspected.

Jane Lussac was the first to speak up. 'How much detail do we need to put into our lesson plans? I often change what I'm doing depending on how the lesson goes.'

It was eventually decided to produce an in-house form of lesson plan - it had headings such as 'aims', 'resources needed', 'introduction', 'method', 'possible extensions' and 'evaluation'. Staff could fill in and adapt as necessary.

The meeting eventually broke up, somewhat gloomily.

Tom had been working out the best way to introduce design technology and went along to Liz's Bursar's Office for a discussion on the content of a paper he was preparing on the subject. Bursar's Office was a rather grand title for what was really not much more than a cubbyhole at the end of a dark corridor. There was just enough room for a small desk flanked by a computer, a couple of chairs for visitors and a large filing cabinet. One wall was completely taken up by shelves filled with files and the window looked out onto the street. Liz was not one to complain as in some ways it suited her - being at the end of a corridor meant the children did not rush past between lessons, so it was quiet. Also she could keep an eye on people coming and going through the main door of the building. Liz liked to know what was going on and often used to pass on useful snippets of information she had gleaned on her travels around the school.

Tom told her how his visit to the schools had gone the previous week and they wondered which parents might be useful as sponsors. Liz had seen Charles Mason, the manager of Astley's, the firm which did most of the school's minor building works and he had given her a quote for the structural alterations needed - this included quite a bit of electrical work to provide power for both tools and computers. Tom left after an hour with enough information to prepare a draft plan – which, once agreed, they'd send to the Governors in time for the meeting later in the term.

Chapter Five

The girls' secondary school exam season was about to begin. This was a nightmare for children, parents and prep school teachers but considered essential by all the local girls' secondary schools. Each school would set its own exam on a particular day and any girl who was going to be eleven by the following September 1st could enter. This meant that popular schools which might have say sixty places for the following September could have two hundred and fifty or so candidates sitting their exam. The top sixty would be offered places and the next forty or so put on a waiting list. The rest would not be offered places; some parents would not be too surprised but others would be devastated. Most girls would sit several of these exams and the more able ones would be in the enviable position of turning down second choices. The school's job was to prepare the girls as well as possible, sometimes trying to persuade parents of less able girls to aim for more realistic choices. All schools set papers in maths, English and some sort of verbal reasoning. Many also interviewed the girls they thought they might offer places to - this was often a crucial part of the selection process.

Mary Teale, one of the Year Six teachers, was in charge of girls' entries. This involved writing reports, talking to parents and completing all the necessary paperwork required. She also ran mock interviews for the girls to get them used to the type of questions they might be asked by scary Headmistresses!

Mary was a rather meek and mild-looking lady - at rising forty she had rather given up the idea of getting married. This was a pity really for she had a petite figure and liquid brown eyes that could certainly have enticed the right man. But now she had come to terms with that, she concentrated on 'her girls' of whom she was extremely fond. They in turn recognised her commitment and liked and respected her.

This morning she was giving her usual chat to all those poor girls who were due to sit exams during the next month or so. Tom went along and sat at the back of her classroom.

'So, make sure that you are tidy. There's nothing worse than a shirt hanging out or hair all over the place. It gives a very bad impression. And don't forget to clean your shoes - Mrs Wood at St Catherine's always looks and, by the way, she may ask you who cleaned your shoes - don't say your mother!'

A feeble tittering went round the anxious faces of the sixteen girls perched on desks. They swung their legs and shifted their bottoms as she went on, 'Now, quite a few of you will be asked for interviews. They usually ask the same sort of question so be prepared. Things such as what is your favourite book or what do you like doing in your spare time. For goodness sake, don't say some book you have not read or can't remember and don't say you like watching "Neighbours" on television even if that's all you do do at home!'

'Miss Teale?' A small hand went up. 'Could I say that I go to dancing lessons – they're not at school - and would it be boastful to say I won a cup last year?'

'Of course not, Rachel, you should certainly mention

anything that you are interested in and of course say what you have achieved. But do it modestly. It will impress the interviewer. Be confident. Who's going for The Lady Jane School?'

Several hands went up.

'Well, the Headmistress, Mrs Rosse, who as you may know is one of our Governors, always asks questions to do with the Royal Family. So you had better know the names of the Queen's children and where her houses are. She probably won't ask you the name of your favourite pop group!'

Pity, thought Rachel and her friends. Tom quietly slipped away leaving Mary in full flow.

Most parents Tom had come across so far were easy to deal with and generally charming but there were others who were the opposite; Mr Summers turned out to be one of this minority. Tom had heard from the staff that he could be difficult. He was a lecturer at the local further education college and was very ambitious for David, his only son. David was a very able boy in his last year and would shortly be sitting the scholarship exam for St Peter's. Precisely on time for his appointment he came in to the office and shook hands coldly. Tom smelt trouble.

'Good morning, Mr Summers. What can I do for you?'

Mr Summers settled himself carefully in the chair opposite. He was a wiry small man in his early forties. His hair was grizzled and wispy and his face pinched. He did not smile very often.

'Yes, Mr Thorne, I wonder if you can tell me what you are doing about the absence of your Latin teacher? My son, David, is taking a scholarship exam very soon and this cannot be doing his chances any good. My wife and

I are really most concerned.'

Tom sighed inwardly. 'As you know, Mr Begg has had to go to hospital for some tests. We are not sure how serious it is and I don't know when he will be returning. I very much share your concerns and am trying to find a temporary replacement - but that is not easy. There are not many Latin teachers available at short notice, though we do know of someone who may be able to help us out in a week or two when she returns from holiday.'

Mr Summers looked at Tom stonily.

'Meanwhile, in the short term we have re-organised David's timetabled Latin classes so that he and the rest of his group are doing profitable work in other subjects.'

This did not seem to satisfy Mr Summers and he went on to say that it was the school's responsibility to prepare pupils properly for important exams. Tom assured him that the school was trying to do just that. It was a relief when he could finally usher him out into the corridor.

'That man is not my favourite parent!' Tom looked at Barbara. 'We are doing what we can about Alastair.'

'Ah, yes,' said Barbara, 'that teacher Mike knows rang just now. She is back from holiday and says she might be prepared to take over Alastair's Latin for a few weeks. Shall I get her on the line?'

'Definitely! Right now please, Barbara. What's her name?'

Unfortunately, it was not long before another problem appeared. Mike put his head around the door in a bit of a panic.

'Where's Paul? He hasn't turned up this morning and no one seems to know where he is. I've had to cover his classes until break. I'm not happy with him at all.'

Paul had been sailing quite close to the wind recently and Tom wondered if this would give him the opportunity to dispense with his services at last. He certainly hoped so.

'Make a careful note in your records please, Mike. We may need evidence!'

Mike went away grumbling. Ten minutes later he returned.

'Would you believe it!' Mike, normally a very even-tempered person, was spitting with rage. 'I've just had a phone call from Paul. He says he's frightfully sorry but his car's broken down and he'll be in after lunch. I don't believe him - I distinctly heard people ordering pints of bitter in the background. He's in a pub somewhere. Bloody nerve!'

Tom shook his head slowly. 'I'm not surprised, but we can't prove it very easily. I'll talk to him when he comes in.'

Just after lunch Paul appeared. He didn't seem at all worried and greeted Tom affably.

'Oh, hallo, old boy. Frightfully sorry to be late. Car broke down - I came as soon as I could. Who's been looking after my classes? I must buy them a beer.'

'Paul, have you been drinking? Mike says you called him from a pub.'

'Well, yes actually, I did have to walk to the nearest pub to make a phone call but I'll be fine for this afternoon's classes. Don't worry.'

'What's happened to your car? How did you get here?'

'I was lucky. There was a chap from the local garage at the pub and he sorted me out. The car's going fine now.

And there was no charge. Just had to buy him a pint or two!'

With that Paul departed, as he called it 'to educate', leaving Tom grinding his teeth.

Batches of Year Six girls had been away all week, taking various entrance exams. Mary came in to see Tom with a final list of which girls were sitting for which schools and their preferences. She was flustered - a normal condition at this time of year according to Barbara.

'Some of these parents are being too optimistic. I've tried to put some of them off when their daughters really are unlikely to be offered a place at the difficult schools, but they won't listen. It's tough for some of the girls.'

Tom sighed. 'Well, don't worry. You can but try - and the same goes for the girls. It's a pity the schools can't agree on one common exam and then make their offers on the basis of that instead of insisting the girls go off to each school one after the other.'

They spent some time looking through the list and working out how to deal with those parents likely to be difficult if their daughters didn't get the desired offers.

Tom continued to enjoy Saturday morning games. On this crisp, clear February day there were about forty boys out on the soccer field practising in different age groups as well as a couple of home matches against other schools. It was a pity that Alastair was still away. Robin Bartlett had taken over his second eleven soccer team with great enthusiasm, though not with quite the same motivational skills as their usual coach. Meanwhile the girls were playing netball on the school playground. A goodly sprinkling of fathers were walking briskly up and down the touchlines shouting encouragement and thinking how lucky they were that they had a good excuse not to go shopping with their wives. As matches and other games came to an end the children were scooped up and removed with many a 'well played' and 'good game' being exchanged by the adults. It was a jolly atmosphere.

Mike and Tom went back to Tom's house to have a spot to eat and watch England playing Wales at rugby on TV. Mike, although an Australian, supported Wales - some distant cousin was born in Cardiff. Being a true blue Englishman, Tom, of course, supported England.

Just as the whistle went for the kick-off, the front doorbell rang. Tom swore briefly and went out to see who was disturbing them. A smartly dressed woman stood on the step outside. Tom knew she was a parent but couldn't place her.

'Ah, Mr Thorne. We have just had a very disappointing letter from St Margaret's - Karen has not been offered a place and is only on the waiting list.'

Tom realised it was Karen Rowe's mother - normally a very pleasant and placid lady; she didn't look too placid right now though!

'Oh dear, I am sorry. I did hear that there were many more candidates than usual for St Margaret's this year. I expect there will be some girls who have been offered places who won't take them up so Karen should not lose hope.'

'Couldn't you ring up now and say how keen we are for Karen to be offered a place? We'd certainly take it. Also you could say what else she has to offer, such as sport.'

You certainly could not fault Mrs Rowe for enthusiasm - or nerve for that matter.

Tom was tempted to say that he was occupied with some very important business, but just at that point a roar came from the television as a try was scored. Mrs Rowe looked over his shoulder in a disapproving fashion.

Hastily Tom said, 'I am sure there will be nobody to talk to until Monday, Mrs Rowe. Don't worry, I'll ring first thing on Monday morning. Of course, I will speak very highly of Karen - she certainly has a great deal to offer.'

With that Mrs Rowe retreated and Tom went back to the serious business of watching Wales lose again!

Results from the various girls' schools exams were beginning to come through and no doubt telephone wires were humming between the competing sets of parents. Tom hoped that the school would not come in for too much flak, but some would be inevitable. Following up his promise to Mrs Rowe, he rang St Margaret's and rather surprisingly the Headmistress was not in a meeting and was prepared to talk to him.

'I am very sorry to bother you, Mrs Reed, and I know how busy you must be, but I did promise one of my parents that I would call you. A girl called Karen Rowe sat your entrance exam the other day and was not offered a place - I think she is on your waiting list. I'm sure that you will have had lots of excellent candidates, but I did say to her mother that I'd put in a good word for Karen - she is very good value. I hope you don't mind me ringing.'

Tom realised he was speaking in an ingratiating manner. He didn't know Diane Reed very well but she was known as a tough and capable Head who was extremely anxious to move her school further up the league tables; it was already high enough to make it one of the most popular secondary independents in West London.

'Oh, Mr Thorne, don't worry, I quite understand you are in a difficult position. In fact, as you may have heard, we have had many more applications this year and only the usual number of places to offer. I can't offhand remember exactly where Karen came in our lists but I think I can say there's a reasonable chance that she might be offered a place when we get replies to our definite offers back in a couple of weeks - but don't for goodness sake make any promises to Mrs Rowe!'

'Of course not! Thank you very much for talking to me - my duty's done!' And he rang off to make a quick call to Mrs Rowe. She was guardedly grateful.

Mike and Tom were wondering how they could get Janet Salter to run an after-school club. It was generally accepted by all members of the teaching staff that everyone would make some contribution of this kind after the school day had finished. All new staff had been appointed on that understanding - it was always discussed and made clear at their interviews. However some of the longer serving staff, like Janet, who had been employed just to teach a specific subject were none too keen to extend their day. Janet also had for years run the school skiing trip in the Easter holidays; this obviously needed a good deal of time and effort to organise and she rather felt that was her contribution to 'after-school activities' for the year. Since she got a free skiing holiday out of it the rest of the staff didn't quite see it that way. There was a dry ski slope opening shortly nearby and so Mike and Tom decided to try to get her to take some children along on a weekly basis during the winter.

Mike ran a squash club after school - he was a very useful player himself. One of the parents owned a sports club down the road and Mike had persuaded him to let the school use their three courts up till 5.30 pm when the members would begin to arrive wanting to work off their office frustrations. Tom ran a photographic club - rather cushy really because although the school had a darkroom next to the science labs it was small and you could only take three or four pupils at a time. It was well-equipped with a sink, plenty of shelving for storing chemicals and trays and a large work surface illuminated by a darkroom lamp. On the work surface was an ancient but reliable enlarger. Someone had donated an old camera and the children would go round the school taking shots until the film was finished. The members would then retire to the darkroom and develop the film, hanging up the strip of negatives to dry until the following week when they would attempt to enlarge and print selected shots. It was a slow process but the children seemed to enjoy themselves and eventually produced some reasonable results.

It was decided that Tom would speak to Janet at the first opportune moment.

One evening Tom was fully engrossed in the photographic club; there were three keen young photographers - Esta Kegode, a very lively girl from Zimbabwe who was full of fun, together with Ben and Charlie, Anita Wolff's boys. There was a gymnastics training session going on in the hall after school and some of Esta's friends were involved. Esta suggested taking some action shots so they trooped off to try and take some pictures. The photographers were not too popular - the girls did not want to be photographed by the boys and the few boys taking part were not happy with Esta. So Ben and Charlie took some shots of the boys and Esta snapped away at the girls doing exercises on the mat. After twenty minutes they retired to the darkroom and the three of them managed without too much help to develop the film. They looked at the dripping strip of negative - surprisingly most of the shots were in focus and with good contrast; they'd be able to print a few at the next session.

For those boys and girls at the older end of the school Valentine's Day was an important day. In general the girls were terribly keen to be sent Valentine cards, even if they were from other girls but the boys varied. As expected, Rachel Billington, a tall good-looking girl, who was much admired by the older boys, had collected quite a pile of cards. On the other hand, James Bland, (who incidentally was doing very well in class, having been promoted just as his mother had wanted) was most put out to receive a rather sloppy card from the brightest girl in his form. She thought he was rather sweet and actually said so on the card. The other boys had looked over his shoulder and seen what had been written - they wouldn't let James forget that for a while!

Later that day Tom was standing by the gate watching the children stream out towards waiting parents. Thank goodness it was the end of the week.

A voice from behind made him jump. 'Well, Mr Headmaster, I bet you got lots of Valentine cards today!'

It was Anita Wolff, carrying two school bags and a pair of football boots. Her two lazy sons were still in the changing room arguing with a friend.

'Actually, no, Anita. Too old for that, I fear.' Tom laughed.

'I wouldn't say that! By the way, the boys are frightfully keen on photography - they say they have taken some good pictures - maybe you could teach me as well?'

'Of course, I'd be happy to show you what we do. We'll fix a time.'

Anita appeared to be very eager. 'Okay, next week maybe? The boys are out on a sleepover on Thursday night; what about that evening?'

'Fine.' Tom was already looking forward to it!

The following Thursday Mr Withey, leader of the inspection team, was expected for his preliminary visit. He arrived spot on time, shook Tom briskly by the hand and got straight down to business. Tom quickly realised this was not a man to waste time, nor was he too bothered about small talk. His dark suit was neatly pressed and his white shirt and blue tie immaculate. He wore rimless glasses through which his grey eyes regarded Tom steadily.

'Now first of all, Mr Thorne, I'd like to get our domestic arrangements clear. Am I right in understanding that you have booked us into the Lime Tree Hotel for Sunday, Monday and Tuesday nights?'

Tom confirmed this to be the case. Inspections were not cheap and on top of the fee payable (based on the number of children of each age group in the school) the extras consisting of hotel bills, meals and travelling expenses made up a considerable cost to be paid.

'We'll need a room in the school for ourselves - which preferably should be lockable - where we'll keep all our books and documents. And could tea and coffee be available whenever we want it - if that's possible?'

These Inspectors were certainly keen to get their comforts sorted out, Tom thought.

'Yes, we can certainly arrange that. Will you be working late at night? I ask because I will need to arrange for someone to lock up after you have gone.' Tom was informed that the Inspectors would be finished at the school by ten o'clock each evening and would then continue working at their hotel.

Mr Withey then asked to be shown around the school. He had with him the plan which had already been sent to him and, as they progressed, he made notes. Tom introduced him to as many of the staff as he could and eventually they returned to the study. Mr Withey said little on his tour and Tom decided he didn't take to the man.

Once settled back into their chairs Mr Withey pulled out his notebook again.

'Mr Thorne, tell me, what do you feel are the strengths and weaknesses of the school? I know you've not been here for long, but you must have formed some impressions by now.'

Tom thought very hard before replying. 'Well, the school is financially quite strong and has a good academic reputation - I think the teaching is generally sound. We could always do with a few younger members of staff, though. I think we should boost the sport a bit - it should be stronger and our facilities are not great. The other thing we could do is extend the range of subjects available - in particular I'm thinking of design technology, which we don't do here at the moment. I'd like to introduce that as soon as possible.'

Mr Withey nodded, Tom hoped in agreement.

He stood up to leave. 'Very well, thank you for your time. I'll see you again on the tenth of March. I think we have everything we need, but if not I'll call you. Goodbye.'

With that he strode off to his smart Rover parked outside.

The time had come to approach Janet Salter regarding after-school activities. Tom spied her marching off home with a pile of exercise books to be marked under her arm. She was not keen to be delayed - and who could blame her.

'Janet, could you spare a moment?'

'I've got people coming to dinner tonight and I need to do some shopping.'

'It won't take a moment, just a couple of things.'

Somewhat reluctantly Janet reversed, followed Tom into his office and settled herself in one of the chairs in the study. Tom started by trying to sweet-talk her a bit.

'I was looking at some of the Common Entrance boys' maths books the other day - they were most impressive; I'm sure the Inspectors will like what they see.'

Janet's face softened a bit and she actually smiled.

'Yes, I'm pleased with that lot - they work well and have made good progress this year. They were quite behind, you know.'

Tom broached the thorny subject of after school activities. 'Janet, I see that they are opening a new dry ski school in Hampton - do you think it would be a good idea to take some children along so that they can get off to a flying start on your ski trip? It might be possible to arrange for a regular time each week after school.'

'Well, Tom, I do have quite a lot of commitments after school, you know. I have to keep an eye on my mother who is getting on now and needs help - she can't drive any more. But I will look into your idea and see whether I could fit it in. Leave it with me for the moment.'

That, Tom thought, would probably be as far as we would get. So much for union-minded teachers. Still, he had better things to look forward to that evening.

By six o'clock everyone had gone home, the cleaners had finished their work and Tom was in the study drafting a tricky letter to some parents who had complained about the food provided for their daughter who seemed to be allergic to most school meals. The front doorbell rang. It was Anita who had come to learn what secrets the darkroom had to offer.

'Come along in.' Tom cast his eye appreciatively over her. She was holding a couple of envelopes in her hand. 'What have you got there?'

'These are some old negatives I thought we could enlarge. Come on then, where's the darkroom?'

They made their way through the empty building, turning on lights as they went. The darkroom was on the first floor.

'Let's have a look at your negatives. Which ones do you want to print?'

Trying hard to ignore the closeness of Anita's trim figure, Tom filled two trays with developer and fixer and then showed her how to hold the negative in place in the top part of the enlarger. He switched on the bulb, which threw the enlarged image of the negative onto the baseboard. Moving the enlarger head further up the supporting column made the image much bigger. They adjusted the focus. The photograph was of Ben and

Charlie standing in front of what looked like a waterfall. Anita was impressed.

She breathed close to his ear. 'Wow, that's great. Can we cut out that tree on the left?'

They fiddled about with the composition and then checked that the focus was as sharp as possible. With only the faint orange glow from the safelight illuminating the room they placed the photographic paper carefully onto the baseboard and switched the enlarger bulb on for a few seconds. Then the paper went quickly into the developer tray until the faces of Ben and Charlie stared clearly up at them; a quick wash and then into the fixer. They had both been concentrating so hard on what they were doing that they hadn't noticed that elbows and hips had been making gentle contact.

'I think that is an excellent result.' Anita looked at the watery faces of her two boys in the fixer. 'I enjoyed that.'

'So did I.' Tom slid his arm around her waist. 'We should do this more often!'

They didn't do any more photography that evening.

Chapter Six

The postman usually delivered early so Tom was able to look through the mail well before school started. Most of it was mail shots from educational companies trying to sell something or get the school to join some scheme or other and government bumph full of regulations and requirements about equal opportunities, health and safety and so on. Tom tried to throw as much as possible straight into the waste paper basket.

Hand written letters from parents however had to be treated gingerly and opened with care. One Tom opened was a bit rich to say the least.

'Dear Mr Thorne,' it read, *'I understand from Stephen that you are currently testing potential new seven-year-old children for entry next September into Stephen's year. While I appreciate that you wish to expand the school I would like to point out that our son joined the school at the age of four and has made very good progress both academically and socially. My wife and I are concerned that an influx of children from the state sector might dilute the quality of education our son has received to date. I hope you understand our concern and look forward to hearing from you. Yours sincerely, David Davenport'.*

What a disgrace! How could anyone actually sit down and write a letter like that! Tom took a piece of paper and started to draft a reply.

'Dear Mr Davenport, Thank you for your interesting

letter. I am glad Stephen has been making such good progress. We do indeed expand the school in Year Three and we have always been able to recruit some excellent children from local primary schools. We interview them and also give the candidates some simple activities to carry out and I can assure you that the quality of intake usually raises our existing level. This year I have written to all prospective parents of seven-year-olds entered asking whether they object to joining a school where some existing parents are snobbish to the point of being offensive, but none has withdrawn. You may therefore feel reassured. Yours sincerely.....'

Tom put a pile of letters plus drafted replies on Barbara's desk and went for a wander around the school. Some bright sparks had already arrived and were kicking a football about on the playground. The caretaker, George, was unlocking the music room; piles of chairs were stacked outside, waiting for him to set them out for orchestra practice.

'Mr Thorne.' George seized his opportunity to catch him. 'I'd like you to see what I picked up around the school last night.'

He led Tom round the corner to the boys' changing room where there was a large pile of dirty rugby shorts, old socks, odd trainers and other abandoned clothing in the corner. There was also a pair of girl's knickers - what was she wearing when she went home, Tom wondered.

'It's too bad, Mr Thorne. It's getting worse and worse - these children just don't seem to care. Will you have a word with them?'

Tom assured him that he would and managed to move on.

Back in the office, Barbara was looking through the

pile of mail on her desk. She peered quizzically over the top of her computer.

'You can't send this.' She waved the draft letter to Mr Davenport. 'I don't think you would get away with it! Mr Black always used to leave letters like this for at least a day before thinking how to reply!'

'You are quite right of course, Barbara, but don't you think he's a complete nuisance? We do have to put up with some dreadful parents. Leave it for the moment and I'll look at it again tomorrow.'

After the session with Anita in the darkroom, Tom was beginning to find it increasingly difficult to concentrate on his job. Routine things needed to be done but he seemed to lose concentration and his thoughts would turn to his next meeting with her. She tended to be very formal when she came into the school during the day and sometimes almost ignored him. At other times she was, well, forward – to say the least. Tom didn't know how he stood with her and this unsettled him. He had always thought of himself as a very stable type. No. There was no way round it. He was falling for her and that was the truth.

Results from the various girls' schools had nearly all come through and Mary Teale bounced in to see Tom - she wanted to tell him that Karen Rowe had been offered a place at St Margaret's and wasn't that good news. Mrs Rowe was now thinking about whether to accept it or not.

'What! Do you mean she might not take the place after I rang Diane Reed?'

Mary hurriedly explained. 'Well, Karen has also been offered a place at St Mary's and they have got used to the idea of that school - and they like the Headmistress there. I think it's possible they may turn down St Margaret's offer.'

If that happened then Diane Reed wouldn't be listening to any of Tom's pleas in the future. How very annoying! Mary went through her list of offers, waiting list places and not offered places for all the other girls. Sixteen had sat a variety of exams - nine had been offered places at their 'first choice' schools and the other seven had all been offered places at second or third choices. Four were still on waiting lists. Mary was pleased with these results and with justification - competition was tough for these eleven-year-olds. Tom congratulated her and thanked her for all her hard work and coaching. Most parents would be happy! The next results due were the boys' scholarship exams. Always something to worry about!

'It's the second master of St Peter's on the line, can you speak to him?'

'Of course.'

Barbara put the call through to him.

There were two scholarship candidates for St Peter's, David Summers and Hitesh Patel. Tom picked up the phone.

'Ah, hallo, Tom.' Henry Bodkin was the genial St Peter's number two. 'I've got some results for you, just a moment. Summers and Patel are yours, aren't they? David Summers did very well and we've awarded him a major scholarship worth half fees. Hitesh Patel wasn't so strong and I'm afraid he just missed out on an academic award - he won't need to take Common Entrance. We were impressed with both of them and will be delighted to take the pair! We are sending letters out to parents today. Well done to you - some good teaching in evidence!' And he rang off.

Splendid, thought Tom - that should keep Mr Summers quiet. A scholarship of half fees would save him a good six grand a year. Pity about Hitesh - a very nice boy but not quite good enough as we feared; still, they will get a very promising cricketer who should get plenty of runs on that wicket of theirs.

Alastair arrived back just before the inspection. He told Tom that there had been quite a scare and they first thought he had cancer; after extensive tests this was finally ruled out. His doctor had finally come to the conclusion that his back pain was a muscular problem and not serious. Alastair said he was feeling much better and was keen to return.

Then Tom reminded him that the Inspectors were due at the beginning of the following week and that he would have to be properly prepared for his lessons, including written lesson plans.

'Right, I'll be off back to the hospital then!'

Tom assumed he was joking!

Later that afternoon Tom went down to the games fields and watched the second eleven soccer team defeat Colt Court 3-1. The team had obviously been encouraged by the return of their regular coach, Alastair. It also appeared they would have a full staff team on board for the dreaded inspection week.

Inspection day finally dawned. Tom and Mike were in early for the first day which was just as well as Mr Withey was ringing the door bell at 8.00 am, laden with two heavy-looking leather briefcases.

Tom greeted him brightly. 'Good morning. How was your hotel?'

'Fine, now where is that room I asked for? I've just got to finish off some paperwork. The others will be arriving in half an hour.' Tom had forgotten Mr Withey was a man of few words.

He escorted him to the Junior Library which had been set aside for the three day visit.

His co-inspectors were a much jollier bunch; they arrived in a taxi chattering away and clearly intended to enjoy their work.

'Hallo, John.' Tom greeted John Wallis whom he had met and liked on a rugby coaching course they had both attended a few years before. 'It's good to see you again.'

Tom took them all down to the Junior Library to join Peter Withey. He looked up from the table where he was working.

'You'll find all the exercise books on that table over there,' he instructed his team. 'We'd better get started.'

Tom left them to it.

Oddly enough it was a very quiet morning - everything seemed to go like clockwork. Jane's classes were unusually ordered and Paul did not even bring the Daily Telegraph into his classroom. Inspectors carrying notebooks roamed the corridors, occasionally asking the children for directions. At morning and lunch breaks some teachers tried to buttonhole an Inspector while others did their best to avoid them.

Tom was taking his maths class just before lunch when John Wallis, clutching his notebook, slipped in and sat at the back of the class. They were working on probability, which involved much throwing of dice and then recording the results. John chewed his pencil and grinned. As the lesson finished and the children went off for their lunch, he came up and said that he was glad to see the children were being taught the basics of bookmaking.

It was 11 o'clock that night before Tom could lock up the school.

Simon seemed very chipper the next morning.

'I thought that it was going to be awful having a woman inspect PE. Actually Felicity's quite knowledgeable - she's an FA qualified soccer coach.'

'Oh, so it's Felicity now, is it?' teased Mike. 'I thought you were getting on well yesterday afternoon during your games lesson on the next pitch. Maybe we should be looking for another female sports teacher to help with the rugby next year.'

'No, I don't think it will be necessary to go that far.' Simon beat a hasty retreat.

The rest of the staff seemed to be taking things quite well - Tom was keeping his fingers crossed.

On the last day of the inspection Mr Withey came in to confirm the arrangements.

'We'll finish looking at lessons by lunchtime today, and then my team will be having a meeting in the Junior Library for a couple of hours or so. After that we'd like to meet you and the Chairman plus anyone else on the staff you would like to be present. Would you like Mr Dawson to be there?'

'Yes, please, that will be fine.' Tom had previously arranged with Ted Whittaker to come in that afternoon. However, it wasn't until six o'clock that Ted, Mike and

Tom were called in. This was to be a debriefing session summarising what they had found. A full detailed written report would follow in about two months time, a copy of which would also go to the IAPS, the prep schools' association.

Peter Withey did most of the talking; only at the end did he ask the other four for their specific comments regarding the subject teaching they had seen. He emphasised that his report could only be based on what they had actually seen or heard at that time and that it was not possible in three days to discover everything that went on.

Tom was relieved to find in the first few minutes that they were clearly going to receive a generally favourable report. The teaching was basically sound - though they were not too happy with some of the safety aspects in the science lab. They also thought that the French teaching could be a bit more imaginative. Latin they agreed was especially well taught. Tom looked across at the Chairman at this point and Ted grinned.

They were happy with the pastoral arrangements but suggested that the school should be more prepared to take the children out to museums and so on. Development and expansion of the curriculum should be a consideration - perhaps the introduction of design technology would give a wider variety of children the opportunity to shine. Again Tom looked across at Ted. He was nodding! Mr Withey eventually brought the meeting to a close.

Quite a good three days, Tom thought, and breathed a deep sigh of relief as the Inspectors packed their briefcases and themselves into their expensive-looking vehicles and departed.

Tom, Mike and Ted spent another half an hour discussing the inspection findings. Tom was pleased at Ted's reaction. 'Well done, Tom! We seem to have come out of that pretty well. We'll talk about today's verbal report at our next Governors' meeting.'

A couple of days later, just as everyone was going home, Tom was passing the boys' changing room. What was Anita doing in there, he thought.

'Ah, Tom, I'm looking for Charlie's tracksuit top – he's always leaving his things lying around. You have no idea what we mothers have to do.' She laughed. 'And I haven't even thought about supper yet.'

Tom looked up and down the corridor. It was empty.

'Er, Anita, why not get the boys organised for their supper and come out with me for a quiet meal later? I know a good place. We could chat about this and that!'

'I'd very much like that.' Anita looked at Tom. 'I expect my neighbour Frances will come and sit with the boys. We have Sky TV and she likes to watch that! I'll give you a ring and tell you if I can as soon as I get home.' And with that she disappeared carrying an assortment of the boys' sports gear.

Later that evening the two of them were sitting at a table in the corner of a little Italian restaurant that Tom knew. It was in Barnes, a good twenty minutes drive from the school; the last thing Tom wanted was to be recognised by other parents - or staff – chatting up one of the mothers.

Spearing the last of his pasta and chicken with a fork, Tom looked across at Anita. In the soft light of the restaurant she was certainly very attractive. They had hardly stopped talking all evening and had increasingly found many things they had in common. Photography, for instance. Tom smiled, remembering the enjoyable time they'd had in the darkroom.

'Why are you smiling?'

'Nothing, just thinking we might do a bit more enlarging some time. Shall we go back to my place for coffee?'

'Good idea,' said Anita.

Later, looking out of the same bedroom window Anita had inspected after delivering those PA minutes earlier in the term, Tom's mind was racing. He'd had quite a few girlfriends in the past but had always backed off if they got too close - always wanting to keep his independence and not be too committed. If anyone had dared to mention the 'M' word, he'd have run a mile. Now though, he was beginning to wonder if there wasn't something to be said for family life. During term time he'd always been so busy that he hardly had time to think. But in the holidays, time had dragged. Maybe it would be nice to have someone to talk to, share thoughts and your life with. Someone, maybe, like Anita.

Anita's mind was also whirling. She'd always thought men were a waste of space. Peter was never around – always 'away on business' and she had often wondered what sort of business kept him away, leaving her to look after the boys - although he was keen enough to come back and see them now he'd moved on and out of her life.

And a good thing too, she thought.

Running her own business kept her busy enough, along with looking after Ben and Charlie. But the fact was she did miss someone to cuddle up to on the sofa in the evenings. And someone to talk to. Maybe she shouldn't dismiss all men. She wondered what Tom would be like to live with.

Anita did not get home till late.

The next Governors' Meeting had been postponed in order for it to take place after the inspection but seeing as the school had only received an informal verbal report from the Inspector and his team the discussion was rather brief. Ted Whittaker did most of the talking and relayed the generally positive impression given the week before. The meeting approved proceeding with plans for the introduction of design technology and also with the rental of the local cricket club's field for much of the sport.

Back in the office next morning, Barbara was opening the mail. 'You won't believe this, Tom! Just read this letter from Mr Summers.'

Tom had thought that the school might get a thank you from the awful Mr Summers for managing to get his son a scholarship, but not a bit of it apparently. His letter informed Tom that in order to prepare his son properly for the Latin exam he had engaged a tutor at home. The cost had been £200 and would the school please reimburse him since his Latin teacher at school had been unavailable! Tom took a deep breath and later that morning drafted a negative reply, trying to remain civil.

It was nearly the end of the spring term and Tom had just finished reading the 'short form' reports written by the class teachers on each pupil. It was the worst task of the term - very tedious and took hours! Also too many of the teachers had been educated themselves at a time when it was not considered important to learn how to spell, therefore they couldn't! Tom had to hand lots of reports back to staff to rewrite them.

'Please could you remember that 'practise' has an 's' when it's a verb and a 'c' when it's a noun?' he asked one teacher.

'How do you mean?' came the reply. 'A verb?' Enough said!

Chapter Seven

Every so often teachers have a moment in their working day when something happens which makes them feel just great. Shortly after the beginning of the summer term there was such a moment. The religious part of morning assembly had just finished, some rather tedious notices had been given out and next came the bit where the music department often arranged for a pupil or group to play something for everyone. Normally this was a performance to be politely listened to and then applauded.

On this occasion a remarkable boy called Greg Kokri was to play for them. He came from a very musical family and his instrument was the cello. As a player he was special - and he also had a weird sense of humour. When prevailed upon to play he would choose a piece of music which he thought would remind people of a particular member of staff.

'I am going to play you a piece called "The Flight of the Bumble Bee" by Rimsky-Korsakov.' Greg settled himself down on his chair with his cello between his knees. 'This piece particularly reminds me of Mr Begg - he's always buzzing around the place like a bumble bee.'

Alastair grinned broadly as a titter ran round the children sitting cross-legged on the floor. Then Greg began to play - and how he played! He had total command of his instrument and used it to express himself with great feeling - the clear sound filled the hall, soaring up to the high ceiling and then down again to the enraptured audience below. No one moved for five minutes, even the youngest listeners. It was a masterly performance and left many of the adults wondering what was to become of this talented child.

That afternoon Mike and Tom conducted one of the school's Open Afternoons, showing around a group of about twenty motley prospective parents. The following morning a letter arrived from one of the parents who had attended the previous day.

'Dear Mr Thorne,' the letter ran, *'Thank you very much for showing us around your splendid school today. We would very much like our son, Christian, to come but we understand that he is quite a way down the waiting list. My husband used to work on the "Jim'll Fix It" programme and has "fixed it" for people to meet gorillas in the jungle, to swim with whales and to meet Princess Anne. What can he do, he wonders, to "fix it" for Christian to come to your school? He says it is probably the most difficult of his challenges! He says he would love to buy the school cap for Christian and for you to fill what's below it! We just hope for some good news from you!*

PS. We were the couple in the front row wearing red sweaters!'

Barbara read the letter and laughed. 'What a pity, they're quite a long way down the list.'

'They are just the sort of people this school needs,' Tom said firmly. 'Make a note on the file to "take if poss" – hopefully we'll be able to shift Christian up a bit when the time comes.'

This being the summer term, the inevitable clash

between sport and the academic side of school life was being raised yet again. Tom saw that on the agenda for the next staff meeting Jane Lussac had added 'lessons missed due to sports fixtures'. This problem became even more of an issue at this time of year – not only were there cricket matches which took lots of time, but there were also other events, such as inter-school athletics meetings, in which Simon was keen for the school to participate.

Tom began the meeting. 'Before we move on to matters on the agenda I would like to mention one or two things. Firstly, as I am sure you may have heard, we have just received the final written inspection report. I am very pleased to say that it is extremely positive as well as supporting the changes we are or will be making, such as in sporting facilities and the introduction of design technology. The teaching was generally rated as very sound and I'd like to thank you all very much for your expertise and hard work. Next – rather more mundane – tidiness! Please could those taking games or lessons where children have to change make sure that the changing rooms are left without clothes on the floor? George is always complaining to me about this. In fact, not so long ago I found a rather grubby pair of girl's knickers in the boys' changing room! Enough said.'

Tom continued, 'Now to the agenda – sports fixtures. As you know, Mike has adjusted the timetable so that lessons on normal match days are switched around. This will mean children won't miss the same lesson each time. I can see it is most annoying for teachers though. Have you any suggestions, Jane?'

'Well, as I've said before, I'm not against sport. It's just that it does make it very difficult to complete the syllabus if people are away all the time. Could we restrict the number of fixtures perhaps?'

Simon responded, 'We are trying to upgrade our fixture list at the moment so I agree there are some extra matches which we have fitted in. There are some schools we could stop playing but it will take time to get the balance right.'

The discussion continued in this vein for a while until Tom finally brought it to a close by asking Simon to let him have a reduced fixture list for the following autumn term; the summer term's matches would, of course, have to be honoured – though rain often put paid to quite a few.

'The Chairman is on the line, shall I put him through?' Barbara's voice came through on Tom's internal phone. 'He sounds a bit worried.'

'Hallo, Tom.' Ted Whittaker was rather abrupt. 'I just thought I'd let you know that I've had a copy of the letter Mr Summers sent to you. He says that because Alastair Begg was away his son David didn't get enough Latin lessons before his scholarship exam and he is claiming compensation from the school. Do you think David has missed out? We don't want unhappy parents.'

Tom explained how difficult it had been to replace Alastair at short notice and how he had rearranged the timetable as best he could until a temporary replacement had been found. He also pointed out that David had won a scholarship so maybe Mr Summers ought to have been grateful to the school. He told Ted that he had replied, politely saying that the school would not be prepared to pay any compensation.

'Quite right, Tom, but I think if something like this

happens again you'd better let me know so that I'm in the picture.'

'Yes, of course Ted, I will. I'm sorry.' Tom felt rather foolish.

'No problem, Tom - don't worry about it.'

Ted rang off leaving Tom feeling as though he'd just been told off and wondering why he had ever applied for the job in the first place!

A fly on the wall of a Head's study would certainly have some unusual tales to tell and this appointment would surely qualify. Barbara came in halfway through the morning saying that Mrs Gregson was outside, rather upset, and would Tom see her for a moment. Of course, he said.

'Please come in, Mrs Gregson,' Tom greeted the rather gentle and friendly lady as she came nervously through the doorway. She did not look at all happy. Her son Michael in Year Six was doing quite well and Tom was not aware of any problems.

She began rather hesitantly. 'Thank you for seeing me, Mr Thorne. It's rather an embarrassing and delicate matter.' She paused and looked down at her hands twisting in her lap. 'You see, it's my husband, Tony. But before I continue, I think you ought to know I don't want this to be spread around the school. You see,' she paused for a second or two, 'Tony has decided to become a woman. He hasn't been living at home for the last month or two and Michael knows something is wrong but not exactly what. Tony is going to change his name to "Toni" and is planning to stay nearby and see Michael as much as he can. He may, for example, come and watch Michael playing cricket for the under elevens - and he'll come in a dress. I don't know how Michael will take this or how his friends will react. What do you think?'

For a few seconds Tom was stunned. This was something he really had not expected. Michael was a very normal ten-year-old - he was a popular boy with plenty of friends.

'Well,' Tom took a deep breath, 'children can be cruel to each other. Michael is a sensible and well-balanced boy but I think he will find this very difficult to cope with. Is there is any chance of persuading your husband to avoid embarrassing Michael at school? I think I ought to let Michael's form teacher and also his games teacher know what has happened; it may well be that he'll need some quiet support for a while.'

Mrs Gregson agreed to this and after a bit more discussion left sadly. Poor Michael, Tom thought.

Most of the Shaftesbury parents, Tom had to say, were a bit dull and conventional. Molly O'Farrell, however, certainly did not fall into that category. She was a feisty Irish lady whose son Sean was in Year Seven. She and her husband used to run a school in Cork but one day he upped and left leaving her to look after their two children. Molly tried running the school on her own for a while but it didn't really work so she sold up and came over to England to live. Molly tended to wear startlingly bright clothes and her bouncing red tresses of hair were not easily missed as she sailed in to collect her son at the end of the day. She often popped her head around the office door to say hallo. Today, however, she came to see Tom looking uncharacteristically businesslike.

'Now, Mr Tom,' she began in her Irish lilt, 'you know that I'm inventing a new method of teaching reading?'

Tom smiled because she had already told him about this project of hers several times. It involved the production of various new teaching aids and persuading a suitable publisher to take up her ideas. Tom knew she wasn't making a great deal of progress with the latter.

'Yes, of course I know. How's it going?'

'Brilliant! I've found the most wonderful little man who says he'll publish my scheme - but he says I need to try it out on a variety of children to give it more credibility. Now, surely you have a few young children who would need a bit of help?'

'Well, most of ours can read pretty well I'm glad to say, but I'll certainly give it some thought and put you in touch with anyone who comes to mind,' Tom assured her. 'And how is young Sean coping with the family finances?'

Sean was a remarkable boy. Only eleven, he ran much of the family's financial and everyday affairs - Molly being full of ideas but poor at organising. Sean had a younger sister aged six and he found time after school to do the shopping and some of the cooking, as well as looking after young Ellen when Molly popped out to meet her colourful friends. He also seemed to fit in time to do his own homework - which he did very well being an able boy. He would go far, that Sean!

'Oh, Sean's just fine. He's a good fellow and I don't know what I'd do without him. Well, I'll be leaving you now - don't forget what I'm asking you, will you?' And with that she hurried off in search of her talented son.

Eileen, who ran the Pre-prep department often organised interesting outsiders to come and talk to the children about their work. Ann Tucker, one of the Year Two teachers, was married to a policeman stationed nearby and Eileen had persuaded Ann to ask George if he'd come in and talk to the children about police work. George was not at all keen but agreed to come on Ann's promise of his favourite steak and kidney pie for supper that night. Tom went along to listen and sat at the back with the other teachers, the children arranged in neat rows on the floor in front of the surprisingly nervous George.

'Now, what do you think this is?' George held up a truncheon.

The children were reluctant to say anything, fearing perhaps that the friendly but very large policeman would demonstrate what it was for! Eventually various hands went up and all sorts of suggestions were made. George began to relax. He brought out his walkie-talkie and, much to the delight of the children, contacted his local station. Then he persuaded one brave boy to talk into the device and say hallo to the station sergeant. That would certainly be something to tell Mum about on the way home!

George then held up a pair of handcuffs. 'Now these are something that we have to use now and again. What do you think they are?'

A forest of five-and six-year-old hands shot up. George selected that of a very small girl called Henrietta sitting right next to his size twelve boots. 'Yes?'

'Well, I'm not sure what they are called,' said Henrietta, 'but I do know that Mummy and Daddy keep a pair in their bedroom.'

A slow grin spread across the face of the policeman and he had to turn away from his audience. The staff tittered to each other on the chairs at the back and Marion Shaw, who taught a Year One class, leant over towards Tom and whispered in his ear, 'I've always thought Henrietta's parents were rather strait-laced. It's amazing what we get to hear about parents down here, you know!'

This was obviously a successful visit and George was clearly earning his steak and kidney pie. Tom quietly extricated himself and returned to the dull business of signing correspondence in the office.

He was just pouring himself a small glass of whisky after what had been quite a good day - two lots of very pleasant prospective parents had signed up their children - when there was a sharp tap on the front door. It was Mike.

'I think you'd better come straight away,' he hissed at Tom urgently. 'There's someone in your office going through the drawer in your desk. It looks like Paul. Should he be there?'

'Certainly not! Let's go - we may have got him now.'

Tom must have carelessly left the study unlocked. They moved quietly out of the front gate and along the path outside the study. Sure enough, there was Paul looking through some files on Tom's desk.

As they opened the main school door there was a scurrying noise from inside and, by the time they had entered the hallway, Paul was standing outside the study.

'Ah, there you are, I was just looking for some French books that I wanted to mark this evening.'

A likely story, thought Tom - Paul's marking was seldom up to date. He noticed that there was an open file on the desk, which had certainly not been left like that by him.

'What's this file you have been looking at then?'

The confidential file was one that Mike and Tom had been keeping on Paul. They had already collected quite a bit of evidence through meetings they'd had with him regarding timekeeping and his methods of teaching and so on. He must somehow have got wind of the existence of this file and was attempting to remove some of the more incriminating documents.

'Paul, I think we'll have to discuss this tomorrow, maybe after school. Meanwhile, if you don't mind, I'd like to lock up the building.' Paul retreated and then Mike and Tom secured the school and went back next door for a drink.

Mike couldn't wait to ask, 'Now can we get rid of him?'

'That I'm not sure of. Maybe. I'll talk to Ted Whittaker tomorrow morning and get his opinion. I think Paul might have overstepped the mark this time.'

Mike and Tom then spent some time working out how they could cover Paul's teaching if he could be persuaded to go at the end of term. It was now a bit late in the school year to advertise and find someone good for the beginning of the next school year in September. Teachers working in the independent sector would normally expect to have to give one term's notice to leave their present job and that would mean a new person not being able to start until next January. There were two current members of staff who had taught some French in the past and who might be persuaded to do a temporary job until then.

Ted Whittaker was extremely helpful. First of all he said that he was all in favour of moving Paul on. He had heard several murmurings from parents he knew about the slack French teaching and was keen to strengthen the staff. He asked how many warnings Paul had been given and what evidence there was. He said if necessary the school would pay Paul a term's wages in lieu of notice. Armed with this support, Tom asked Paul to come and see him and asked Mike if he would also sit in on the meeting.

Tom spoke first. 'Paul, I know that we've spoken on several occasions about the French teaching and that you have rather different views to myself and Mike. In particular we have discussed the content of lessons, marking pupils' work and timekeeping. I was also not at all happy to find you going through and removing some of my confidential papers last night.'

Paul did not deny this and was clearly rattled; he was wondering what was coming next.

'What do you have to say?'

'Well, as to last night, I said I was just looking for those books. Can I have them, please?'

'Of course.' Tom handed them to him.

'What papers did you take from my desk?' There was no reply. Tom continued, 'I have spoken to Mike and to the Chairman, Mr Whittaker, and we consider that your conduct amounts to a breach of your contract with the school. We are proposing to terminate your contract at the end of this term. The school is, however, without prejudice, prepared to pay your salary until the end of December. Also, provided the rest of this term's teaching is completed satisfactorily, I will be happy to write a reference for you if you wish.'

Paul looked stunned and said nothing for a while.

Eventually he spoke slowly, 'I see. This has all taken me rather by surprise. Maybe I'll have to do as you suggest. I'll have to think about what to do next.'

Paul then got up and left, closing the door quietly behind him. Mike breathed a sigh of relief. He didn't like confrontations.

'Thank goodness he didn't turn nasty, though maybe he'll think of some way of getting back at us before the term is out.'

Tom agreed and then they turned their attention to drafting a suitable advert for the Times Educational Supplement to go in as soon as possible.

This was the cricket season - or at least it was supposed to be. There seemed to be a permanent rain cloud positioned right over the school waiting until everyone got changed for games in the afternoons before releasing its contents over the unfortunate participants. Tom had successfully negotiated with the local cricket club to rent their facilities for school matches when not in use by the club's teams. Simon's first eleven was due to play their first match on the new games field.

'It's really annoying, Sir.' Timothy Gower, the newly appointed captain who was sitting next to Tom at lunchtime, was definitely disgruntled. 'The match has been cancelled.'

'Why is that, Tim?' (It hadn't rained yet that day.)

'Mr Bragg says the pitch is unfit. He says it would be

dangerous to let us play, but we don't mind, Sir.'

Tom went in search of Simon.

'I'm sorry to hear you've cancelled the match today, Simon. What's the problem?'

'Well, Tom, the wicket itself is playable but there is a very wet patch just where square leg would be and the boys might easily slip over and hurt themselves. I didn't think we could chance it - if somebody was injured we'd probably get sued.'

'Could we not mark out that area with cones and say 'dead ball' if the ball was hit in there? It would be better to play some sort of a game than nothing at all.'

Simon shook his head and said that it was a bit late now but that he would try to rearrange the match for later in the season. Tom went away thinking that so-called Health and Safety policies had a lot to answer for and, with this attitude in England, it was no wonder that the Test team was beaten regularly by South Africa and Australia.

A few days later the first under eleven cricket match was due to be played and Michael Gregson was in the team. Tom wondered if Mrs Gregson had managed to persuade her former husband to keep away from the boundary, certainly if he was proposing to come in a summer dress and matching handbag. To keep an eye on things down at the cricket field would be a good excuse to get out of the office for a while so, after lunch, Tom told Barbara where he was going and escaped into the fresh air. Contrary to what he had said to Mrs Gregson, Tom had confided in Barbara about poor Michael's family troubles. Even Barbara, who had come across all sorts of situations in her years as school secretary, admitted that this was something new.

As it turned out there was no sign of Mr or, should one say, Ms Gregson and Michael was able to concentrate on his game. He opened the batting and made a very cautious twelve runs before being run out by a frustrated partner. Shaftesbury lost the game but there were some encouraging signs and the few loyal parent supporters went away happy.

Common Entrance was getting close – the exams were in June. There were eighteen boys sitting CE, as it was known, and parents had to make up their minds which school was to be their 'first choice'. Timothy Gower's parents had yet to make a final choice of secondary school and they came in to see Tom.

'We've entered Tim for St Mark's in Barnes and also my husband's old school, Wellington, though I personally don't want to send him away to boarding school.'

Mr Gower took over from his wife. 'We feel that St Mark's may be too academic for him - his practice Common Entrance results were not so hot and we are keen for him to go somewhere where he can develop his sport. What do you think, Mr Thorne?'

It was true that Tim was a questionable candidate for St Mark's, which set a strict 65% pass mark for candidates in the main subjects. Tim was borderline. Wellington would be easier - and would be more likely to make allowances on academic results if they thought a boy could contribute to school life in other ways, for example sport - an area where he would have much to offer. On the other hand, the cost of boarding was much more, though in Tim's case Tom knew this would not be a major problem for his banker father.

After a long discussion, in which Tom tried to cover himself and the school in case Tim didn't make it, the Gowers decided on St Mark's as their first choice. As they left, Tom promised to keep Tim's nose to the grindstone as much as possible for the next few weeks. He would need to keep his fingers crossed, as CE failures would have to be explained.

At about quarter past four in the afternoon, Barbara put her head round the door and told Tom that there had been a parking problem and that a local resident, a Mr Brind, was on the phone and wanted to speak to the Head; it appeared he was rather angry.

'Are you the Headmaster?' A rather loud voice barked at the other end of the line.

Tom agreed that this was the case. 'Can I help you?'

'My name is Brind and I am fed up to the back teeth with the way your parents treat us local residents, parking all over the place. They just do not care where they leave their cars. I have been taking video evidence and will be showing it to the police. Today was the final straw. One of your parents, who refused to give his name, parked right across my driveway. It really is too bad. I asked him to move and he wouldn't. My wife needs to go out shopping.'

'I am extremely sorry, Mr Brind.' Tom realised he could have an impending war on his hands if he did not deal with this quickly. 'I will certainly come straight down and see what the problem is. You understand that I cannot force parents to park with consideration, though I do send out circulars from time to time. What number is your house?'

Tom went off down the road. Outside Mr Brind's house

was Mr Summers. His rather smart Audi had been covered with branches, which looked as if they had been torn off a nearby tree. Tom suppressed a grin. Mr Summers was beside himself with fury. 'Look what this man has done to my car! It's a new car and if there is any damage I'll sue!'

'Why do you have to park in front of my driveway?' It was a reasonable enough question from Mr Brind. 'Can't you be bothered to walk a bit further to collect your precious children?'

Tom started to remove some of the branches from Mr Summers' car - there didn't seem to be too much damage.

'Maybe you could park a bit further down the road, Mr Summers,' he suggested.

It took some time but eventually Mr Brind calmed down and accepted Tom's apologies on behalf of the parents and Mr Summers, with a scowl, moved his car a few feet further down the road. Meanwhile his son, David, had arrived and said breezily, 'Collecting firewood, Dad?'

Serve the old fool right, Tom thought as he walked back to the school to share his amusement with Barbara.

For once the day dawned without a cloud in the sky - summer had at last arrived! And the timing was good since Tom was due to take the under ten cricket team away for their first match against his friend Mark Rowland's school near Epsom. He always umpired his boys and there was usually a fair amount of banter during the games.

It was an unwritten rule that umpires did not tell their young captains what to do all the time - boys needed to make mistakes now and again and hopefully learn from them. Mark, however, had developed a cunning method of letting his captain know who he ought to have bowling at each end. He would carry a number of different coloured biros in his top pocket. Each of his bowlers would be represented by a colour - and Mark used to arrange the pens so that the two favoured bowlers' coloured biros were at each end of his top pocket. One became used to the captain, who had to be a smart young lad, looking intently at Mark's top pocket at the end of each over before saying, 'You are still bowling, Stephen,' or whoever!

For this match, the Shaftesbury opening bowlers were a fast, rather inaccurate, left-armer called Ben Boon and the captain, a steady off spinner called Andrew Mills. Andrew, having won the toss, decided to put the opposition in. Unlike in Test Matches, prep school boys tend to want to field first - so that they know the score they have to get when batting.

The opposition scorer, a very small boy in glasses perched on a chair in the pavilion, called out, 'Bowlers' names, please?'

Tom had been waiting for this and replied at once, 'Mills and Boon!'

The scattering of adults around the ground laughed but the boys did not understand why. It was a very pleasant afternoon, even though Shaftesbury eventually lost by twenty odd runs.

Georgina Tingle was a splendid girl in Year Six who had just gained a place at her first choice secondary school. She was good at lots of things and much liked around the school. Tom wondered why Mrs Tingle had made an appointment to see him.

She made herself comfortable in the office. 'Mr Thorne, let me first say how much Georgina has enjoyed her time at Shaftesbury - Frank and I are delighted at how well she has come on here. We have been discussing what we could do to say thank you and came up with the idea of presenting the school with a cup. We thought it might be for the best girl swimmer. What do you think?'

'How very generous of you.' Tom realised immediately that Georgina herself, easily being the best of the girl swimmers that year, would be the first recipient. He thought quickly and went on, 'Actually we don't have a cup for the winning house at the school swimming gala later this term. I wonder if you would like to donate the Tingle Cup for that? It would be wonderful if you would like to make it a House swimming cup.'

This was not what Mrs Tingle had in mind. She had made careful enquiries from her daughter as to who might be possible winners of her cup and had come to the same conclusion as Tom; however, she could hardly back out now so she forced a smile and agreed. Tom thanked her profusely and said that the gala would be on the 10th June and enquired as to whether the cup would be ready for then. She promised it would be.

'I think Georgina's house, Neptune, have a good chance of winning the cup this year,' Tom said as Mrs Tingle went off – not entirely happy.

Some parents treated their children appallingly. Joshua Gough-Hill was in his last year and was one of those boys who always tried hard but wasn't very good at anything. He was extremely keen on sport and though not very talented had eventually managed to get into the second eleven cricket team. It was the first time he had been selected to play for the school so naturally he asked his parents to come and watch.

Mr Gough-Hill, who was not a keen sports watcher, arrived in his dark blue Bentley. It was a chilly day so, instead of sitting wrapped up in a deck chair alongside the other parents on the boundary, he opted to stay in the comfort of his car and watch from fifty yards back. Joshua's team were batting and the boy waited by his father's car for his turn. When eventually a wicket fell Joshua waved to his dad and walked onto the pitch. At that moment Joshua's father's mobile phone rang. Joshua's innings was brief but he had his moments. He snicked a ball through the slips for a single and then a rather wild swipe actually went for four. Shortly afterwards he was bowled by a straight one. He had scored five runs - not bad for a first effort. He proudly walked back to his father's car anxious to discuss his performance with his dad.

His father had missed everything. He had not looked up once to watch his son playing for he had been totally engrossed on the phone with some very important deal.

'Did you see me batting, Dad?'

His father had no answer.

Chapter Eight

Tom was busy one Thursday morning before Barbara had arrived, working through the mail and discarding as much as possible of the junk mail into the wastepaper basket when Mike came into the office, grinding his teeth. 'That woman, Valerie Eales, is off sick again. I suppose she'll be away tomorrow as well - it gives her a long weekend. She just doesn't seem pull her weight, that one.'

'As a matter of interest, Mike, do you keep records of the days people are away? It would be interesting to know who is away the most.'

'I certainly do. In fact, since Valerie joined us two years ago she has missed fifty days - that is easily the most of any of the staff. I'll put up a note on the staff room board covering today's lessons; it will mostly be Robin to sit in.'

Mike's usual 'cover' notice went up on the board in the staff room - on the bottom he had added 'Polite clapping for a well constructed fifty went round the ground.'

Valerie came storming into the office first thing the following Monday morning. 'I wish to complain about Mike. I'm not going to stand for this sort of thing. He has been making sarcastic remarks about me on his notices in the staff room and I don't like it.' She wagged her finger at him as she spoke.

She really had only herself to blame, thought Tom, and

pretending to know nothing about it, asked what the problem was. She had seen Mike's notice and some malicious person had explained to her the meaning of his cricketing footnote. Tom couldn't defend Mike obviously and he promised to see him and get him to apologise. Still, Mike had made a good point and maybe this laid-back art teacher would think twice next time before ringing in to say she would be 'off' for a day.

The beginning of June was crunch time for eighteen Year Eight boys who were sitting the 13+ Common Entrance exams over the following three or four days. The Junior Library was set aside and Hugh Broddy, a former maths teacher at the school, came in to invigilate. He loved this job - he would make a great deal of fuss of the boys and make sure they all had the right pens, pencils, geometry instruments and so on. Everything that could possibly be wanted would be laid out meticulously on his invigilator's table, including biscuits and drinks which Hugh would provide for his charges during the morning break each day between papers. Just before the first exam was due to start Tom went in to wish them all good luck. 'Good luck, chaps. Do your best!'

A muted chorus of 'Thank you, Sir' rumbled around the room. They were not looking forward to the next few days. Tom left them to it, crossing his fingers that all would perform as needed.

Later that day a delightful couple came in to see Tom with their six-year-old son. The boy's father was Danish and had just been posted to London with his company. The mother was English and had been working as a secretary in Copenhagen. Their son David was a capable-looking boy and joined in confidently with the discussion as they went on the usual tour around the school.

Mrs Peterson was extremely enthusiastic as they returned to the office. 'We love the school; do you think you could find a place for David? We should say that the school system in Denmark does not start to teach the children reading formally until they are seven. David has not yet started; would this be a problem?' Tom had to admit that yes, it would be a problem - the pushy English system started teaching children reading at least by the age of four so by the time they reached David's age most would be quite fluent readers. David would be at a considerable disadvantage if he joined without any preparation.

Tom was however keen to take this boy because he was clearly an able child and he had the feeling he would be a willing contributor. He then thought of the school's eccentric Irish parent Molly O'Farrell and her claim to be able to teach anyone to read in less than a month - this could be her opportunity. David would be an ideal candidate.

'We'd certainly like to take David but I think it would be better for him to have a "crash course" in reading first. We do have a parent who is an ex-headmistress and who has invented a new way of teaching reading. I am sure that she would love to take on David as a pupil. Would you like me to contact her? We could then arrange to have a look at him after say a month or so.'

Mr and Mrs Peterson agreed at once that this would be fine and after a brief phone call to Molly the first lesson was organised.

The house swimming gala was one of the big events of

the term and most parents would come and support their offspring. Shaftesbury didn't have a swimming pool and had to rent The Lady Jane School's pool for the evening. The promised Tingle Cup had been delivered the previous week and stood gleaming on Tom's desk. The children all went home at the normal time and then had to be transported by parents to the pool for a seven o'clock start. The Headmistress, Eileen Rosse, was scurrying briskly out of the entrance when Tom arrived.

'Hallo, Tom, I think everything is ready for you. Have a good evening. Terribly sorry I can't be with you - I have a Finance and General Purposes Committee meeting in half an hour.'

'Rather you than me,' replied Tom, though which of them would have the more pleasant evening was by no means certain - Tom didn't enjoy the screeching racket that always accompanied competitive swimming.

Simon was in charge assisted by virtually all the teaching staff. It was a three-line whip - all hands were required for the various jobs - even Valerie Eales, the expert at work avoidance, was there dressed in a very smart tracksuit. The children were all lined up on one side of the pool and the spectators crammed together on benches opposite. Simon, on the microphone, welcomed everyone and the races began.

Tom held a stopwatch and was in charge of timing lane two. A very important job! All went pretty smoothly until the girls' Year Six breaststroke. It was a very close race and Fiona Clegg in lane one and Tamsin Peters in lane four were neck and neck; the resonating high-pitched voices urged them on and they both stretched out for the final touch. The place judges gathered around Simon who after a short consultation announced the winner as

Fiona Clegg of Neptune. There were cheers and groans alike from the spectators. Out of the corner of his eye Tom saw a large man rise ponderously from his seat near the finish and walk towards him. It was Mr Peters - who had a reputation as capable of being 'a bit awkward'.

He spoke quietly, 'Mr Thorne, I have no wish to be difficult, but did you not see that Tamsin was the first to touch? And also, I thought that you had to finish by touching with both hands at the same time in breaststroke - which I don't think Fiona did.'

He had a point.

'I was looking at lane two so I didn't see those two finishing.' Tom avoided agreeing with him. 'I'll have a word with Mr Bragg. Just a moment.'

Tom went over to Simon and repeated what Mr Peters had said. He, naturally enough, was not pleased to have his decisions queried; he said that in the judges' view Fiona was the winner and that although her finishing was not perfect it satisfied the panel. The decision would stand. Tom returned to Mr Peters.

'I'm sorry, Mr Peters, but the judges have made their decision and, though they understand the points you have made, they won't change.'

Mr Peters returned scowling to his seat and in due course the final relays came to an end. The winning house turned out to be Neptune which meant that Georgina Tingle and Lucas Steele, being the house swimming captains, came up to receive the Tingle Cup for the first time. Mrs Tingle beamed graciously and all the spectators clapped - except Mr Peters who had not enjoyed his evening.

Alastair, though perhaps eccentric, was no fool. His after

school club was rather cunning. He ran a 'stock exchange' club which involved recruiting as members a number of youngsters who were interested in money. Each member would be allowed to 'invest' up to £5,000 in stocks and shares of their choosing at the beginning of term. They would follow the progress of their 'investments' throughout the term by looking each week at the financial pages of the Daily Telegraph. They would draw graphs and use calculators to work out the value of their 'portfolios'. It was an excellent way of improving their maths skills. At the end of term the club member who could show the best gain would be the 'winner' and would be presented with a prize - much coveted.

Of course, both children and parents were extremely competitive. One or two parents were stockbrokers or bankers and were very well informed - even, dare one say, with access to 'inside' information. So naturally they would pass on any hot tips to their offspring - a perfectly above board thing to do. Alastair was well aware which boys would have the best information and once all the members of his club had told him what their choices were, he would ring up his 'Man in the Midlands' (as he called his broker) and buy a variety of shares suggested by the boys' fathers. Most terms he would make a nice profit, which supplemented his salary. Alastair was very busy on the staff room phone at lunchtime as Tom went in to find someone. He finished his call and jotted down some figures in a notebook, chortling. 'Excellent fellow, Mr Bransby, I thought he'd come up with something good this time after last term's disaster.'

'Are you up this term, Alastair?'

He pretended not to understand but he patted his notebook and grinned as he replied that it was most important to keep up to date with what the market was doing. He went back to his marking happily.

A recent addition to the after school clubs list had been provided by Janet Salter. As a result of gentle pushing by Mike she had agreed to run an activity, but had neatly sidestepped the idea of dry skiing which Tom had suggested - that would have involved taking pupils in a minibus and waiting for at least an hour during the lessons. She had suddenly developed an interest in chess. Her chess club met once a week in her classroom, which enabled her to do her marking as the various games went on. It turned out that Sean O'Farrell was a keen and proficient player and Janet was happy to let him run the club. All parties were satisfied!

The day of the Common Entrance results arrived. If a school was going to fail a candidate they would normally ring up the Head of the prep school and warn them in advance so that alternative arrangements could be made; Tom had not had any such phone calls so he was hoping for the best. He and Mike pounced on the post when it arrived and extracted the likely looking envelopes. All the boys had passed, some with rather disappointing grades, some with surprisingly good ones. Timothy Gower had done better than expected and his parents would be especially pleased. Usually the popular London day schools marked strictly in order to give them the option of turning down the weaker candidates if they had too many names on their list while the boarding schools tended to be more lenient.

Mike went off to assemble the eighteen boys. One by one they came in to the study, not knowing their results. What a pleasure it was, thought Tom, to shake each boy's hand and congratulate him on passing. They reacted in different ways - some just took it in their stride and smiled confidently, asking him if they could see their grades. Others couldn't contain themselves and cried with relief. It was difficult not to do the same oneself! As the last boy went off to phone up his parents with the good news, Tom was left happily thinking that he could report 100% success in Common Entrance in his next Governors' report.

Molly O'Farrell and Sean were hurrying down the corridor on their way out of school at the end of the afternoon - no doubt for Sean to do the shopping - and Tom waved to them as they passed.

'Hi, you're in a hurry. Who's doing the cooking tonight?'

Sean looked at Tom and shrugged his shoulders.

'It'll be me, Sir. We'll be having bangers and mash, I expect.'

'I'm sure it will be delicious - tell me, Molly, how is young David Peterson getting on with his reading?'

'Ah, now there's a bright young boy. He's just forging ahead - you should definitely take him. He's a good lad.'

'The two of them are crazy, Sir,' Sean chipped in. 'They were both on the floor with their feet in the air last night, playing some sort of game. I suppose David's learning something but it's difficult to tell.'

'Now don't you worry, Tom,' said Molly. 'That boy will surprise you when you see him again. That will be the beginning of next month, won't it?'

It would indeed be interesting to see how David had progressed as a result of a month or so of Molly's odd teaching methods. Molly and Sean scurried off.

The school had advertised for a French teacher to replace Paul in September but there had been a poor response. Not surprising, as it was so late in the school year. Glumly Tom sorted through the letters with their CVs and picked out the best three of a bad bunch. Before calling anyone for an interview, he always made a quick informal phone call to each candidate's referees; they were asked to provide at least two. Before him on the desk Tom had his list of questions. The most important was probably to the current or former employer: *'Given what you now know about the candidate would you now appoint him/her to the job?'* It was amazing how many referees, who had written the most positive of references about a candidate, when asked that question, couldn't bring themselves to say 'yes, they would'. Written references might easily not be worth the paper they were written on but verbal ones over the phone were usually quite truthful.

Tom rang the Head of one school whose name was given as a referee for the best qualified candidate, on paper at least. Tom explained what the job was and asked if he could tell him something about the candidate.

'Well, since you ask,' he started, 'I was not asked to act as a referee for this chap - hardly surprising really since I sacked him a fortnight ago. But I could certainly tell you a bit about him if you like.'

Not much point in going further! But Tom did ask why he'd been sacked and it wasn't for anything too ghastly; nevertheless a blue pencil line had to go through his name. That left two to follow up and fortunately there were no more skeletons to be unearthed. Tom rang up both candidates hastily and made appointments to see them the following week.

They arrived promptly for their interviews. They had each been asked to prepare a half-hour lesson with a Year Six class. Mary Teale, as an experienced Year Six teacher, would observe how the lessons went and report back to Tom and Mike.

Both candidates were women, neither of whom had experience of teaching in the independent sector - not that it mattered, but they did need to know how the school worked and what would be expected of them - including duties such as supervision at lunch times and breaks. This might put them off!

A half-hour chat with Tom was followed by being shown around the school by Mike who also explained how the house and discipline system worked. They then taught their lesson, which was followed by a further session with Tom concerning possible salary (Shaftesbury paid national rates plus eight per cent). Eventually they were asked if they would be interested in the job if offered. Both replied yes like a shot, which was encouraging.

Mike, Mary and Tom met when they had departed.

'So, what did you think?' asked Tom.

'I thought the first one, Miss Bracken, was confident and well prepared,' began Mary.

Emma Bracken was thirty, had taught for six years in a middle school in Buckinghamshire and wanted to move to London for 'personal' reasons. She was an impressive, slightly frightening figure standing nearly six foot tall with rimless glasses. She probably wouldn't have too many discipline problems. The other candidate was completely different. Jenny Toyne was short and friendly and not so confident. She had been brought up in France where her father had been working and after qualifying in England had worked for two years as a class teacher at a primary school in West London. She now wanted to broaden her experience in an independent school.

'Miss Bracken's lesson went well and she obviously had a good grasp of the language,' Mary continued, 'and the children seemed to enjoy it. The second one, Miss Toyne, was OK but she started hesitantly. Once she got into the lesson though she really got the children involved. She finished strongly. I did notice that at the end of the lesson Miss Toyne immediately went up to the children and started to chatter away to them. She seemed very much at ease, whereas Miss Bracken seemed to be quite glad that her lesson was over and came over to me to find out what was to happen next.'

They spent the next half an hour discussing the pros and cons of each and eventually plumped for Miss Toyne as their first choice, mainly because she seemed to get on better with her prospective pupils. In the evening, Tom rang her and offered her the post, to start in September. She accepted at once. A good job done, thought Tom as he wandered out onto the empty school field and down to the pond in the corner where the frogs were plopping in and out of the water. It was a peaceful spot to come after a day's work.

The effectiveness or otherwise of Molly O'Farrell's unusual teaching methods were about to be revealed as Mrs Peterson brought David into school to spend the morning with the class he might possibly join. Ann Tucker's Year Two class would be moving up to Year

Three in September - would David be able to cope? Tom needed Ann to answer by the end of the morning. David himself looked a bit nervous but went off happily enough with the two boys who would be looking after him until after lunch when his mother would be returning.

David's guides duly returned him to the study - Ann meanwhile told Tom that David was quiet but did read quite well enough to join her class next term.

'What did you think of the lunch?' Tom asked David. First things first!

'Fine, but there weren't any seconds. I could easily have had more!'

Not a faddy eater - good. There was a tap on the door and Mrs Peterson appeared. When told that David had got on fine and the school would really like to sign him up for next term she beamed.

'Excellent news, Henning will be delighted.'

The two of them went through to the office to fill in various forms and, of course, to hand over a cheque for the deposit. Year Three for the following term was now full - splendid, thought Tom. He rang Molly and told her how well her pupil had progressed.

'Well done, Molly. You've done a fine job with that boy. How are you getting on with your publisher?'

'Just great!' She sounded extremely pleased with herself. 'I told him about David and I'm seeing him again this week. We hope to sign a contract soon - and then I'll be rich!'

Tom laughed. 'I doubt that! You'll spend any money you earn as soon as you get your hands on it!' She was a very happy bunny!

Paul came in to ask for Thursday and Friday off to attend

two interviews at schools in Hampshire and Devon.

'No problem, Paul.' Tom was grateful he would not be around for the last day of term. 'Good luck!'

The next morning Mike met Tom outside the school gates on their way into school; Mike was obviously not pleased.

'When I got home last night, there was a chap waiting to see me. He turned out to be a wig salesman! Someone had contacted his firm and said I would be interested in his services - gave my address. Who do you think might have done that?'

Mike, though a very fit and healthy fellow, did have a receding hairline about which he was rather sensitive.

'One name springs to mind,' said Tom. 'Do you think Paul is having one final go at authority before he moves on? I wouldn't be surprised.' Mike ground his teeth and described what he would do to Paul if he caught up with him again.

Later that morning Barbara came through on the internal phone.

'There's a man on the line who says he's calling about your car. Do you want to speak to him?'

What about my car, Tom wondered, and asked Barbara to put him through.

'Good morning, Sir,' said an Irish voice. 'Would you be the gentleman who has the BMW for sale? I'm very sorry about the drinking - I know from my own experience it's that easy to get caught out.'

Tom was particularly fond of his car and had no intention of selling it. 'Yes, I do have a BMW but it's certainly not for sale. Who are you and how did you get my number and what are you talking about?'

'Well, Sir, it's in the local paper - here I'll read you the advertisement:
FOR SALE - RED BMW 3 SERIES TWO YEARS OLD. HEADMASTER MUST SELL OWING TO DRINK DRIVING CONVICTION £3,500 PHONE 411 7342.'

This had to be another of Paul's 'jokes'. He was going to have to whistle for any reference from me, thought Tom. The man was very disappointed when told that the advertisement was a hoax. He went on about how such a fine car would have suited him - just the ticket. Tom put the phone down. There were another dozen such calls that day but Barbara intercepted them courteously, smiling at Tom and asking him what he had been up to. Tom made a terse call to the newspaper's advertising department, complaining bitterly that they had not verified the details in this advertisement before publication. They amounted to libel. He received an abject apology and rang off wondering whether to take the matter further. Probably nothing would be gained and maybe it would be better to let sleeping dogs lie.

The summer term finished with prize-giving. This was to take place at seven o'clock in the evening in the Assembly Hall. The guest speaker was Hugh Waters, Head of a West Country boarding school to which Shaftesbury sent a few pupils now and again. Tom had met him at his school when he had hosted a meeting of prep school heads and liked him a lot. He had agreed at once to come and give away the prizes at Shaftesbury - something he no doubt did very often at prep schools. He might pick up a few more customers if he made a good speech.

With great care Barbara arranged all the cups and

prizes on a long table covered with white sheets - they had to be in exactly the right order if things were to run smoothly. Behind the table on the stage was a row of chairs for those Governors who could spare the time to come plus Hugh, his wife Diana, Barbara and Tom. Mike and the staff all had seats dotted about the body of the hall arranged so that they could keep a sharp eye on the children - good behaviour being essential at this last event of the term.

The temperature climbed into the eighties - it was the middle of a heatwave - and inside the hall packed with parents, children and staff it was oppressive. The staff suffered especially as they, on this one occasion of the year, wore academic gowns. It would be a bonus to get through the proceedings as quickly as possible. After Tom's summary of the year, the Chairman welcomed the guest speaker and Hugh stood up to address his sweltering listeners. He began with the 'lion making the speech' story - in the Roman arena the lion is about to eat the Christian when the Christian whispers something in the lion's ear. The lion stops, thinks for a moment and then slinks off to the side. The watching Emperor is amazed and calls for the Christian to ask him what he said to the lion. 'Oh,' says the Christian, 'I just told him that he would be expected to make a speech after dinner.' Hugh paused for the obligatory laughs and promised he wouldn't speak for long. He was true to his word. The prizes were handed out and in just over an hour from the start prize-giving was over.

Everyone was now ready for the summer holidays!

Chapter Nine

Tom looked back on his first year as Headmaster of Shaftsbury Prep. He had survived at least, remaining on reasonable terms with the Chairman. Ted Whittaker had not said much to him during the year, except occasionally wanting to be kept more informed of what was going on. Exam results had been good. Tom had upset one or two parents and one or two staff along the way but on the whole, after Mr Black's long reign, he had been accepted and the school was moving forwards. The parents became more confident in the management and turned their attention to earning enough money to pay the ever-increasing school fees. A large new area for design technology had been developed and equipped with a wide variety of tools and several computers. Tom had found a splendid young girl, full of enthusiasm, to run the department. The pupils loved this new subject and were soon producing all sorts of weird and wonderful contraptions. The Governors had agreed to employ a second sport-minded gap year student to help with games. Shaftesbury started to win more matches than it lost. Tom felt that school was now more 'fun'.

Tom's Deputy, Mike Dawson, was a strong supporter of his and the two of them often met for a beer either at Tom's house or at the Red Lion in Twickenham.

Mike took a long gulp of what he called 'the amber liquid'. 'Well, Tom, I think we've had a pretty good year.

Have you enjoyed it? I can think of one good reason why you will have!' Here Mike grinned a knowing grin. They were sitting in the garden of the Red Lion with almost full beer glasses on the table in front of them.

'Okay, Mike, yes I have.'

'Will you two be going off somewhere for the holidays?'

Tom had tried to keep his friendship with Anita low-profile but in the gossipy school world this had been beyond even his skills of deception.

'Probably. What about you and Debbie?'

'We're off to Spain to get a bit of sunshine, it's always raining in this place - not good for us Aussies!'

The long holiday stretched ahead.

This is more nerve-wracking than making an end of term speech, thought Tom. He and Anita were walking across a deserted meadow in Somerset, near to Tom's mother's house. It was very hot and they were in T-shirts and shorts. As they came up to a locked gate leading to the next field, Tom quickened his pace and climbed over first. He turned ready to help Anita, putting his arms out towards her. 'Anita, I was just wondering something.'

Anita paused, her suntanned leg halfway over the top bar. She looked down at him. 'What's that, Tom?'

It came out with a rush. 'I love you, Anita, and I want to marry you. Will you marry me?'

Anita laughed, lifted her other leg over the gate and fell into Tom's arms. 'Of course I will! I've been waiting for you to ask me for weeks now.'

Tom held her at arm's length for a moment and then

drew her towards him and kissed her, gently at first, and then with a passion which surprised them both.

They were married during the Easter school holidays. Mike was best man and made an amusing speech, only mentioning 'whinging Poms' once. Anita and the twins moved into the Headmaster's house, which filled it nicely. Ben and Charlie accepted Tom – they did, after all, know him pretty well already – they just had to remember when to call him 'Sir' and when to call him 'Tom'! Anita changed the bachelor style of furnishings and made the whole place much more cosy and homely. Naturally she became involved in all sorts of school events. As a result she found that she had less time for her Employment Agency business and decided to take on a partner.

The question of which school the twins should move onto after Shaftesbury was much discussed. Anita was still keen for them to stay living at home, while their father, Peter, favoured boarding school. Eventually the impasse was resolved when both Ben and Charlie said firmly that they wanted to board as they could play more sport at Oundle. Anita accepted this and the boys were entered for Common Entrance the following June.

Over the next two or three years, there were some staff changes. Barbara, the school secretary, decided that it was time to move to the country and retire. She was sorely missed. Simon applied for and was appointed as Deputy Head of an expanding school in Suffolk. Robin Bartlett did not go into teaching and started to train as a lawyer. Valerie Eales, having accepted that too much time off work did not go down well, left and took up a part-time post at another school. Alastair, Mike and Liz carried on as before except that Liz had to become full-time.

David Peterson, who had been taught to read in a month by Molly O'Farrell, joined the school and rapidly rose to the top of his class. James Bland, having proved he was capable, was promoted to the year above and after two years' hard work, won a minor award at Charterhouse, delighting his parents. Ben and Charlie Wolff passed Common Entrance and moved happily on to Oundle. Other former pupils also did well - Greg Kokri won the top music scholarship to St Peter's and then was selected for the National Youth Orchestra. Karen Rowe moved on to St Mary's where she was very happy, played plenty of sport and represented the London Schools at netball. Sean O'Farrell left school early, founded a computer company and, Tom suspected, was well on his way to his first million.

One February morning Tom was sitting at his desk looking out at the stark bare brown trees and watching specks of snow falling gently down onto the path. There was a good deal of winter to endure before the sun would begin to get warm again. Tom was not looking forward to donning his tracksuit and braving the cold for games that afternoon. The new school secretary, Jane, put her head around the door. 'There's a chap on the line who says he knows you - he's speaking from Kenya, shall I put him through?'

It must be Dave Rivers, thought Tom - Dave was an old cricketing friend of his who had gone to live in Kenya and had, quite successfully, started a travel company there. The previous Christmas, Tom, Anita and the twins had been out to Africa and had stayed with him and his family.

'Put him through, please, I wonder what he wants.'

'Hi, Dave,' began Tom, 'how's the batting going - still getting out slogging?'

'Listen,' replied Dave, 'you might be interested in this. You know The Kora School which our two attend? Well, I know the Chairman of the Board, Peter Mallinson, and he says that Mr Forest, the Head, is retiring and they will be looking for a new Head for September. It could be just up your street - and you could play cricket for the Kongonis! Why don't you apply?'

Tom looked again out of the window at the snow - what would Anita think, he wondered.

'Where's this job being advertised? I'll look at the details and yes, I'm certainly very interested.'

'It's a great school, both ours love it and you'd like the outdoor life. I've taken the liberty of mentioning your name to Peter and he was very interested to hear about you. Go for it!'

Dave arranged to send the details.

Anita and Tom sat for hours discussing the pros and cons of moving to Africa.

Tom was concerned about the boys. 'What about the twins? What would they say if we went off to Nairobi?'

'They're happy enough at Oundle and I'm sure they'd love coming out in the holidays. Think what safaris we could do with them.'

'What about your business? You and Frances are making quite a success of it.'

'Frances is taking on more and more these days - I've

been quite involved here, you know, Tom. I've been thinking recently that she might like to take over completely – no, I don't think that would be a problem.'

'What about you? Do you mind snakes and wild animals?'

'I'm not keen on snakes but don't forget, I spent part of my childhood in India so I'd cope. Hey! Would we have servants?'

'I expect so - you would certainly not be doing much washing up or cleaning! The shopping would hardly be Oxford Street though.'

Anita hesitated. 'I suppose not. We would come back to the UK for the summer holidays, wouldn't we?'

'Of course.'

'Then, if you're offered the job, I think you should go for it,' said Anita firmly.

So Tom sent in his application. Not long afterwards Peter Mallinson came over to the UK. He rang up and asked if he could meet Tom and then have a look around Shaftesbury Prep. After an exhaustive tour Peter questioned Tom closely about all the recent developments and how the place was run in detail. He said little in reply.

They then spoke at length about The Kora School and where Peter saw it going. There were many similarities to Shaftesbury, together with some added problems one needed to deal with, such as work permits and currency variations. Peter was keen to make sure his school was well up to date with the entire recent curriculum and other educational developments in the UK and he had clearly been impressed with what he had seen at

Shaftesbury. There was new construction being planned and the next Head would be in a position to be fully involved in the design and use of this development. The academic and sporting side of the school was already strong but other areas such as music, art and technology needed better facilities. Tom warmed to the way Peter said with great conviction that he wanted The Kora School to be the best prep school in Africa. Perhaps it could be.

A few days later, Peter rang and offered Tom the job of Head of The Kora School in Nairobi to start in September. Though he would be sorry to say goodbye to Shaftesbury, Tom felt he had done as much as he was going to do there and that it was
time for another challenge - which Africa would surely provide. He accepted the post.

The next few months were extremely busy. Tom went along to see the Chairman and explained he had been offered another job and handed in his notice. Ted was disappointed but understanding and thanked Tom for all he had managed to achieve at Shaftesbury Prep. Ben and Charlie knew about the possibility of a move to Africa and, when Anita told them that it was definite, they were excited by the prospect of trips to Kenya which they thought would be more fun than Twickenham. Anita discussed with her partner, Frances, the future of their business and Frances, who was already taking the major role at their office, decided to buy out Anita's share. Tom and Anita went shopping for short-sleeved shirts, shorts and safari jackets. The post of Head of Shaftesbury Prep was advertised. Despite Tom's prodding, Mike Dawson did not apply.

At the end of Tom's last term, Mike arranged a leaving party and the staff presented Tom with an Australian bush hat made by Akubra, which they thought would be most suitable for the wilds of Kenya.

Chapter Ten

The big jumbo jet circled over the Nairobi Game Park preparing to land at Jomo Kenyatta International Airport. Anita leant over Tom to look through the window. Below them the reddish-brown dusty plains were dotted with small green areas marking the water holes. They could make out herds of zebra and impala grazing quietly and a few giraffe were nibbling the tops of acacia trees. The plane touched down and soon they were at the airport exit, looking through a sea of black faces for the familiar profile of Peter Mallinson.

The school was about twenty minutes drive from the centre of Nairobi and a house had been rented for the use of the Headmaster and his family about a mile down the road. It was a large, not very beautiful place but with a pleasant garden, well stocked with bottlebrush bushes, hibiscus and jacaranda trees. A purple bougainvillea entwined the entrance porch. Beyond the fence was the Ngong Forest and behind the house were the African servants' quarters - a couple of bare rooms and a toilet. This was where Irene, who looked after the house and her husband David, who was the gardener, lived.

They emerged expectantly as Anita and Tom arrived in Peter's car, beaming warm welcomes. Irene, although still quite young, was a large and motherly figure and she shook hands with both of her new employers and then insisted on taking the cases inside. David, whose thin face was also wreathed in smiles, was small and wiry. He didn't say much and Irene told him sharply to help her with the bags. He did so immediately. It was clear who was in charge!

Parked in the driveway was a smart-looking Mitsubishi which, it emerged was to be the Headmaster's car. Peter showed Tom and Anita round the house and then departed.

Their new life in African had begun.

'You'll have to go to the prison,' said Veronica Mabete, the school secretary.

What on earth for, Tom wondered - this was his first day at The Kora School and he certainly did not wish to have anything to do with Kenyan prisons which, Tom had heard, made Pentonville look like Butlin's.

Veronica went on to explain. 'Our taekwondo instructor works as a prison officer at the Langata Road Prison. His name is Paul Olongo and he doesn't have a phone - at the beginning of the year we have to go down to the prison and tell him when we want him to come. He's not very reliable so you'd better write it down for him. We'll need him for an hour at three o'clock on Friday afternoons.'

The idea of an unreliable prison officer did not fill Tom with confidence but he agreed to go and look for him. Various activities were organised on a Friday afternoon instead of the normal games sessions. Sport being taken very seriously in this part of the world: cricket, rounders, hockey, rugby or netball was played every other afternoon for an hour or so. Friday activities included cubs and brownies, Swahili, Scottish country dancing, photography, squash, golf, pottery, gymnastics and, of course, taekwondo - if the teacher could be found. Tom did not know much about taekwondo apart from the fact that it was a martial art similar to judo and karate.

The Langata Road Prison seemed to be a pretty laid-back establishment. There was a guard of sorts on the gate but plenty of people appeared to be free to wander in and out. Tom thought they were probably relatives of the inmates bringing them food and other supplies. He asked the guard, who was leaning up against the small gatehouse, where he might find Paul Olongo.

'Yes, *bwana*. You will find him over there.' He waved an oily rag with which he had been cleaning his ancient rifle in the direction of a group of huts.

Well-trodden tracks criss-crossed the baked mud compound connecting the various huts with the gate and each other. Small groups of men, presumably prisoners, were gathered squatting under trees; some were cooking, some mending clothes and some doing nothing except watching. Tom walked in the direction the gate man had indicated, feeling particularly conspicuous as the only white face around. Three uniformed guards were chatting to each other and laughing.

'I am looking for Paul Olongo,' began Tom, 'can you tell me where to find him, please?'

'You have found him, *bwana*,' replied a small powerful-looking man. 'I am Paul. I think you have come about the taekwondo; is that so?'

Tom assured him that it was so and introduced himself as the new Headmaster of The Kora School. Would he be able to come and take his classes on Fridays at three o'clock?

'I can come,' he said, 'but I will need to get permission from my boss. I think it will be no problem. If I come for one hour, how many shillings?'

'It will be eighty shillings for one hour,' said Tom, 'but you must agree to come for the whole term - starting on Friday the 12th September until December 12th which would be the last day.'

Paul smiled broadly and agreed he would come. His two companions had been listening intently to the conversation.

'I know The Kora School,' said one. 'It is a very good school. I could come to your school and teach the boys to play football. I am a very good player.'

Tom replied quickly, 'Thank you very much, but we already have a football coach - in fact several teachers for sport. But if we need one more I will ask Paul to ask you to come and talk to me.'

The man nodded and seemed happy with this, so Tom said goodbye to the three of them and made his way out of the compound, wondering if Paul would appear the following Friday.

When Tom returned to school and told Veronica that the taekwondo teacher was all organised, she just looked at him and said, 'We'll see!' Veronica, as Tom was to discover quickly, was inclined to be cynical, having adopted a 'seen it all before' attitude. Her father was a well-known Kenyan politician and, although shielded from the real world for a time when she was sent off to England to a boarding school, she was well aware of the pitfalls of life in Africa. She had worked at the school for a couple of years and was a key person – though Tom rather doubted that he would be able to build up the same sort of relationship he had had with Barbara. Veronica was a bit more distant, though she was certainly efficient. Tom retired to the study to prepare for a meeting next day with his Deputy, John Hutton.

At ten o'clock next morning, Tom stood in the middle of the games field thinking how lucky he was to be there. The sun was beating down from a cloudless sky but, as yet, it was not too hot. Towards the south-west it was just possible to make out the shape of Mount Kilimanjaro with its white topping of snow shimmering through the heat haze. Over fifty miles away it was the highest mountain in Africa and often visible from the playing fields. Just across the road a row of five giraffe ambled along inside the game park fence, their long necks and purple tongues reaching out for the tender top shoots of the acacia trees. From the low classroom block John Hutton came walking purposefully across the field. 'Good morning, Tom. I've got the timetable, duties and games lists for you to look at and we need to make a decision on where to use the two extra computers which arrived yesterday.'

John, or Jonny as he preferred to be called, was a white Kenyan. He was born and brought up near Nanyuki out in the bush where his father had a farm and was sent away to boarding school in England at the age of thirteen. He had found England to be terribly cold, but he was a tough character and good at rugby so he was respected and eventually did well. Not really knowing what he wanted to do after school he trained as a teacher. His first post was in a Birmingham inner-city comprehensive - he lasted a year and then applied for and was appointed as history teacher at a prep school in Dorset. Remembering his own prep school days in Africa when the children did what they were told or were given six of the best with the 'tackie' or gymshoe, he found the modern laid-back attitude to discipline far too lax. It wasn't long before he was applying for teaching jobs back in Kenya. So here he was, very much in his element - he had gained quick promotion at The Kora School where everyone hoped he would stay for some time before he inevitably took over as Head somewhere else.

'Okay, Jonny,' said Tom, 'let's go back to the study - I was just enjoying the wide open spaces here!'

'You should have seen the fields three months ago before the rains - they were completely brown. It's amazing how the grass grows after the rains.' Jonny pointed to some men who were working on the other side of the field. 'I think Gideon wants to have a word with you when you have a moment.'

Gideon was a very important person - he was in charge of the ground staff who looked after the games fields and in fact all twenty acres of school grounds. He had worked for the school for fifteen years and knew everything there was to know about the grounds and how they should be managed. He had sixteen men working for him - rather more than the one caretaker cum groundsman, George Millar, who had looked after the Shaftsbury Prep school grounds in London! Probably their combined wages equalled that of George.

Tom made a mental note to speak to Gideon as soon as he could.

Jonny and Tom spent the rest of the morning going through various documents that had been prepared most efficiently. The beginning of year staff meeting was fast approaching and they needed to be armed with all necessary information.

The next morning found Tom deep in conversation with Gideon who was rather annoyed by the latest problem to face him. The school had some permanent cricket nets made out of chicken wire tied onto metal poles. The playing surface was '*murram*' – hard baked red earth - on top of which coconut matting was laid. Gideon explained the problem.

'You see this post, *bwana* Thorne,' he said sadly. 'It has been knocked sideways. It is the warthogs living on the *shamba* over there.' He pointed to a group of huts surrounded by bushes and open grassy areas. 'They come over at night and dig holes and scratch themselves on my posts. It is very annoying.'

You could not argue with that, though what could be done about it was beyond Tom.

'Can we not make our fence stronger to keep them out?' he asked naively.

'We have mended the fence often, but the warthogs are very determined. They easily break through the fence.'

Not knowing much about warthogs, Tom just made a sympathetic grunt and asked if Gideon had all the equipment he needed for sport facilities during the coming term. It would be the cricket and rounders term - with plenty of swimming, tennis and athletics as well. Gideon promised that all would be ready for the start of term and went off to supervise his men.

The school Bursar, Major Jim Broom, came in to brief Tom on what he expected. The Major had retired from the army after a moderately undistinguished career in The King's African Rifles and had taken up an offer made by the then British colonial authorities to purchase at a discount some farming land in the North West of the country. He and his delightful wife, Doreen, were making a good go of this when Independence came along and soon pressure was put on Europeans to hand over their farms to Africans. The Major wisely sold out and looked around for something else to do. After a number of false starts he ended up as Bursar of The Kora School, a job he was quite well suited for since much of his time was spent chasing up the African ground, maintenance, cleaning and kitchen staff - all of whom were charming but lazy if given half a chance.

The trim figure of the Bursar, his white moustache neatly brushed, came straight to the point. 'Now, Tom,' he began briskly, 'the most important thing at the beginning of term is to get the fees in as soon as possible. There are some notorious bad payers and it would be a great help if you could back me up on this one.'

'Of course, Jim, I will certainly do that. Just give me the names of those who are a problem and I'll contact them personally.'

'Good. We had some problems regarding this with your predecessor who was rather laid-back.'

They went on to discuss the history of the school and the set-up of the Board and administration generally. The Kora School had been up and running for about thirty years or so; it had originally been set up by an old Kenya hand, Fred Thompson and his wife Vera, who had bought what was then the old Kora Hotel on the edge of the Nairobi Game Park. The Kora was a pleasant old-fashioned watering hole used by a wide variety of customers from local African businessmen to European doctors and professionals as well as game wardens; not too many tourists though - it was not very sophisticated and did not have a swimming pool. The day Fred and Vera bought the place they went around inspecting the rooms. These were in a number of wooden huts dotted around the compound. Vera was horrified to find a dead body in one of the rooms.

Naturally enough she immediately refused to move into the place and so she and Fred had to return to the Muthaiga Club for the night while the police investigated. It turned out that the corpse was a bona fide guest who had suffered a heart attack; the owner of the hotel, not wishing to pay more wages than necessary, had dismissed his staff the previous day and hadn't bothered to check the rooms before handing Fred the hotel keys.

This little hiccup sorted, Fred and Vera set about altering the premises so they could run it as an English prep school and within a few months had acquired a dozen pupils. The school had prospered and by the time Fred retired seven years previously the number of pupils had risen to over three hundred with at least twenty different nationalities represented. The curriculum was exactly the same as provided by other IAPS schools in England - except that Swahili was also taught. The school had been sold a couple of times since then and now the owner was an Asian businessman who kept himself out of the limelight. He was apparently keen to contribute to 'education' in the country but was also not averse to making a profit. He had appointed a Board to oversee the general running of the school and left things to them. Tom had been appointed by the Chairman of the Board and would deal on a day-to-day basis with him, but as yet had not discovered the identity of the real owner. Tom presumed that would come with time. Jim clearly knew a good deal more but was certainly not divulging other than what was absolutely necessary at the moment.

The Bursar's department comprised quite an assortment

of people. There were several book-keepers and assistants who, it seemed, were required to do the same job carried out by just one lady - Liz Freeland - at Shaftsbury Prep and she was part-time at first. Tom did not mention this to Jim. The Major was not one for small talk so, once he had completed his briefing, he stood up to leave. Tom thanked him for his time but he was already out of the door. A moment later, he could be heard berating some unfortunate cleaner for not doing something he should have done. He obviously kept things in order did the Major.

Tom did not know quite what to expect at the pre-term staff meeting. Jonny had filled him in regarding some of the characters on the staff and he had met most of them informally during the previous few days. He had been made most welcome but he was still a bit nervous going into the large assembly hall, where a table for himself and Jonny had been set out facing a double row of chairs for the staff. They proved to be a frisky lot and quite ready to put forward their particular points of view. Presumably this was partly because they were a lot younger and more adventurous - why else would they drop a perfectly safe job in the UK and come out to Africa?

There was only one absentee - a new teacher by the name of Gerald Minster, who had been appointed to teach science by Tom's predecessor. Gerald was a South African and the Major had said that there had been some difficulty getting him a work permit - white South Africans were not popular here. Someone said that he had been seen in Nairobi so he was around. It was not a good start for him though.

After much backslapping and 'How was your safari?' to each other the motley collection of teachers settled themselves in the two rows of chairs. Various documents were handed out - timetables and other vital lists which were inspected hastily.

All sorts of routine matters were summarily deal with - including Tom's statement that there were to be no 'physical' punishments - the days of six of the best with the 'tackie' were long past. Not that there was any need for that sort of thing - relations between staff and pupils were generally recognised to be excellent. Because they were mostly pretty young, the teachers were able to remain on relaxed and easy terms with their pupils, while at the same time retaining their respect. It was one of the great strengths of the school, Jonny had said.

Jonny went through the 'duties' list; Fergus Glover, the man in charge of the stationery cupboard - a very important job - gave complicated instructions on how to order more exercise books, pencils and the like. Fergus was one of the longest serving members of staff and was a most fastidious character. He liked everything just so. He had taught most subjects in his time and now took a large portion of the geography as well as running the cub pack with huge dedication. His khaki shorts were always neatly pressed and, equipped with a collection of different coloured biros stuffed down his long socks, he was prepared for any scribing requirement that should arise. Fergus was a fixture and a character.

Ross Pelling and Angela Hughes, in charge of boys' and girls' games respectively, told everyone about equipment and the games programme. Ross was young and keen and had played rugby to a very good standard in England. He had abandoned his original ambition to play rugby at the highest level and arrived two years earlier at The Kora School to develop his teaching career where he had made an immediate impact. Angela was also a fine games player and had once been ranked number one tennis player in Kenya. She was an excellent games coach and had produced a series of unbeaten netball and hockey teams.

Through the assembly hall window Tom was relieved to see Anita who had arrived to join everyone for lunch. The meeting broke up and they all moved to the dining room for a buffet eagerly devoured by the staff. Since most of them had been catering for themselves during the holidays they needed no invitation to tuck in.

That evening Tom and Anita sat outside in the garden, sipping their drinks, chatting about the events of the last few days and watching the sun go down.

It was the first day of term. Rather surprisingly Gerald Minster arrived early, smartly dressed, and apologised for missing the staff meeting. He had misunderstood the time, he said. Jonny told Tom he had heard that Gerald had been seen in The Thorn Tree - a well-known hotel much used as a meeting place in town - talking to someone from the film crew who were in town to make a movie. Nairobi was sometimes used as a base for film-making due to the sunshine and cheap cost of locally recruited labour although this was counterbalanced by the hassle involved in obtaining permission to film and work permits for actors, technicians and so on from the authorities. Maybe Gerald fancied a career as an actor. Almost all the children who were expected arrived and greeted each other noisily as they made their way to the low brick classroom blocks. A purposeful low buzz settled on the place and the term commenced.

In England one tended to assume that the phones would work, that water would come through the tap when it was turned on and that the electricity supply wouldn't break down - well, at least not that often. This certainly was not the case in Nairobi. On the second day of term the telephones wouldn't work. It didn't worry Tom too much - less communication meant less hassle - but it did upset the Major who was already on the warpath for those hapless parents who hadn't sent the fees in on the first day of term. He was pacing his office like a caged tiger when Tom went down to see him.

'What's the matter with the phone system, Jim?'

'It's the usual problem. Giraffe moving out onto the plains - they knock the wires down; it often happens and it takes the telephone people days to repair the damage. I'll have to get Joseph to go into town and talk to his cousin.'

Joseph Waljema was an invaluable person to have in the office. His official title was bookkeeper but in fact a more accurate description would have been 'Mr Fix It'. He came from a large family and had relations working in almost all the government departments the school needed to deal with. This was most useful. Joseph would surely be able to pull a few strings and get the phones back working again. This sometimes required an appropriate palm to be greased but the Major had a fund for that sort of thing and dispensed cash when needed. Joseph was duly briefed and departed into town.

The Major was out in the school car park first thing next morning still trying to catch those parents who owed fees. He was particularly pleased with one success.

'That chap Walji has pots of money but it's difficult to catch him.' The Major looked at Tom and nodded towards a swarthy-looking man climbing into a smart black Mercedes.

'He's had five sons through The Kora; three of them are with us now. He runs a transport business with at least a dozen lorries supplying goods to Somalia and bringing all sorts of stuff back. I got him to pay in cash - he doesn't deal in anything else. Look!'

The Major delved into his pocket and withdrew a large wad of used five hundred shilling notes. Tom was suitably impressed and congratulated him accordingly.

'Do you know, Tom, he also has five daughters but he doesn't think they need to be educated - well at least not here anyway. He could well afford it. Poor show really.'

Tom was surprised that the Major had such liberal views. One would have put his politics somewhere to the right of Ghengis Khan!

The Kenyan postal service being a bit erratic to say the least and the fact that most people in this part of the world had better things to do than writing complaining letters to their child's Headmaster meant that it didn't take long to deal with the mail. Usually there wasn't any. There were other problems though of an administrative nature. Or at least that originated in the office. Veronica, the school secretary, was efficient but she could not get on with the Major and his sidekick, Joseph. She regarded the Major as a throwback to the bad old days of the colonialists and Joseph as a bit too sharp for his own good. She spent quite a bit of her time trying to catch the pair of them out.

The Major, for his part, thought that Veronica was too self-important for a mere school secretary and that his position of Bursar should be shown more respect. To say that relations between the Bursar's office and the school office were strained was an understatement. Fortunately they were situated at opposite ends of the school compound, so the two camps could avoid each other easily enough. Tom, however, had to keep on good terms with both sides and this would involve some taxing of the diplomatic powers!

One morning Veronica had some lists that had to be copied and given out to the teachers. Predictably, her photocopier broke down and she immediately blamed the Major for not getting a new one the previous term.

'It's so typical of that man. I told him this machine was on its last legs years ago but he wouldn't do anything about it. I'll have to go down and use his.'

Tom thought it wise to keep the two offending sides apart. 'Don't worry, I'm going down to see Jim myself - I'll take the lists and get Joseph to do them.'

When he arrived at the Bursar's office everyone was having tea and some excellent home-made pizza. The school kitchen was run by an eccentric Welshman by the name of Roddy Jones. Roddy made a point of providing the staff each day with tasty 'elevenses' which were always freshly cooked and hot from the oven. He was an extremely popular man in the staff room.

Tom placed the lists which needed to be copied on Jim's desk.

'Jim, I wonder if Joseph could make twenty copies of this list for me? Veronica's photocopier has broken down and they are needed today.'

Jim finished munching his pizza and offered Tom a slice. He accepted.

'Needed today, eh?' The Major brushed away a piece of pizza from his moustache. 'Wonder why she didn't get it done a bit earlier. She always leaves things to the last minute. Yes, okay.' He called a loud 'Joseph!' and a moment later an earnest dark face appeared in the doorway. Joseph was despatched to do the copying.

Every Friday after lessons were over in the afternoon 'other activities' were organised. The games fields would be covered by miscellaneous groups of children engaged in all sorts of activities. Budding gymnasts would be performing outside the assembly hall on mats laid haphazardly on the grass. A large group of girls would be seen Scottish country dancing - an incongruous sight in the middle of Africa. The cubs would meet under a tree, earnestly organised by Fergus, always immaculately kitted out in his khaki shorts and scouting shirt. On this first Friday of term, Paul Olongo, the taekwondo teacher, rather surprisingly arrived on time for his session and began to explain the rituals of his sport. The children entered enthusiastically into the spirit shouting high-pitched cries and performing what looked like karate chops. Paul spotted Tom and greeted him with a broad white-toothed grin as if he was an old friend.

At the end of the day Tom and the Major were standing in the school car park watching the stream of slightly grubby children find their parents' cars while a load of others waited patiently to be sent off to the four buses hired by the school to carry children back to various outlying districts of Nairobi.

The Major knew most of the children and said goodnight to one lanky fair-haired eleven-year-old as he strolled past.

'Goodnight, Jim!' came the easy reply. It was not too formal here.

Anita found her new life very strange at first – she had been used to doing her own washing and cleaning in England, but here all these mundane tasks were carried out by Irene. Shopping was certainly an experience and it took quite some time for her to work out which *duka* or shop in the little Karen shopping area sold what. As soon as they had arrived, Dave Rivers and his charming wife Rani had invited them round for a meal. 'It's great to have you two out here!' Dave had welcomed them warmly and very soon the two men had become immersed in the subject of cricket. Meanwhile Rani began to brief Anita on the delights and pitfalls of living in Nairobi. Anita quickly accepted her offer of trips together around the various places one needed to know about in town. However, even though she thoroughly enjoyed Rani's company, Anita found herself with time on her hands. Although a very social person, she was not at all inclined to join the hard-drinking, bridge and golf-playing wives who frequented Nairobi. She began to cast around for something interesting to do. This was a problem, for without a work permit you could not take a paid job if you were a foreigner. Work permits were only granted to those with a particular skill not available from Kenyans. She had heard that there was an animal refuge centre next to the Nairobi Game Park where volunteers were welcome. She resolved to look into this at the earliest opportunity.

Tom was sitting at his desk when Veronica arrived at eight thirty one morning; she greeted him with a little more warmth than had been apparent at the beginning of term - he was slowly making progress!

'The Chairman of the Board, Mr Mallinson, wants to come and see you. I've made an appointment for him tomorrow afternoon. Is that all right?'

'Fine.' Tom was looking forward to talking to Peter again.

Peter was a white Kenyan and had lived all his life in Africa. He was a partner in a firm of lawyers in Nairobi and had lots of useful contacts. An influential and well-known character in the business world, his two children had attended The Kora. He kept a close eye on the running of the school and was held in some awe by the staff.

Tom went into the staff room at morning break to let everyone know that the Chairman would be paying the school a visit the following afternoon. Maybe their respective programmes for the after lunch and games sessions could be planned more carefully but Tom doubted it. The staff were a pretty easy-going and confident bunch. At least the new teachers seemed to have settled in well and the South African science teacher, Gerald Minster, was present and correct. The

Major had assured Tom that Gerald's work permit was now in order.

Peter Mallinson slipped in to have a word with Jim before coming up to Tom's office. He was apparently always keen to know the latest financial state of the school - and presumably had to report this back to the owner at regular intervals. The Major and Peter had known each other for years and played golf at Karen Country Club together - the Major played off a handicap of eight and Peter off six. They usually took the money in their regular Sunday four-ball. Karen, the district close to the Kora School and named after the Danish writer Karen Blixen, who had lived there for many years, boasted a small shopping area, some smart expatriate occupied houses and the immaculately maintained Country Club.

The tall figure of the Chairman made his way through the outer office where Veronica was unusually busy; he greeted her and then came into the study and with a friendly smile he lowered himself into a chair. 'Well, Tom, how is Anita settling into life here? It will take a bit of adapting for her, I expect. Is the house all right?'

'Well, it is a bit strange but Anita is beginning to find her way about. The house is fine although we do have a problem with the water - there isn't any sometimes!' There was supposed to be mains water supplied to the house Tom and Anita were living in but it was quite often switched off; there was a large storage tank in the garden but the water level was getting low.

'If you need water, just ask Jim to organise a bowser for you,' said Peter.

Many people seemed to rely on bowsers or water

lorries to top up their supplies – expensive but necessary.

Peter continued, 'Everything seems to be going quite smoothly. Jim tells me that the numbers are more or less as expected and that the fees are coming in well. I hear you have had a bit of trouble getting a work permit for one teacher?'

'Yes, I'm afraid so. It's Gerald Minster - Jim says that they don't much like South Africans but his came through in the end.'

'If you have any legal problems, don't hesitate to get onto me. I do know some useful people who may be able to help.'

Peter leant his long frame back in the chair and rubbed the side of his nose with a finger. He gave the impression of someone who usually got what he wanted and that it would be unwise to get on the wrong side of him. He and Tom spent the next half an hour talking about the teaching staff and how Tom had found them so far.

'You have some strong characters in the staff room. Don't underestimate them. Jane Hogan is one - she can be charming to your face but work against you behind your back. You need to watch her.'

Jane was the teacher in charge of what was called the Junior School - Years One and Two. So far she had been delightful and most welcoming. Tom raised his eyebrows but thanked Peter for the warning.

'Jonny Hutton is absolutely straight,' went on Peter. 'I know his family well and he will always be loyal - you can confide in him.'

This conversation was beginning to sound like a briefing by M to James Bond but Tom nodded, trying to take in as much as he could. Eventually they came to a pause and Tom suggested they had a wander around the school. They were just in time to see Ross Pelling take the first game cricket. There were some very useful players left over from last year's side. One in particular, Jasrinder Singh, a large Asian boy, was an outstanding cricketer for his age. He bowled slow left arm and turned the ball sharply. His father had played for East Africa in the old days and his son had certainly inherited his talent. Jas, as he was known, was also a powerful batsman with a tremendous 'eye'. Tom and Peter moved on to watch the girls playing rounders - Tom was amazed to see so many athletic children compared to those he was used to in London. Of course, it was hardly surprising considering the outdoor life children led here. There was not much in the way of TV to watch and they were blessed with good weather for most of the year. Tom was confident that the Chairman went off happy with what he had seen.

Boys will be boys, it is true, but one day a twelve-year-old boy called Jeremy Duckworth went somewhat over the top. Jonny had dealt with this incident, which had happened first thing in the morning. There was a girl in Jeremy's class called Rose Best. Rose was a very correct and charming English girl whose parents had recently been posted to Nairobi – her father worked for the World Bank, which had a large office in the Kenyan capital. Rose was a little prim for the likes of Jeremy who was a bit of a 'lad'. He had always lived in Kenya and was very much at home at The Kora which he had attended since the age of six. One break time Jeremy and his sidekick, William James, had found a dead rat in the grounds and had thought up a good wheeze to play on poor Rose. The classrooms were equipped with old-fashioned desks with lids that lifted up. Books and pens etc were kept inside.

After Rose had gone home, Jeremy and William opened her desk lid and pinned the end of the dead rat's tail to the underside with a drawing pin. They carefully closed the lid with the rat inside.

The boys made sure they were in the classroom when Rose came in the following morning. Being a conscientious girl she went to her desk to get her books out for the first lesson. As she lifted the lid the dead rat swung out towards her face. She let out a piercing shriek much to the delight of Jeremy and William. Unfortunately for them Jonny happened to be passing their classroom at the time.

'I have made the boys apologise to Rose,' said Jonny, relating the incident to Tom, 'and given them plenty of work to do in detention, but maybe you should also have a word with them? I have to give them full marks though for initiative!'

As Tom spoke to the two miscreants later that morning he found it quite hard to keep a smile off his face.

As Anita and Tom were sitting on the terrace after school enjoying a quiet drink, Irene and David appeared.

Irene as usual spoke for the two of them. '*Memsab*, David and I would like to know if you and *bwana* are from the same tribe.'

This was a perfectly reasonable question since Kenya is a very tribal place and it was unusual for people from different tribes to marry. She and David were both Kikuyus.

Tom and Anita looked at each other. He was from London and she from the West Country. Hardly the same tribe.

'Yes, of course,' replied Anita. 'We are from the same tribe though it is a big tribe which spreads through the south of England.'

'Ah, that is good.' Irene and David went off, satisfied.

Chapter Eleven

Tom had just put away his hymnbook after Assembly when there came an urgent knock at the door. It was a Year Six girl called Christine Haithar whose dark face was creased with worry.

'Please, Sir, there's a snake in the art room!'

This certainly didn't happen in London, Tom thought as he went with Christine to the door of the art room. An excited group of children were gathered outside - with their new teacher carefully not getting too close to the door. Linda O'Shea had recently arrived from Ireland and was proving to be an inventive art teacher but she clearly did not like snakes. Maybe that had something to do with the fact that they don't actually have any in Ireland. Tom wondered fleetingly what had made her come out to Africa.

'Move back from the door, please. Let's have a look.'

In the far corner of the room, a large brown-coloured snake was curled up underneath a table. Tom had no idea what it was but it was big - about four foot long - and it had a diamond shaped head; could it be a puff adder?

One of the boys outside said should we call Gideon. But none of the African staff would go anywhere near a snake - sensibly, Tom thought. There was one teacher on the staff, however, who kept snakes as pets and knew all about them. She would deal with this little problem. Christine was despatched to find her.

A few minutes later Molly Brown arrived. Molly, one

of the Year One teachers, had lived out in the bush for years and was something of an expert on snakes. She took one look at the invader and pronounced that it was quite harmless - just a 'house snake'. With that she picked the unfortunate snake up by the tip of its tail and carried it outside accompanied by much squealing from the boys and girls who had been following events with great interest. Art was popular but this had been much more exciting. Linda led her class back into their lesson, looking carefully under all the tables in case the snake had a friend still hiding.

Anita was settling quite well into the African lifestyle - and the fact that the electricity and telephone didn't always work was acceptable; anyway, not to have the phone ringing all the time was sometimes an advantage. She had gathered together a varied collection of candles in case the lights weren't working and there was also a large stone fireplace in the living room for cold evenings; even just south of the equator it could be very chilly at night. One of David's jobs was to keep the wood basket full.

Lack of water was however a pain! You couldn't really do without it for long and in Langata the water supply was often cut off for days at a time. There was a large water tank at the back of the house, which could slowly be filled up when and if the 'mains' was working. During the rainy season the tank would be quickly filled up due to a complicated system of pipes from the guttering which had been put together by their resourceful gardener. When it rained he would stand outside admiring his handiwork as the water poured into the tank - he himself would be soaked but happy; however during the long dry season the level of water would drop quickly.

Anita, getting more confident, went off in a determined mood to have a word with the Major; she was determined to get him to arrange for at least one water lorry or 'bowser' to fill up the tank. The Major, as ever, was busy ticking off some unfortunate school employee but, seeing Anita marching into his office in a mood that clearly meant business, he dismissed the man and asked her what he could do for her.

'Jim, our water level is right down again and we need topping up. Can you arrange for some to be delivered?'

'Didn't you have some delivered the other day?'

'Yes, but it's finished, Jim.'

'I hope you are not flushing the lavatory too much - these bowsers are not cheap.' Anita gritted her teeth. 'Only when necessary, Jim!'

'Okay, of course you must have some more - I'll get Joseph to arrange it. We don't use the council supply any longer - it's better to pay the army to deliver water. They have access to the mains and Joseph knows the officer in charge - for a fee he'll drop off a load or two to your house instead of the barracks. I'll let you know when to expect a delivery.'

Later that evening Anita was telling Tom about her encounter with the Major. 'Do you know he wanted to know how many times we went to the loo? Ridiculous man! I don't much like his attitude, Tom.' Tom could hardly disagree. Still, the next day two bowsers arrived filling the tank - so their ablutions could continue unabated.

Tom didn't get much in the way of mail in Kenya, certainly not from pupils. So he was amazed to receive a splendid letter one morning, written by three ten-year-old boys. It was neatly typed and left on his desk. It read as follows:

Dear Mr Thorne
I hope you like Kora School. Mr Forest is glad you have come to take over his job. Congratulations that you have become the new headmaster of the Kora School. You are doing a very good job here. You are just made for this kind of job. I hope you like your job. There is only one complaint to make, that is you should talk more about sports than work. If it is sunny and there is puddles please make it games. If there is wet games please can we do something more interesting than reading our books.
Yours sincerely
Dhruv, Karan and Shaun.

Of course, Tom resolved to spend less time worrying about unimportant matters such as academics and concentrate on the really important things such as sport. Well, not entirely!

Ignoring the request from his three well-meaning pupils, Tom continued to teach maths - he took the lower Year Five set who were delightful but not geniuses. They understood all about animals, sport and many practical things but were not too hot on their tables. The sums they did meant nothing unless they were related to things they liked. So they had questions such as 'How many legs do three giraffes, a warthog and a chicken have?' Or 'Australia score three tries and two penalties in the World Cup Final. How many points did they score?' Needless to say the girls did know that you get five points for a try and three for a penalty!

Back in the staff room at break time everyone was talking about an incident that had happened the night before to a boy called Daniel. Daniel was a resilient ten-year-old who was often left alone with his mother - his father ran upmarket safaris and was often away in places like Samburu or the Mara with rich clients.

At about ten o'clock that evening some burglars attempted to break into the house. Daniel's mother was, naturally enough, terrified but Daniel coolly got out of bed and collected his 22 rifle from the cupboard in his bedroom. He had been given it for his tenth birthday a few weeks before and had used it for target shooting in the garden. He then went up to the window which the burglars had broken and shouted at them that he would shoot if they didn't go away. He fired a shot over their heads to make his point, quickly reloading. The burglars retreated. When this attempted break-in was reported to the police, they were very impressed with Daniel and advised him that next time, should there ever be a next time, he should shoot to hit the burglars. 'That is what they deserve' he was told. Not the sort of advice he would have been given by the police in England!

The Kora did not have a proper purpose-built music school and the art room, apart from being infested with snakes, was too small and had inadequate storage space. So the Board had decided to build a new block to incorporate two music teaching rooms and several small practice rooms as well as a large art room. The architect chosen was a Kenyan called Richard Maeda who had designed a number of game lodges. Peter Mallinson had asked Tom to go down to his office for a meeting with Mr Maeda to finalise the plans. As always it was pleasant to escape from school for the morning, so Tom drove off cheerfully down the Langata Road into town. This sounds easy but maximum concentration was needed to avoid the enormous potholes in the road and to anticipate the erratic and adventurous driving of the *matatu* drivers racing out of town. *Matatus*, small van-like vehicles crammed full with passengers, were one of the main methods of getting around if you didn't have a car. They were cheap, often unsafe and the drivers could be crazy. Regularly when the inside was full, there would be several extra passengers hanging perilously onto the outside of a vehicle as it threaded its way nimbly through the traffic. Occasionally they might be stopped by the police, but a small payment from the 'conductor' would normally be enough to allow their journey to continue. It was essential to give *matatus* as wide a berth as possible!

Peter's office was certainly not plush but it was functional; neat rows of law reports filled the shelves and there were comfortable leather armchairs arranged around a low table ready for the meeting. The proposed plans were laid out on the table as Richard Maeda explained the layout of the new building.

Richard was a dapper cheerful man with a broad smile and loud laugh - he wore a red spotted bow tie and oozed confidence. His view was that there was nothing which couldn't be done if one used sufficient ingenuity and his good humour was totally infectious. His proposed design for the school building looked very like one of his game lodges; there was a high sloping roof with large exposed wooden beams and very large first floor windows. The first floor was to be the new art room. The outside of the building was striking and impressive. Since the school was right next to the National Game Park, Richard's design seemed to be appropriate. Peter turned to Tom and asked his opinion.

'I think the shape and outside design of the building is excellent,' said Tom. 'I just wonder if there is enough storage space for both the art and music departments. They have to keep lots of bulky instruments and equipment and the teachers always seem to be complaining of lack of storage!'

This point was taken and Richard explained how his plan could be altered in a fairly minor way. After further deliberation, the meeting broke up. Having agreed the final plans, the surveyor would now cost the operation and hopefully building could begin soon. Tom was pleased to be at a school where things were happening and he looked forward to showing prospective parents around the new facilities.

As Tom drove home one evening he was still feeling irritated by a letter he had received that morning. Anita was sitting on the terrace waiting for him.

'Do you know what, that man Paul White has had the nerve to write to me for a reference? Do you remember him at Shaftesbury Prep? He was that useless French teacher who had to be sacked. No bloody chance.' He looked at Anita who was clearly not listening to him. Her face was radiant as she broke into Tom's tirade. 'Tom, I've got some news for you. You are going to be a father!'

Tom took a second or two to absorb what Anita had said and then he threw his arms around her. In his preoccupation with Paul White he had quite forgotten that Anita had had an appointment with the doctor that morning.

'What fantastic news, so that's why you went to see DM this morning! That's wonderful! I'm so proud of you, well done!'

'You did have something to do with it, you know,' said Anita.

'When's it due?' '

'Well, DM said around May 30th.'

'Right,' said Tom. 'Just as well we've got some bubbly in the fridge - let's celebrate!'

'Well, maybe just a small glass,' said Anita.

Their doctor, DM Patel, known universally as DM, had told Anita that all seemed to be well, but that she was to come back for regular check-ups during the first few months. She was not to do anything stupid or go on dangerous safaris. He suspected that Anita might not listen to this advice.

'Do you know if it's going to be a boy or a girl?'

'Of course not - it's much too early. Later on they'll do a scan and maybe then we'll find out. But I don't really want to know - either is OK by me.'

'Yup.' Tom was still grinning from ear to ear. He kept on telling Anita how wonderful the news was and how fabulous she was until, laughing, she had to tell him to shut up!

At the next morning's staff meeting, Tom took Anita along and started off by telling everyone their good news. A spontaneous cheer erupted around the room and the meeting was abandoned in favour of backslapping and congratulations.

Outside the kitchen block Tom found Fergus Glover deep in conversation with the kitchen manager, Roddy Jones. Roddy, like Mr Kipling, made exceedingly good cakes and Fergus had come to an agreement with him. Fergus lived alone in a neat little apartment on the other side of town and he was particularly partial to Roddy's fruitcakes. Each month he would get Roddy to make him a cake, which he would then take home. He ate one slice a day; this meant that in the short month of February he would have slightly larger slices than in, say, October when the cake would have to be cut into thirty-one pieces. It was all very carefully worked out. It seemed that Roddy was proposing to increase the cost of Fergus's cakes; this did not go down well with Fergus who liked to know where every shilling went.

'I'm sorry, Fergus, but there is nothing I can do about it. The cost of nuts has gone up a lot this month. I'll have to charge you a bit more from now on.'

Fergus thought about this for a time.

'Very well, I'll have the cake without nuts.' And so it was from then onwards!

It was about half past five in the afternoon and Jim and Tom were standing in the car park watching the last of the staff and children depart when a very smart Mercedes made its way slowly up the drive. It had a flat tyre. The car limped to a halt in front of them and four distinguished-looking Africans in dark suits emerged looking somewhat embarrassed. It transpired that they were on their way to a wedding party and wondered if they could change the wheel in the school's car park.

'Please go ahead,' said Jim. 'Can we give you a hand?'

His offer of help was politely declined. There was a pause at this point; it was clear that they were reluctant to start the job with these *mzungus* or Europeans watching. Tom and Jim retreated a bit and resumed their conversation. Eventually two of the men went round to the boot and unlocked it; they leant forward and gently lifted out a live goat, which they tethered to the bumper. They then removed the spare wheel and replaced the wheel with the flat tyre. After packing the jack and wheel back into the boot they lifted up the surprisingly unresisting goat and stuffed it back into the small space left. Thanking the two spectators profusely, they proceeded on their way.

'They'll be roasting that goat this evening at the wedding,' said Jim. 'Have you ever eaten goat?'

Tom had to admit that he hadn't and come to think of it wasn't planning to. He hoped they would enjoy it though.

It was Saturday morning and time for the first up-country cricket match. The opposition was a boarding prep school called St Christopher's, which was a couple of hours drive up into the Rift Valley. It was a social occasion for the parents who would come with lavish picnics and plenty of Tusker beer. As usual there was no need for the school mini-bus - there were enough parents to transport players and staff and six cars set off at about 8.30 am. Play would start at eleven, go on for a couple of hours and then there would be an extended break for lunch. The match would resume after lunch and be finished in time to return to Nairobi before it got dark.

The drive was spectacular. The first few miles were through some very scruffy small villages on the outskirts of the city; battered old cars, ancient buses, *matatus* and people on foot as well as miscellaneous goats and cows had to be avoided. The smell was unattractive - a combination of over-boiled cabbage, animal dung and human sweat permeated through firmly closed car windows. It was not long, however, before the convoy of cars was past the townships into farmland and they were looking over the lip of the Great Rift Valley. Directly in front, in the middle of the vast plain several hundred feet below, rose the purple and black cone of the extinct volcano, Longonot. Far away on the other side was the other lip of the valley - a greyish light-blue haze. Beyond that was the Masai Mara, one of the finest game reserves in Africa and to the right the silver gleam of Lake Naivasha twinkled in the morning sun. Further on down towards the lake a gaggle of policemen were waiting by the side of the road. This was a well-known spot where cars could be stopped, documents demanded and, if any opportunity arose, spot cash fines imposed. The police were poorly paid and needed to somehow supplement their wages. This time the cars, being crammed with schoolboys in uniform, were waved on.

Unbeknown to Tom and Anita who were in the leading vehicle, the car carrying the captain and opening batsman broke down behind them. Fortunately, the next car was being driven by a mechanically minded father who quickly set about some running repairs. It meant however that several players had still not arrived when play was due to begin at eleven o'clock.

St Christopher's was set in farmland on the edge of the valley, a few miles from the nearest village. The grounds were a paradise for children. Neatly mown games fields, lots of trees and wild places to explore, tennis courts, a swimming pool and a paddock for horse riding were all well used by the pupils. St Christopher's was a boarding school and discipline was strict. No one dared to step out of line here! Perhaps because of their relative isolation, both staff and pupils were fiercely competitive and did not like to lose matches. This applied particularly to their cricket coach, Roger Ellis.

He approached Ross and looked intently at his watch. 'I think we need to make a start now; it's eleven o'clock.'

Ross Pelling, in charge of The Kora team, looked around and counted only six of his players.

'We're still waiting for our captain and four others.'

Roger was impatient to start the match. 'Okay, then, at least we can toss up.'

Ross agreed to this and one of his players went out with the opposition captain to toss up. They pretended to look at the wicket - which was the usual matting stretched out on top of a *murram* base. The Kora boy lost the toss and the St Christopher's captain immediately decided to field first.

Despite Ross's protest that neither of their opening batsmen had yet arrived, Roger insisted that the match should start.

'They'll be here soon, and it will give your later batsmen a chance to show what they can do.'

By the time the last of the visitors arrived, St Christopher's had removed four batsmen for only ten runs and it looked as though the match would not last too long. Ross was quietly fuming as he stood at square leg, umpiring. Rescue was at hand, however, and Ross was relieved to see his captain, Jas, strapping on his pads.

Jas was soon at the wicket. He managed to hit a couple of fours and the score began to look healthier. But it didn't last. Jas, though a fine striker of a ball, was overweight; he avoided running whenever possible. His partner called him for a quick single and he was too slow. He was run out by yards. The rest of the team scraped together a few more runs but The Kora's final total was only fifty-four. An easy target, thought St Christopher's.

The two teams walked up to the school dining room for lunch while the parents spread out their rugs and opened their picnic baskets. Anita had packed lunch for herself and Tom, which included some excellent egg and mayonnaise sandwiches, cold sausages, lemonade for herself and Tusker beer for Tom. Black kites swooped around the field looking for carelessly held food, which they would eagerly snatch out of people's hands.

The match restarted with St Christopher's only needing fifty-five to win. It should have been easy. However, they had not bargained with Jas's bowling. He bowled beautifully with hardly a bad ball and took seven wickets, only conceding twelve runs as St Christopher's were all out for forty-nine. The visitors knew that justice had been done and as they set off back down to Nairobi they reflected on how much nicer return journeys were if you had won.

Tom was soon to learn that there were all sorts of pitfalls when employing people in Nairobi. As he came out of Assembly one morning Jonny was looking peeved.

'That chap Gerald hasn't turned up yet. He hasn't sent any message so I have covered his lessons until break.'

'Who might know where he is? Maybe Angela knows - doesn't she rent a place next door to him?'

Angela said she had no idea where he was. At that point Tracey Scott, a girl in Year Eight who happened to be listening to the conversation, chipped in.

'I think he's an extra in that film they are doing, "The Master of the Game". My mother is helping with the costumes and she said she saw him the other day on the set.'

Tom knew about 'The Master of the Game'. It was an adaptation of the book by Sidney Sheldon and they had been asking around recently for white extras to be South African gold miners. This probably paid more money than being a teacher.

'Thanks, Tracey,' said Tom.

Gerald turned up after lunch saying he had been suffering from a bad headache and was sorry he hadn't let the school know but his phone was out of order. It was difficult to disprove either fact!

The Kenya Posts and Telecommunication Corporation were not noted for speed of installation of telephones or administrative efficiency. Ten years earlier the school had applied for a telephone to be installed in one of the staff houses on the compound. After nothing had happened for six months or so, Joseph had been sent down to the appropriate office - where of course he had a 'contact'. After the transfer of a suitable cash sweetener a telephone line had finally been installed. Then, nine years later, the school received a letter from KP & T saying that they would be pleased to 'investigate the possibility of providing telephone service' to this house. The 'proper channels' worked a lot slower than Joseph and his contacts!

The school had advertised in the local paper for a part-time librarian. Some of the replies were splendid. This one arrived on Tom's desk:

Dear Headmaster
Re: Part-time Librarian
I hereby sent in an application for the above mentioned position in your school.

Just for the record, I am a 22 year old ambitious and workaholic, with a dying desire to be involved in such areas of academics.

I vaunt of a rather mild experience, having been a librarian assistant with the Jesuits Refugee services and Comboni Missionaries. I conduct absolute fluency in communication. I am armed with two 'O' level certificates.

I fully hope that you'll consider my application. A chance for an interview is welcomed.
Thank you. God bless.
Yours satisfactorily
Tom Konya

There were many other similar letters - Mr Konya did not get his interview, but he did sound a charming person.

It turned out that Gerald Minster eventually came a cropper in rather an alarming manner. Tom was sitting quietly in the office, working out how to answer a tricky letter from a parent about the importance of providing good Swahili teaching, when two large Kenyan policemen appeared at the door. They were looking very serious and were armed with modern machine guns. They were clearly not the normal police and Tom did not much like the look of them. He stood up respectfully.

'Are you the Headmaster?' said one.

'Yes,' Tom replied more confidently than he felt. 'What can I do for you?'

'Is Mr Minster working at your school?'

'Yes, he is teaching at the moment.'

'You will take us to him now.' Seeing as it appeared to be an order and not a request, Tom complied immediately.

He led the two policemen round to the science laboratories where Gerald was taking a class of eleven-year-olds for chemistry. He knocked on the door of the lab and went in, the two policemen standing menacingly in the doorway. The children looked up from their books and went quiet.

'Gerald, these two gentlemen would like to have a word with you.' Tom indicated the two policemen at the door.

Gerald went rather pale as he got up from his lab stool and went out. Tom stayed behind and, as Gerald did not return, looked after the class until the end of the lesson.

'What happened to Gerald?' Veronica was in the office when he had finished teaching.

'I don't know. I just saw him being taken away by those two policemen. I wonder what he has been up to.'

Gerald wasn't seen again that day; it was going to be most inconvenient if there was a problem. Jonny and Tom worked out a way of covering his science lessons should he not return. Jim said he'd get Joseph to make some enquiries with a friend of his who worked in the immigration department. Tom phoned the Chairman to see if he could help. Peter said he'd look into it.

All the Heads of the British curriculum schools in Kenya had a meeting once a term to discuss matters of mutual interest, such as staffing and work permits, educational supplies and external exams. On this occasion the meeting was to be held at a school called Greenways just outside the town of Nakuru, about two and a half hours drive north of Nairobi. Usually the Nairobi contingent shared cars to make the journey more enjoyable; Tom went with David Whetton, the Head of the largest secondary school which was just up the road from The Kora and Paddy O'Reilly, Head of a rather unusual girls' boarding school. David's school, Highbury (nothing to do with any football club!) was run along similar lines to The Kora, only for pupils from thirteen to eighteen. It was a popular and successful school and many pupils went on to university in the UK. Admission was through the Common Entrance exam just as to similar schools in Britain and it was not easy to get a place. It was important for Tom to build up a good relationship with David - he might need to try to talk weak candidates into his school in due course.

Paddy's place was a different kettle of fish. Set in lovely countryside about fifteen miles outside Nairobi, Langata Academy was a small boarding school for girls – whose pupils had to be very self-reliant. The curriculum was basically British, but with a strong 'outdoor' flavour. The academic results were in fact quite good but the girls spent plenty of time doing other activities such as camping, alfresco cooking and orienteering. For the annual school trip to the coast to study marine biology - a journey of some four hundred kilometres - the girls did not go, as one would expect, by bus. They ran - at least part of the way. The school didn't have a bus but what it did have was a lorry suitable for expeditions. Paddy would drive the lorry down the main road to Mombasa carrying some girls while others would run. After a time he'd drop off more girls to start running and then go back to pick up the first lot. By a series of rotations most girls would run for quite a few hours before they eventually made it to the coast. They were a fit bunch, Paddy's girls. It was a school that did not suit everyone, but it certainly produced some characters.

David, Paddy and Tom set off at about eight o'clock. They aimed to arrive at Greenways around eleven; meetings usually started at eleven thirty. In England these types of events were pretty serious and there would be at least an hour or so of lecturing on some educational theme of the moment, followed by discussion groups led by ambitious members. Kenya was a bit more relaxed. There were brief meetings for Junior and Senior schools separately and then everyone would come together for a joint meeting. Great efforts were made to get all business completed in time for an early lunch to enable those members who happened to bring their golf clubs with them to adjourn to the nearest course for a few holes. Getting your priorities right was what it was called!

Apart from a group of caddies who were sitting chatting under a tree, Nakuru Golf Club was deserted when four not so hardworking Headmasters arrived after lunch. They unearthed the secretary who was asleep in his office, paid their green fees, chose four of the more alert-looking caddies and set off to the first tee. David, Paddy and Tom had been joined by Giles Maddock, Head of St Christopher's, who as one might have expected, was a very competitive player of all sports though a bit erratic when it came to golf.

As they came towards the end of a very enjoyable round, they came upon a group of three young African boys, maybe about ten years old, playing in front of them. The boys stopped to let the four players go through. They were amazed to see that the boys were not using golf clubs but had cut branches from trees, which were roughly the right shape. The ends of the branches had been carved to give more or less the shape of the head of a club. The golf balls they were using were fine - they had obviously found these on the course. What was remarkable was that these small boys could play really well with their makeshift clubs. Paddy challenged them to a chipping competition. He and the three boys aimed at the seventeenth green, about fifty yards away. Paddy hit a decent enough shot onto the edge of the putting surface. Each boy, one after the other, swung lazily at his ball and watched as it plopped onto the centre of the green. Paddy lost fifteen shillings.

What would these lads have been able to achieve if they

had the right equipment, Tom wondered as they set off on the road back to Nairobi.

Since having been removed by the two armed policemen, Gerald Minster had not been seen. Joseph, having been given the morning to find out what had happened to him, returned from town with the news that the word was that 'a South African' had been deported that morning. The immigration department had apparently discovered that he had been involved in drug dealing in the past. This struck his colleagues as pretty unlikely since Gerald seemed far too meek and mild to have anything to do with that sort of thing.

'Hmm,' said Jim, 'they just don't like these white South Africans - we won't be seeing him again.'

How irritating, Tom thought - and it would mean that he'd have to take on a good deal of his teaching for a while until a replacement could be recruited.

Now that it was November and well into the dry season, the grass on the games fields was brown and the water in the swimming pool was getting a bit warmer. Nairobi, being about five thousand feet above sea level, although very hot during the day, became decidedly cool at night. The twenty-five metre pool which was uncovered never became really warm. During their swimming lessons, when they were not actually in the water, the children would lie on the concrete slabs around the pool, which had been nicely warmed by the tropical sun. Being able to swim more or less all the year round meant that almost all the children were very good swimmers.

A very popular activity at this time of year was 'Boats'. This was an unusual form of swimming competition invented by someone years ago who had been to Cambridge. Every pupil in the third year upwards was required to be in a group of four swimmers called a 'boat'. This was arranged by forms so that there were usually about four 'boats' in each form with one or two reserves left over. The four swimmers in each boat swam as a relay - one length for each swimmer. The four-lane pool allowed four boats to swim against each other at one time. At the beginning of term all boats were put into order with the best in 'Division One' and the next in 'Division Two' and so on. After each race the winning boat would be promoted, the last boat demoted and the middle two would stay in the same division. Races generated huge excitement and were especially enjoyed because 'Boats' always took place instead of the last few lessons before lunch. Given the choice, which would you prefer to do? Have maths, English and then geography or sit in the sun on the swimming pool steps and take part in 'Boats'? There really was no contest!

It was the first round of 'Boats'; the organisation was taken care of by Ross but the staff were needed for judging and crowd control. Tom was doing the latter armed with a loudhailer and unfortunately made quite a fool of himself, much to the amusement of one and all. He was being rather officious and trotted around the pool to ask some spectators to move back from the side. As he moved the offenders back he stumbled and managed to fall, complete with loudhailer, into the pool. His Australian bush hat was left floating on the surface as he scrambled out trying unsuccessfully to convince everyone that he had gone in intentionally because it was so hot. The loudhailer and Tom had to be dried out and no doubt when they went home that evening the pupils enjoyed telling their parents how their Headmaster had fallen into the pool. You win some, you lose some, thought Tom. Anita, who was watching, could not refrain from reminding Tom about this incident for a long time afterwards!

Anita was in her element. Although sometimes involved in school activities and social life, which took up some time, she had been casting around for another interest. She had previously visited the animal orphanage, run by an intrepid Englishwoman called Daphne Sheldrick, which was situated next to the Nairobi Game Park and close to the school. This extraordinary institution had been set up to care for very young orphaned animals – mostly baby elephants and rhinos. The animals' mothers might have been killed by poachers, died during a drought or just separated from their offspring. These young animals needed a good deal of looking after. As well as being fed regularly, they sometimes needed to be nursed back to full health if they had fallen prey to disease – quite a possibility after having been traumatised by their experiences. The orphanage's aim was to release each animal back into the wild once they had grown sufficiently and were able to cope. Anita had offered her help, which was accepted with alacrity. She would go along two or three times a week and help with feeding and other chores. A particular favourite of hers was Saba, a three-month-old elephant whose mother had been shot by hunters. Saba was suffering from malnutrition when rescued by rangers in the Tsavo National Park and it would be some time before she would recover sufficiently to be returned to Tsavo. Anita became very attached to these young animals and would eagerly recount all the details of her visits to Tom after his school day was over.

There were some larger than life characters around this part of the world. Mrs Doga-Chandili, a prospective parent who came to see Tom one morning, certainly fell into this category. Her voice could be heard quite a time before she herself arrived. It was a powerful voice, which carried easily up the drive as she instructed her ten-year-old son on how it was necessary to behave perfectly when visiting this 'splendid establishment' as she called it. Mrs Doga-Chandili was about six foot tall, dressed in flowing African robes and wore a large flowered hat. She sailed into the study holding her unprotesting son firmly by the hand. The room was immediately filled with the aroma of violets - her perfume for the day. She took Tom's outstretched hand in both of hers and looked into his eyes. 'Ah, Mr Thorne,' she sighed, 'I am so delighted to meet you. This is my son, Ivo. He is ten years old and I have come to see what you can do for him.'

'Please do sit down - here is a chair for Ivo. Perhaps you can tell me what your situation is?'

'Now Mr Thorne, I want to tell you first that I am the Kenyan Delegate to the World Women's League and I travel all over the world with this organisation. I will be flying to Toronto next month for a conference.'

Tom had never heard of the World Women's League and wondered if this was a title she had invented, but he listened as she went on.

'My son, Ivo, is a brilliant student but he has had a problem at the school where he is at the moment.'

This did not sound too good, so Tom asked cagily what school he attended.

'Ivo is at Plumpton College,' Mrs Doga-Chandili informed him. 'The Headmaster there, Mr Bain, is a wonderful man but I fear that his teachers do not recognise what abilities my son has. I do not think he is stretched enough in the classroom.'

At this Ivo looked modestly down at his well-polished shoes. Could he be embarrassed by his mother's gushing eulogy?

Plumpton College was a very well-respected English day and boarding prep school situated near the centre of Nairobi and Bill Bain had quickly become a good friend of Tom's. He would have to tread very carefully here. One of the IAPS rules was that you could not take on a pupil from another prep school if any school fees were outstanding. This happened quite often and might be why this colourful lady was now sitting in front of Tom. He would have to check with Bill later. Meanwhile he made a quick decision.

'Perhaps you would like to have a look around our school?'

'That would be wonderful,' and with Mrs Doga-Chandili still keeping a firm hold on Ivo's hand they set off.

The Head of maths, Neil Watson, was taking the top set in Year Eight. These were a bright bunch, so Tom thought it would be interesting to see what Mrs Doga-Chandili made of the work they were doing. As they entered Neil's classroom the children were so absorbed in their work that they didn't even look up. It was very quiet. Mrs Doga-Chandili looked over the shoulder of Gary Robertson who was due to take his scholarship exam to Rugby the next term. She was duly impressed with the standard of the work and they moved on.

When they were back in the study, Tom hinted that he may have a place for Ivo, subject to a brief test at The Kora and a favourable report from Plumpton College. Mrs Doga-Chandili was not entirely happy with the idea of Tom speaking to Mr Bain but nevertheless made an appointment for Ivo to come in after half term for a test.

Later Tom rang Bill Bain.

'Tom, that woman is a pain in the neck. She's always in the school wanting to see teachers and asking why Ivo is not in this or that team. He is quite a bright boy but not as brilliant as she thinks.'

'Have the fees been paid?' This really was Tom's priority.

'That's another thing, she does pay eventually but our bursar has to get on to her time and again.'

'What about Ivo's father - does he see the boy much?'

'I think he lives in America - I don't blame him! If you want to take Ivo on I have no objection provided this term's fees have been paid - which they haven't yet.'

Tom assured Bill he wouldn't offer Ivo a place until given the go-ahead that all fees had been paid and then rang off.

A few days later Ivo Doga-Chandili came into school to be assessed. He went off with Toni Logan, one of the Year Six form teachers, to spend the morning with her class. Toni was a large jolly lady who had been at The Kora for years. She had never married and the school was her life. Her passion was Scottish Country Dancing and she ran a very thriving group with the children often performing at functions around the town. She also tried to get members of staff involved in the adult section of the Nairobi Scottish Country Dancing Club. The club ran competitions now and again and The Kora School Staff 'Team' had once won a large cup for their interpretation of 'The Spirit of the Dance'! Tom had so far resisted her attempts to recruit him.

Toni pronounced Ivo to be a very capable boy but reserved. Who wouldn't be with a mother like that! When Mrs Doga-Chandili returned Tom said he would be delighted to take Ivo on next term providing there were no outstanding debts with Plumpton College. He only just managed to avoid being kissed.

Jim Broom called Tom to come and see the architect and builders setting out the stakes, which would mark the footings of the new art and music block. The whole building looked pretty small to him but Richard Maeda, the architect, said that people always said that and once the walls were up they'd think it was fine. Tom 'Hmmed' to himself and returned to the office. The site chosen was close to the edge of the school compound and overlooked the game park. A few interested giraffe gazed steadily at the activity from the far side of the road and then turned and wandered off into the bushes.

One of the entrances to the Nairobi Game Park was within a few yards of the school gates and it was easy to nip into the park after school, drive around, see what was happening and unwind after a day's teaching. If you went in regularly you would get to know where the various animals were to be found - and you could, for example, follow the progress of a pride of lions and their cubs day by day. Trips into the game park became a regular habit of Tom and Anita's. After dealing with Mrs Doga-Chandili, Tom thought it would be good to escape with Anita into the park.

They drove slowly through the forested area near the

gate; there were some glades between the trees where shy impala grazed on the sparse grass. They looked up at the car and then trotted casually away. A few monkeys chattered in the treetops but otherwise there was nothing much to be seen. Anita was restless in the passenger seat.

'Tom, I need a pee – just stop here for a minute.'

Tom stopped the car and Anita slipped out and squatted down.

'I think you'd better get back in.' Tom had just noticed a lioness stalking through the bushes not too far away. Zips were done up very quickly and Anita was back in the car in a trice. The lioness, however, took no notice of them at all and seemed intent on something on the plain beyond. Tom drove on slowly, following. As they emerged onto the plain Anita pointed to a dark shape lying in the grass. They realised that this was what the lioness was heading for. The big lion shook his head as the female came up; she rubbed herself against him, flirting. Eventually, after ignoring her for a while, he struggled to his feet and nipping her back gently with his powerful jaws, mounted her. Tom and Anita watched, not saying a word. After a time, the two of them separated and slumped down on the grass.

'Mmm, Anita, that gives me an idea.'

'You must be joking!' Anita patted her expanding tummy. 'Let's go and look for something else.' And so they moved on.

Chapter Twelve

Toni Logan had been having a battle with some of the Year Six girls. Normally the children got on with each other well - there was so much space it was easy for children to choose their own friends and keep out of the way of those they didn't want to mix with. At break times there were always little knots of children congregated under the various trees that were dotted around the edge of the playing fields. Those who disliked each other could easily keep apart.

Zoë Waller was a strong character who had quite a following amongst her contemporaries. She was good at sport and near the top of her Year Six class. Her family had lived in Kenya for many years and her father was a well-respected and successful accountant. Zoë was used to getting her own way at The Kora School.

Then a new girl joined the class. Jessica Fox was a gentle girl who had been at a girls only prep school in Buckinghamshire before her father had taken up a new job in Nairobi.

Jessica, though a retiring, shy girl, was bright - very bright. She rapidly found her feet and began to do better than Zoë in class. She also made friends easily - including one or two of Zoë's. Zoë did not like this at all. Who was this new girl from England challenging her as top dog in the class? Zoë began to try and provoke Jessica, at first with snide remarks and then, when this had no effect, by telling all the girls in the class that if they continued to be friends with Jessica she would be nasty to them. She didn't say what she would do exactly but the threat was enough to make several girls begin to avoid Jessica.

Jessica, mystified at first as to why her friends should suddenly desert her, became very unhappy. She went and had a talk with her form teacher and Toni made some enquiries. A catalogue of small incidents involving Zoë came to light so Toni came to Tom to put him in the picture.

'Zoë is really making Jessica's life a misery. I've spoken to her but she seems to think that she hasn't done anything wrong and wonders what the fuss is all about. Maybe you could talk to her; we really don't want children being as distressed as Jessica certainly seems to be.'

Tom agreed immediately. 'Send her to me now and I'll have a word with her.'

He sat Zoë down and patiently explained that everyone had a right to make friends with whoever they wished and she was not to threaten girls if they wanted to go around with someone else, for example, Jessica.

Zoë hotly denied threatening anyone. She said that she only said a few things to one or two friends of Jessica's 'as a joke'. Tom said it was not a 'joke' if it upset people as, in this case, it clearly had. Zoë went off unconvinced.

The next day Zoë's father arrived at the school demanding to see Tom. Veronica warned him he had a reputation as a man with a short fuse and advised Tom to tread carefully.

Mr Waller strode into the study and, without looking at Tom, shook him briefly by the hand. He sat down and then, lifting his head, fixed Tom with a steady gaze with his clear blue eyes. A reddish vein in the side of his neck throbbed rhythmically.

'Mr Thorne, I'll come straight to the point. Zoë tells me that you have accused her of bullying a girl called Jessica and I'm not at all happy. What has she done and if it is bullying why haven't you contacted me?'

'Mr Waller, I have not accused your daughter of bullying. I have told her that by making snide remarks and telling other girls not to be friends with Jessica she has made Jessica unhappy. I do not want this type of behaviour taking place in my school.'

Mr Waller didn't look convinced. 'So Zoë has made a few remarks, has she? What remarks? Zoë tells me they were nothing much and only made as jokes anyway. Surely this Jessica girl is overreacting. It sounds to me that it would do her good to be toughened up a bit.'

'Mr Waller, we are not here to "toughen up" girls. I want each child in the school to be treated with respect and not to be made unhappy by other stronger children. This sort of behaviour is not acceptable and I would be most grateful if you would explain this to your daughter, as I'm not sure she understood my point either when I saw her yesterday.'

This did not go down at all well with Mr Waller who grunted, muttering something about too much cotton wool not being any use to anyone. Schools in his view were much too protective and children needed a few knocks to grow up. Tom did not agree, but refrained from further argument; he merely repeated his request that he speak to his daughter. Mr Waller finally agreed to ask his wife to have a chat with her - and with that he left - displeased.

It has to be said that irate parents were perhaps less of a hazard than the wild animals, which were never far away. That evening there was great excitement. The Head's house at The Kora School was not actually on the compound - it was just down the road next to the Ngong Forest. There was a fairly high wire fence surrounding the garden but it was not terribly secure. The school employed guards or *askaris* to patrol the grounds and open the gate when needed. There was a small hut just inside the gate where the night *askari*, Joshua, could shelter if it was wet or cold. It was not a pleasant job.

Joshua was a wizened, tough old character armed with a spear, a bow and some poisoned arrows. He boasted that in his last job he had shot at and killed a would-be burglar with one of these arrows. He was commended by the police for his bravery - they were quite happy for the general public to dispose of burglars and other such people breaking the law. Bravery only goes so far, however, and he was about to be tested once again.

It was about eight o'clock and Anita and Tom had decided to have a takeaway curry for supper. This involved phoning in their order and Tom driving up to Karen to collect it. He was away about three quarters of an hour and when he returned he found Joshua locked inside his hut, refusing to come out. Anita shouted to Tom through an open window to be careful and to drive as close as possible to the front door. She told him that an old leopard had come into the next-door neighbour's garden and tried to attack their pregnant Labrador. Leopards apparently have a great liking for dogs as light snacks. The dog had somehow managed to squeeze through the fence into Tom and Anita's garden, but the leopard had jumped over the fence and renewed its attack. The dog had fought back fiercely and eventually escaped leaving a trail of blood across the lawn. The big cat had given up the chase and disappeared back into the forest. Whilst all this was happening, Joshua had very sensibly barricaded himself inside his hut and had watched the proceedings through a crack in the wall while Anita had been looking through a window into the dark garden. Tom was rather disappointed to have missed all the action. They heard later that, apart from some minor wounds to her back leg, the dog was none the worse for her adventure. A very lucky Labrador!

Jim and Tom were taking their usual Monday morning walk around the grounds. The footings were now in place for the new art and music block and the brick pattern indicating where the walls would be was now about two foot high. Richard Maeda was standing looking at the beginning of the walls and scratching his head. 'These builders are hopeless. Look at that room there – it's supposed to be the office for the music department.'

The three of them looked. The walls were very well constructed but the space for a door into one of the rooms was missing.

Jim called over to the foreman. 'How are you supposed to enter this room? Through the roof?' A terse conversation followed. The foreman then went off to speak to a group of his workmen who were relaxing under a nearby tree. After a few minutes two workers, without much enthusiasm, got to their feet and collected a sledgehammer each from a pile of tools. Under the direction of the foreman they started to demolish a part of the construction they had just completed to make space for a door. Tom and Jim left them to it.

Ross Pelling was a splendid sports coach but his driving was erratic to say the least. Before he had come to Kenya he had only just acquired an English provisional driving licence. This he was assured was valid in Kenya and so he had bought himself a second-hand, blue pick-up with a notice on the back, which stated 'Kenya is my country, Datsun is my car'. With various brave passengers, this vehicle was often to be seen travelling at high speed around the suburbs of Nairobi. Ross decided it was time to acquire a full Kenyan driving licence. The driving test contained two parts - in the first the candidate had to go to the testing station and do the 'dinky car test'. Until that was passed candidates would not be allowed out on the road for the final practical test. The 'dinky car test' was taken on a large board, marked out with roads, stop signs, traffic lights and roundabouts (called *keepilefties*). There were various toy cars and buses parked in appropriate spots around the board. You would be told to be the driver of one of the cars and, describing the correct hand signals, show on the board how you would manoeuvre your vehicle along a particular route. You would have to negotiate right hand turns and roundabouts properly, keeping in the correct lane. It had to be taken very seriously.

After his test Ross returned to school very shamefaced - he had failed the 'dinky car test' and consequently had not been allowed to attempt the second part. His friends were intrigued as to what had gone wrong. It appeared that Ross had decided, unwisely, to add some realism to the proceedings and, as he had moved his little car along the board had added his own sound effects – 'brrrm,

brrrm' he had gone, giving a fine impression of a revving engine. The examiner had, not surprisingly, taken a very dim view of this and failed him on the spot. It was not very clever to try to take the mickey out of officials.

Joseph, who had listened to all this with interest, spoke to Ross. 'Ah, *bwana* Pelling. You should have told me you were taking your driving test. I have a friend who works in that office and he could help you. Would you like me to speak to him?'

'Joseph,' said Ross gratefully, 'I think I'll need your help.'

A couple of weeks later, armed with an adequate supply of shillings, Ross went for his second attempt at his test with Joseph's friend - outside office hours on a Saturday morning. Needless to say, he appeared the following Monday with a brand new licence. 'Very easy this time,' he told everyone.

Tom was a keen golfer and he had been trying to persuade Anita to take up the game - she could hit a pretty mean ball on the tennis court and Tom thought she could become a useful golfer as well.

Anita screwed her nose up in distaste. 'It's too slow for me, rather a boring game. I prefer more action.' Eventually, however, he managed to persuade her to hit a few balls on the Kora playing fields after school one day. He had borrowed some ladies' clubs from the Major's wife - who was a demon player. He threw down a collection of practice balls on the edge of the field and showed Anita how to grip the club. Putting his arms around her growing waist, he showed her how to swing. It must be quite enjoyable, being a golf pro, he thought.

Anita's first effort was a quick heave, missing the ball

completely. She was not pleased. 'Okay, I'll try again - I can't believe I missed altogether.'

After a few more tries she began to get the idea and hit the ball quite well, despite the bump in her tummy. Anita beamed. 'I'm getting the hang of this, I think,' she told Tom as they went off to collect various balls sprinkled around the field. As they walked towards one of the corners where the grass grew longer under a pepper tree, a loud scolding whistling noise stopped them in their tracks. A pair of outraged birds with black heads topped with a white ring ran angrily along the ground, clearly defending their territory.

'They must have a nest with eggs in that grass,' said Tom. 'We'll back off - let's leave that ball.'

Anita's interest in golf waned. 'How beautiful those birds are - what are they?'

'They are crowned plovers - lovely birds - we get lots of them round here.' A gravelly voice spoke from behind them.

Leaning on the fence at the edge of the field was an old man. His sunburnt face was shaded by a battered old straw hat and he wore a safari jacket, khaki shorts with long socks and a pair of dirty old suede shoes - 'Bata Bullets.' He looked like what he was - an old Kenya hand.

'You must be Bill Weston,' Tom held his hand out to the old man. 'Jonny Hutton was telling me all about you and Polly. You live just over there.' Tom pointed to an old house on a small plot adjacent to the school grounds, which could just be seen behind some eucalyptus trees. 'I'm Tom and this is my wife, Anita.'

A broad smile crossed Bill's face. 'Delighted to meet you both. Tom is a lucky chap, Anita, but I'm afraid your golf swing needs a little more practice! Would you like to come over for a quick snifter and meet Polly?'

Anita was quite happy to give golf a rest for a while and they quickly accepted Bill's invitation. It would be good to meet his wife - Anita needed a friendly female face nearby, not connected with the school. They climbed over Gideon's non-warthog proof fence and walked down the dusty track to Bill's place. As they went through the gate a small bird-like woman greeted them from the front porch.

'This is my wife, Mavis.'

'I thought you said your wife's name was Polly,' said Anita.

'Ah, no,' Bill laughed. 'You'd better come and meet Polly - come along inside.' A parrot perhaps, thought Anita. They went through into the living room. Anita froze. Lying in front of a well-used sofa on the hearthrug was a large beautiful cheetah, licking its front paws delicately with a moist pink tongue.

'This is Polly,' said Bill proudly. 'She's very friendly; we've had her since she was a cub - about five years it is now. She was abandoned by her mother for some reason and we rescued her. She's very tame - you can stroke her.' Anita, overcoming her initial surprise, went up and gently patted Polly's head. Polly purred contentedly.

'We had some friends visit us some time ago,' began Mavis, 'and they knew we had a pet cheetah. So, when they arrived and found this beautiful cheetah sitting on the lawn they went up and started to stroke it. All was fine until they came on into the house and found Polly sitting quietly here. The other cheetah was a wild one, which had come to see Polly. Oddly enough those people haven't been to see us since.'

Mavis was a delightful, sociable woman and she and Anita soon became firm friends - Anita always felt she could escape across the road for a cup of coffee and a girlie chat. Essential if one was not to become too school obsessed.

The last event of the autumn term was the barbecue and Christmas Disco. All day the African ground staff, carefully supervised by Gideon, had been using bricks and mud to construct two large barbecues on the paved area outside the assembly hall. It was amazing how much trouble was taken when they would be used for just one evening. All the staff and pupils attended, which meant about three hundred and fifty people would be needing food. Roddy, the catering manager, was in his element, first filling up the wire trays with large quantities of charcoal and then lighting it. The kitchen staff brought out home-made hamburgers, chicken legs and steaks in large steel containers and, as the flames from the charcoal died down to glowing embers, Roddy started to cook. The delicious smell of wood-smoke, garlic and sizzling meats of various sorts wafted across the courtyard. The African sun went down and in a few minutes it was dark.

The children, having gone home at the end of the school day, began to return, dressed in party clothes. Some of the more eager teachers arrived and started to sample the Tusker and other beers and wine supplied in fairly generous quantities by the Bursar. Jim himself kept a low profile, putting his head out of his office from time to time to see how things were going. Later he would judge the right time to cut off the supply of alcoholic refreshment to the teaching staff. By eight o'clock the barbecue was in full swing and the children were beginning to ask when the Disco, which was all set up in the assembly hall, would start. Ross Pelling, who was an enterprising fellow, had bought himself the amplifiers, speakers, lights and decks needed to set up a disco as a part-time business with a mate of his from the rugby club. He had persuaded Jim to let him run it for a reasonable fee.

It was traditional during the Disco for both pupils and staff to provide some form of entertainment - known grandly as the 'Cabaret'. This consisted of a series of sketches invented mostly by the children. Any new member of staff was also expected to perform for everyone's amusement - and that included Tom. He had been persuaded to join up with Angela Hughes and another young teacher, Fran Mayes, to mime one of the tunes from 'Grease'. In great secrecy they had practised their performance, which could only be described as dire. The dressing up involved Tom squeezing into some extraordinarily tight trousers belonging to Angela and a leather jacket borrowed from Roddy.

The Disco started and the children and most of the staff disappeared into the noisy interior of the hall. Angela, Fran and Tom prepared themselves for the ordeal of being laughed at by the mob. Fortunately they were on first and could get it over with quickly.

If you are a teacher and are prepared to get up in front of your pupils and do something silly you cannot fail to get a laugh - that's what they kept telling themselves. In the end they did their bit, the pupils fell about laughing and they were forced to do an encore. Thank goodness we don't have to do that again, Tom thought as they finally retreated backstage. Other members of staff were not so reticent, however. Neil Watson, who was normally a quiet sort of chap, had made a habit of inventing and then reciting a poem as his contribution to the Cabaret. His poems were always about the senior pupils - their oddities, likes and dislikes - including mainly invented bits about boyfriends and girlfriends. He would sit on a chair in the middle of the stage, wearing a wide-brimmed cowboy hat and recite his poem in laconic style. The audience would listen intently, immediately picking up any references to girl or boyfriends and hooting with laughter. On this occasion Neil settled himself down at the front of the stage, took out his poem and fixed his gaze on Jeremy Duckworth who was standing at the front of the audience with his arm around a girl.

Neil began:

I'll tell you a tale about a lass and a lad
They weren't that good, but they weren't that bad.
The boy was a sportsman and his name was Jerry
He was full of such fun and was always so merry,

He couldn't find time for studying much
Since he was hoping his girl would melt to his touch.
This lass was fair haired and Mara by name
Fiery she was and far from being tame!

Now Mara's a sport and keen on her rounders
But she's choosy about men and doesn't like bounders
So Jerry got nowhere with all his advances
And his rugby exploits were no good for his chances

He tried and he tried but she wasn't impressed
Even though it was reckoned his lines were the best

Until one night and purely by chance
He found the right formula just here at the dance.

He swirled her around with twinkling feet
And danced like Nureyev, using steps - Oh so neat!
She could not believe he avoided her toes
'My goodness,' she thought, 'his dancing just flows!'

All evening they danced, together as one
That Jerry and Mara, what wonderful fun!

The moral is clear if you're a young boy
This is the way to find favour and joy
Forget all your sport, with the cheers and the roars
Take lessons in dancing and success will be yours!

Amidst the uproar that greeted each line, Jeremy squirmed and Mara hid her face with her hands, although secretly enjoying the limelight!

The children's sketches which followed, mostly arranged by the girls, were mainly dancing - copied from Top of the Pops most likely. Tom noticed that Zoë Waller and Jessica Fox appeared together in one girls sketch and was glad that his meeting with Mr Waller had been fruitful. A group of boys did a sketch trying, fairly successfully, to take off a Fergus Glover lesson. They devised a simple skit involving numerous biros being extracted and replaced down people's socks. Highly droll. The pupils loved it.

At eleven o'clock the Disco ended - Tom asked Jeremy Duckworth what he thought of it. He didn't say much - he just flicked his hand as if shaking off water, a characteristic white Kenyan mannerism, and said 'Way, man' as he and Mara wandered off looking for their transport home. They had enjoyed the term and so had Tom.

A voice came out of the darkness from behind the staff room.

'Tom, I'm going to need your help here, I'm afraid.'

It was the Major who, shrugging his shoulders, pointed to a dark figure slumped on the ground beside the table which earlier in the evening had held large quantities of bottled soft drinks and beers. Now there were only empty bottles. The staff, including those who worked in the office, had been invited to the Disco - and to partake in the beverages provided by the Major. Unfortunately Joseph, normally the most polite and correct of employees, had gone too far. He was drunk, very drunk indeed and couldn't stand.

Tom was aghast. 'What are we going to do with him? Where does he live? I think we'll have to take him home.'

'Bloody nuisance,' grunted the Major. 'Can you get your car, Tom - I'll help you get him in the back. I know where he lives.'

Tom moved his car as close as he could to the prone figure of Joseph and they lifted him, with some difficulty, onto the back seat. They set off down the Langata Road towards town. After a short distance the Major directed Tom down a side road into a rather seedy-looking estate. There was rubbish everywhere and all the box-like houses looked the same. Amazingly the Major soon found the right place. They stopped and opened the car door to extract the figure slumped inside. Taking an arm each they walked the staggering Joseph up to the front door and rang the bell. Almost immediately the door opened and a large woman wearing a brightly-coloured headscarf and apron peered out.

'Joseph, is that you? Don't tell me you have had too many beers again. That is not good. I will speak to you about it.' With that she cuffed him smartly on the side of his head. Joseph groaned and was then gathered inside by this rather frightening woman. She ignored Tom and the Major who retreated.

The Major chuckled to himself. 'He'll regret this evening's performance I should think. She's a tough woman his wife - serves him right really.'

The two of them returned to school, the Major to supervise the clearing up and Tom to explain to Anita where he had been.

Chapter Thirteen

The start of the spring term was low-key. Not many new children had started; there were no staff changes and no one was ill - that was a good omen. Mrs Doga-Chandili provided some amusement when she arrived driving a very smart blue Mercedes. Her much adored son Ivo was looking very neat and tidy in his new school uniform of khaki shorts, blue short-sleeved shirt and school tie. His mother, her multi-coloured robes flowing behind her, sailed up to the classroom block dragging young Ivo, firmly grasped by the hand. Toni, Ivo's form teacher, saw her coming and didn't get a chance to take evasive action. She was immediately enveloped in a warm hug.

'Ah, Miss Logan, how delighted I am to see you. Now you will look after my Ivo, won't you?' she pleaded. 'He is *so* looking forward to joining your class.'

Mrs Doga-Chandili proceeded to collar any other staff she could find and introduced herself, asking them all to look out for 'my son Ivo who is so glad to be at your school.' She eventually dragged herself away from the classroom area and, without dropping into the Bursar's office to pay the fees, left, no doubt to attend an important meeting.

It was Saturday morning and Tom and Anita were having breakfast on the terrace. There was a large umbrella on a stand under which they could sit to avoid the tropical sun. This is definitely the life, thought Tom, as Anita poured him coffee and passed him another slice of mango. He looked up as a pair of turacos called 'kaw, kaw, kaw' to each other as they flitted between the branches of the trees in the garden. As their wings fluttered they could see the crimson flash of their under-feathers - what beautiful birds they were.

'Hey!' exclaimed Anita suddenly, 'what's that?' She pointed towards the edge of the terrace. Tom looked and there, poking out of a crack underneath the stone, was a small snake. It lifted up its head in the characteristic shape of a cobra on the attack. It was small, but both Tom and Anita knew that baby cobras were just as poisonous as adults and they backed off hastily.

'Keep an eye on it, I'll deal with it.' Tom, not knowing exactly what he was going to do disappeared into the house and returned carrying one of his golf clubs.

'I'll get it with this,' he said as he advanced into the danger area. This was not the time for an air shot but Tom's first swing at the snake missed and the 5-iron whistled over its head. The snake took a dim view of this and began to hiss aggressively as Tom took a second shot. This time he connected perfectly and the snake's head was neatly removed by a shot that would have been approved of by Tiger Woods himself. Anita approached warily.

'Well done, Tom, but I wonder if he has any brothers or sisters lurking in that hole.' They looked but there were no other snakes to be seen. The two of them retreated to the centre of the lawn to finish their breakfast, though Anita said she was no longer hungry. After thinking for a while, she came up with a plan.

'I think what we should do is get David to build us a shelter on the lawn, away from that terrace, you know a sort of *banda* made out of palm leaves on a frame. Do you think he could do it? We need a larger area to sit outside in the shade anyway – well away from snake holes. Cheetahs and elephants I like but I'm not too fond of snakes – especially poisonous ones!'

David, when this idea was explained to him, immediately said it would be no problem. It would be more interesting than his normal duties of cleaning the car, picking up leaves and making bonfires of rubbish. He would just need some money to buy the necessary wood and other materials. Anita drew a sketch of what she had in mind and David went off happily to purchase the materials with the cash Tom gave him.

It took a couple of weeks to build - David recruited Joshua, their old *askari,* as his assistant and the two of them spent hours constructing a wooden frame with a thick central pole from which a large umbrella shaped structure grew. Irene appointed herself as advisor and critic and would stand watching, telling the pair of them where they were going wrong. Finally palm fronds were tied onto the frame and David called Tom and Anita to approve his work. He beamed as they told him it was splendid and just what they wanted. David's shelter was the ideal place for entertaining outside in the tropics. It was first used by Anita when she invited Mavis Weston for lunch one day while Tom was busy at school. Both being keen animal lovers, they had much in common. Anita had overcome her initial fear of cheetahs and made friends with Polly. She was telling Mavis all about her work at the animal orphanage and how she would spray Saba, the baby elephant, with water to keep the animal cool in the heat of the day.

Tom looked out of his office window at the games fields, burned brown by the African sun. This was the hockey term - played by both boys and girls. Gideon and his ground staff were busy on the field putting up hockey goals and marking out the pitches. Marking the lines for the sides of pitches was not done by pushing one of those machines with a wheel on the front which dips into whitewash. That was much too complicated. Gideon just organised eight men with eight buckets of whitewash and eight paintbrushes. It was all done by hand - labour intensive but then, there was always plenty of labour available.

The school buses, used by about a third of the pupils, could be a problem. Behaviour by the pupils was not always what it should be and the volunteer parents who acted as 'bus escorts' had their work cut out. Tom received a letter one morning, which ran:

Dear Mr Thorne
We must make a strong protest against the use of skateboards in school buses even when stationary. Their use in such confined spaces can cause accidents.
Our son Richard was on the Westlands bus on Friday afternoon near the back talking to a friend when another boy on a skateboard ran into him and knocked his face into the handrail on the back of the seat in front of him. He ended up with a black eye and some bruises. We would prefer that this not be repeated on any occasion in connection with school buses.
We are not against skateboards and we are not looking

for any publicity. Just cutting down on unnecessary accidents.
Yours sincerely
David Street

A very restrained letter, Tom thought and a not unreasonable request! He asked the bus escort who was on duty on Friday afternoon whether this was true. She confirmed that some boys did bring their skateboards to school but she couldn't remember anything untoward happening that day. Tom asked her to keep a sharp lookout for silly behaviour and then wrote a placatory reply to Mr Street.

The staff room was not very politically correct. A corner of the room which was usually used at break times for coffee and chatting by the more experienced lady teachers was known as 'witches corner' by the younger male members of staff. There was no lack of banter. For instance, the local newspaper 'The Nation' often published letters which would hardly be accepted in England. There had been quite a bit of correspondence about the lack of discipline in Kenyan schools. An unknown, probably male, member of staff cut out the following letter and posted it on the board:

Dear Sir
These are my views concerning poor teaching in primary schools.
To discipline teachers, the following are some of the measures the Ministry concerned should implement.
Teachers who report late after 10.00 should be given verbal warning by their headmasters and the area

education officers informed.

Teachers caught looking for chang'aa (illicit liquor) *or spreading bush politics to old men and women should get summary dismissal.*

Teachers found roaming in girls' boarding secondary schools looking for 'green pastures' should get a month's suspension.

Teachers reporting for duty with uncombed hair or wearing tight trousers or drunk should be refused entry by head teachers and be served with warning letters.

Teachers' love affairs with pupils should end.

Teachers caught making love with their pupils should be forced to marry them and lose their jobs.

Forcing schoolgirls to cook for the unmarried teachers should end.

'Faithful Reader,'   Mombasa.

Someone had written 'So watch it!' underneath.

Tom went down to the Bursar's office to have a word with the Major. The four bus escorts who had arrived that morning were standing outside, chatting and waiting to be given lifts back to their cars which had been left at the various bus pick-up points around Nairobi. Tom greeted them.

'Well, ladies, was there any skateboarding on the buses today?' They all laughed.

The Westlands bus escort reassured Tom. 'Not today, no! Mr Street says thank you for your letter.'

Inside the Major was chuckling over a letter he had just received from Peter, a new employee who had just started work in the kitchens. The school had organised a savings scheme with the Prudential for any staff who wished to take advantage of it. Peter had written as follows:

'Please do not deduct 100 shillings per month from my salary as life insurance premium to the Prudential. On Kenyatta Day I was saved by Jesus and I do not need to be saved by the Prudential also.'

'Fair enough,' said the Major. 'Who's to say that he hasn't made a good decision?'

The security situation in Kenya had always been a great concern and one evening, without realising it, Anita and Tom drove past a car hijacking involving parents and their children. It was after school had finished and the Hopleys had collected their two children and were on their way home along the Langata road to Karen. It was about five o'clock; Ben and Sarah Hopley were standing by their fairly new Toyota Land Cruiser, which was parked just off the road, apparently talking amiably with three African men. The children were still in the car and a battered old saloon car was parked in front of the Land Cruiser. Tom and Anita waved and drove on thinking nothing of it.

Later they discovered that one of the Africans had a gun and had been aiming it at Ben the precise moment they were driving past. Apparently the three men had overtaken the Hopleys and forced them to stop. They had then climbed into the Land Cruiser along with the family and forced Ben, with a gun poking in his ribs, to drive off into the forest up on the Ngong hills. Wisely Ben did exactly as he was told and eventually, when they were well inside the forest, they were ordered out of the car and the robbers drove off - most likely across the border to Tanzania where they would be able to get a good price for the four-wheel drive vehicle.

The Hopleys were, fortunately, not too far away from a village and they managed to find a telephone to call for help. They were a very scared family but lucky - no one was hurt.

This sort of thing was now happening too often. Jonny had been telling everyone in the staff room how one diplomat had recently fought back. Apparently he was a Norwegian who had a very desirable four-wheel drive vehicle. He decided to fill an old whisky bottle full of rat poison and kept it in the glove compartment. Not long afterwards he was hijacked and his car stolen by four men. A couple of days later the car was discovered along with an empty whisky bottle. Four dead policemen were still inside the vehicle. An interesting legal point - what crimes had actually been committed?

As a result of the general deterioration in security in the Langata area, a group of local residents decided to set up a 'Neighbourhood Watch' scheme. The idea came from a group of Catholic nuns who ran a thriving nursery school at the end of the road where Tom and Anita lived. They were a tough bunch these nuns and stood no nonsense from anyone. Sister Barbara visited all the houses in the area canvassing support and shortly afterwards about twenty people, including Tom and Anita, assembled around a large low table in the nursery school garden. Sister Barbara took charge of the meeting. 'We cannot go on living in fear of lawless thugs. There have been too many incidents recently and the police don't seem to be able to do anything about them. They always say they have no transport and can't patrol our area. I have spoken to the Inspector at Karen police station who is sympathetic but not able to do much. I do think we are quite lucky having Karen as our local station – the police there are reliable, I've known them for years. Anyway, the Inspector did say that he would release an armed constable to keep an eye on our area each night if we were prepared to collect him from the station each evening and then return him the following morning. What do you all think of that idea?'

A general murmuring of assent went round the circle of black, brown and white faces. James Wood, a grey-haired man in his seventies who had lived in Kenya for years and had been quite a successful film actor in his day (he was in 'Born Free' with Virginia McKenna many years before), agreed. 'Excellent idea - but what about transport? Presumably we'd have to take it in turns collecting and returning this fellow and I'm afraid I don't drive any more. And we would also need to provide him with a hut or some sort of shelter.'

Some thought if he had a shelter he'd just go to sleep and not bother to patrol at all, but of course it did get very cold at night. What about the rainy season? Would his gun actually have any bullets? All these points and more were discussed but it was eventually decided that they should give it a go. Tom volunteered to do the first week's transport run once the hut had been built.

A tall distinguished-looking African stood up at the end of the meeting. 'My name is Olyongo. I am a colonel in the Kenyan Army and I think what you are proposing is splendid. I think also it would be most wise if many of you could learn to shoot a pistol - I am very happy to teach all those who would like to learn.'

The colonel explained where his house was and said he would be pleased to see any pistol shooting pupils the following Thursday evening at six o'clock. Sister Barbara thanked him and everyone wondered who would take up his kind offer. Tom didn't plan to!

A week or so later in the evening, a small hut having been built at the corner of the road, Tom took his old Land Cruiser up to Karen and collected the policeman. It was obvious they had not been allocated the pick of the force but the man was keen and armed with an enormous ancient rifle, which looked as if it had last seen service in the Boer War. He clambered with some difficulty into the back of the vehicle and, ten minutes later, Tom deposited him by the hut for his night's duty.

The following morning, on his way to school, Tom collected the guard. Wiping the sleep from his eyes he assured Tom that there had been 'no problems, *bwana*,' and Tom returned him to Karen police station. The fact was that for the next few weeks there were no problems, but unfortunately after a time it became apparent that only a few of the residents were able or willing to take on the transport rota and the system fell by the wayside.

Residents then had to rely on the few brave souls who had responded to the colonel's offer of pistol training - maybe potential burglars got to hear about that too for there was a long period of 'no incidents'.

The end of the spring term school play was to be 'Toad of Toad Hall' produced by Will Jones (no relation to Roddy the Chef) who was the Head of English. Will was a very capable young teacher who had been at the school for several years and had made his mark in all sorts of ways. He was a useful games player and coached hockey, cricket and rugby. He was a good-looking fellow and had recently been approached to do some modelling - much to the amusement of his colleagues who gave him quite a bit of stick when his picture appeared in the local paper in an advertisement for an upmarket safari lodge. If the truth be known they were also rather jealous.

Assisting Will in this production were Ross and Marion Peacock who ran the music department. Rehearsals had been taking place during break times and after school for several weeks. When school had finished Tom went along to see how things were progressing. Will took everything very seriously and he was berating the unfortunate boy who was taking the part of Toad. He hadn't yet learned his lines properly and this had not gone down too well with the producer. The boy, James Olindo, had a marvellously expressive face and when he was in full flow, actually looked very like a bumptious, though black, toad. James's father was the Minister for Energy in the government and an important man. Will was always one to keep on the right side of people who matter and maybe this had something to do with who was asked to take the important parts. Marion was busy getting the cast to run through one of the songs and Ross was fiddling around with the stage lighting. All seemed to be progressing just fine, so Tom left them to it.

There was great excitement one morning during lessons; five lionesses had escaped from the game park during the night and were roaming around the area. Three of them were padding their way slowly across the playing fields as the children were working. A rather naive but enthusiastic Year Two class teacher suggested to her little charges that they should go out onto the pathway outside her classroom to have a better look. Fortunately Gideon was passing by at the time and in no uncertain terms pointed out the error of her ways. They retreated back into their classroom and the Major phoned the Wildlife Department at the gate in Langata. They already knew the lionesses were loose and promised to send game rangers at once. Meanwhile the cats wandered off into the scrubland behind the school. A couple of hours later a message came through that all five lionesses had been returned to the park and that the children could be allowed back onto the field again.

It appeared that two months earlier eight lions had broken out of the park and roamed the area around Karen and Langata. They had eventually been captured and returned to the park but not before killing six horses and a cow and injuring a dog. The rangers clearly had some serious fence mending to do.

The school had been having quite a few power cuts and Will Jones, who was already getting incredibly stressed about his play, was worried that a power cut in the middle of the performance would be a disaster. He and

Tom were discussing this when Will made a suggestion. 'James Olindo's dad is the boss of the Kenya Power Company, isn't he? Can't we ask him to keep the power going in this area for the two performances of Toad?'

Tom looked surprised. 'I thought he was the Energy Minister.'

'He is that as well - I think being a minister doesn't stop you from owning companies that supply your ministry. In fact it's a good way of making money.' Will had quite a cynical and worldly-wise head on his comparatively young shoulders.

'Okay.' Tom agreed to give Mr Olindo a call and see if he could arrange it.

Back in the office Tom eventually got through to James's father on the phone. He could not have been more charming and although he couldn't promise anything he carefully took down the days and times of the performances of Toad.

Every year The Kora School organised a six-a-side hockey tournament for Kenyan Prep schools with both boys' and girls' trophies to be won. Usually about eight schools took part, some travelling from miles up country - Kora parents could easily accommodate those who needed to stay overnight. Ross and Angela were in charge and organised the programme of games, provision of umpires and recording of results. This required a good deal of work beforehand and they usually managed to persuade one of the parents to sponsor the tournament and pay for trophies and medals for winners and runners-up. This year they surpassed themselves and the Serena Hotel chain, whose managing director was a parent, had agreed to provide not only the trophies and individual medals, but also a free bar for parents and soft drinks for the players. This being Kenya their generosity would certainly be put to the test!

By nine o'clock the field was surrounded by parked vehicles and the various teams were beginning to assemble. Hockey balls were being hit around with some abandon and Ross went off to tell players where they could practise.

It was a very hot day and all the spaces under the shade of the trees around the field were already taken up. Rugs were laid out and cool boxes opened. Tusker and Whitecap was already being consumed. The first matches began and parents and supporters gathered along the touchlines of the pitches to urge their teams on. The ground was hard and not at all flat but this did not stop the players from whacking the ball as hard as they could. It was amazing how these children could stop and control the ball at such speeds but they did - there were some very skilful players and the standard of play was high.

By twelve thirty the group matches had all been completed and there was a break in the proceedings for lunch. Afterwards the semi-finals and finals would be played. Both the boys' and girls' teams from The Kora School had qualified so Ross and Angela were looking happy but strained!

There was a slight setback at lunchtime. The bar for parents provided by the Serena Hotel was well stocked with a variety of refreshments including Pimms. Pimms is an excellent drink - for adults. Unfortunately The Kora girls team, led by their captain Tanya Chappell, decided that they would sample a jug left unwisely unguarded for a moment by the barman. They liked it - so they tried some more. It wasn't long before the team began to feel rather unwell and a friendly parent whispered in Angela's ear that she had better sort her players out. The hiccupping girls were led away to a classroom for a severe ticking off. Two made their way somewhat unsteadily behind the classroom block and were rather ill.

Meanwhile everyone else was enjoying lunch and trying to keep cool. After time for food to settle, the competition continued with the semi-finals. The Kora boys' team lost in extra time to St Christopher's in one match and in the other St Anstell's emerged victorious, urged on by their coach Angus's loud Scots voice. The Kora girls amazingly enough recovered in time to win through to their final.

There must have been something unique in Pimms, for in the girls' final Tanya Chappell scored twice as The Kora team played superbly to win the trophy. Angela was not sure whether to go on being angry with her team or to congratulate them.

A microphone had been set up for announcements and as Ross read out the final results to the assembled company, behind the semi-circle of parents and children he saw a warthog trotting across the field with its tail pointing straight upwards, as they do.

'Congratulations to the boys winners, St Christopher's, but I should warn them that next year we may be playing our secret weapon on the left wing. There he goes training behind you.'

He pointed over the crowd's heads to the warthog in the distance. Ross didn't win a trophy but he did get a laugh.

As the dates for the production of 'Toad of Toad Hall'

approached, the number of rehearsals increased as did the general level of tension. There was a cast of about forty children and the producer recruited almost everyone on the staff to do a job of some sort. The set, having been built by Gideon and his men, was painted by Linda O'Shea and a selection of her arty friends from Karen. Others were involved in the production of programmes, make-up, tickets, costumes, props and so on. The Major organised a well-stocked bar which was set up in the adjacent dining room area. It was bound to be very well patronised and hopefully would make a substantial profit - 'to go towards the cost of the production'.

The performances themselves went well in front of full houses of well-oiled and appreciative parents. James Olindo as Toad was splendid and only forgot his lines twice. Mr and Mrs Olindo sat in the front row on both evenings and, in contrast to what happened most nights, there were no power cuts. Tom made a special point of thanking Mr Olindo afterwards. He grinned and agreed that they had been lucky, hadn't they. What a good man!

The Nairobi newspapers were always worth reading and as well as news the letters page could be amusing. It was clear from this letter in The Nation that equality of the sexes had not yet reached this part of the world! It read as follows:

Dear Sir
These Pets are a Bore
I have three pets in my house and I am thinking of giving them away to my neighbours if they are interested in keeping them.

The first one is a Zairean parrot who makes a lot of unnecessary noise in the house thus disturbing the few hours of peace that I get. He also incurs a great debt to me due to the seeds that I import from Zaire for him to feed on.

The second pet is a black cat who climbs on my bed at night, spreading fleas and mites which attack me viciously thus forcing me to wake up prematurely.

The third pet is my wife whom I got easily by taking a few goats to her father in exchange for her. After I go to sleep, she goes through all my pockets and makes a clean job of all my money thus forcing me to walk all the way to work the next morning. The journey is painful especially when I am nursing a bad hangover which I occasionally get the previous night from my watering hole.

Julius Kariuki, Nairobi.

'I think I need to go to the hospital now - right now!' Anita nudged Tom with her elbow. They were sitting on the sofa watching a video just before going to bed.

'Are you sure?' Tom was somewhat reluctant to move from such a cosy place, even though he knew their baby was due pretty soon.

'Yes, definitely.' Anita was not joking. 'I need to go now.'

'Of course, darling! I'll just get your things.' He was determined to stay calm.

Tom collected the bag which had been previously packed containing Anita's nightclothes and other essentials, made a quick call to DM, Anita's doctor, and then helped his very large wife into the car.

'DRIVE FASTER!' Anita screamed at Tom as they

made their way down the pitch-dark Langata Road towards the hospital in town. Tom put his foot down.

'NOT SO FAST!' Anita clutched the dashboard of the car. Trying to keep a balance, Tom drove on, now worried that they might not get there in time.

It was eleven o'clock when they drew up outside Nairobi Hospital. DM was waiting for them on the steps.

'Don't worry, Anita,' he reassured her. 'Everything is organised - come with me.'

Within a few minutes Anita was tucked up in bed in a private room Tom had previously arranged. DM set about examining Anita while Tom paced up and down outside.

'All's well.' DM was cool and calm, unlike the two prospective parents. 'I don't think anything will happen for a while - just take it easy. Tom, you sit here while I go and check a few things.'

A delightful nurse called Dolores came in and asked Anita if she wanted anything.

'No, thanks, I'm fine.' Anita did not sound very convincing as she gripped Tom's hand tightly.

'Just you call if you need me, there's the bell.' Dolores gestured towards the push button on the bed and then wandered out, her slippers clacking on the tiled floor.

'Prunes, Tom, get me some prunes.' Over the previous few weeks Anita had developed a passion for dried fruit of various kinds, including prunes. Wisely, Tom had come prepared and he handed her a piece of fruit. Anita chewed on it fiercely.

'Another prune!' Tom obliged.

Eventually Anita fell into an uneasy asleep and Tom managed to doze in the chair beside her bed. It was six in the morning before Anita woke with a start.

She poked Tom in the ribs. 'Something's happening, Tom, get DM!'

It wasn't long before DM was there, supervising Anita's move into the delivery room. Tom followed sheepishly, not knowing what to do. There was a pause while the doctor fiddled with some equipment in the corner. As he did so, Anita heard a noise from the window and looked up - she could see the black face of a man who was working away with a cloth and some soapy water cleaning the outside of the window. The man looked at Anita and smiled, his white teeth glistening. Anita was horrified at being seen in such an undignified state. Here she was, about to give birth and was being watched by the local window cleaner! DM reacted immediately to her screech, quickly waving the man away. The face disappeared and Anita went into the last stage of her labour.

After a great deal of swearing, pushing, chewing of prunes and gripping of Tom's hand, DM was finally able to hold up in front of their delighted eyes a tiny baby girl. Anita had done it.

Tom was completely overwhelmed with so many emotions. 'Well done, darling, you are brilliant! She's beautiful! She's amazing!'

This seven pound eight ounce bundle with straggly dark hair, crying lustily as she waved her little hands in the air was to be the centre of their lives from now on. Samantha had been born.

During the following few days Anita had a stream of admiring visitors. Sometimes the baby would be lying in her arms as she cuddled her most precious possession and at other times, while Anita rested and recovered her strength, Dolores would come and take Samantha to the nursery where there were dozens of other babies being cared for.

Tom would stand at the window, gazing at his daughter - it was easy to identify her since she was the only white face visible. He could not have been happier.

When Tom and Anita returned home a few days later, carrying their precious bundle, Irene and David were waiting.

Irene was the first to greet them. 'It is a beautiful baby, what is her name?'

'She is called Samantha,' said Tom proudly.

Irene did not look too impressed. 'Well, I suppose you will need to try again to get a boy.' Boys were more valued offspring than girls in this part of the world.

'I'm not sure about that!' Tom laughed. 'We are just delighted to have such a beautiful baby.'

Irene's face softened. 'When I have a baby, I will call it Tom - or Anita if it is a girl - if you don't mind, *bwana*?'

'Of course not, Irene!'

Chapter Fourteen

The rains came with a vengeance. For months the sky had been a deep blue each day and the baking sun had parched the playing fields to a dusty brown. Then one evening a few clouds appeared and the next afternoon great towering pillars of black clouds built up in the western sky over the Ngong hills. At six o'clock, just as it was getting dark, there was a great crack of thunder and then it rained. For a couple of hours it came down in a solid sheet soaking everything. Then, just as suddenly, the rain stopped and the clamour of dozens of frogs croaking their delight at the arrival of water commenced. A short while later and the air was full of thousands of flying termites emerging from their mud castles. The rainy season had begun.

The chattering of monkeys in the tree outside the bedroom window woke Tom and Anita early next morning. The sky was still a dark blue black but through the burglar bars could be seen the orange glow of the African sun slowly banishing the night. From the game park a mile away came the whooping of a lone hyena returning from its night's scavenging. Samantha, now six weeks old, was fast asleep in the cot at the end of the bed. Beside Tom, Anita stirred, pushing her foot slowly against his leg. About time we went into the game park again, Tom thought, tickling her foot absent-mindedly.

'Shall we take the car into the game park after school today?'

'Okay,' she answered sleepily. Reluctantly Tom swung his feet from under the warm covers, groaned as they landed on the cold tile floor and made his way to the bathroom. Irene was already clattering away in the kitchen, washing last night's dishes. Tom munched through his bowl of cornflakes and set off for work.

After school Anita and Tom went into the game park for a drive as arranged. They took Samantha with them, tucked into her Moses basket, which they wedged securely on the back seat. If they could get into the park by about five o'clock there would be a couple of hours before it got dark and the park closed. Anita had also become a keen photographer and they would always take cameras and suitable telephoto lenses. There was a certain amount of rivalry between the two of them as to who could take the best shots.

This time, however, they were not so clever. They set off in the car and drove through the forested area by the gate and down onto the plains. Here there were few trees and the savannah grasslands provided wide-open spaces for grazing animals such as wildebeest, impala and zebra. Tom was looking for a family of lions they had watched the previous week in a dried up river bed. There were several young cubs and it would be unlikely they would travel far. On the way they stopped off at a waterhole edged with palm trees where animals often came for an evening drink.

Tom drove up near the water as they watched some storks fishing. Forgetting about the recent rain he edged a bit closer. The front driving wheels sank into a mud patch and suddenly they were stuck. This was not good. The wheels spun as he tried to reverse, drawing them deeper into the soggy ground. He got out of the car to assess the situation when a very large black object rose up out of the water a few feet away. It was a hippo and it obviously did not like its waterhole being disturbed by intruders. It opened its cavernous mouth, displaying two huge curved tusks and, beginning to heave itself out of the water, angrily bellowed its annoyance. Tom hastily retreated back to the safety of the car. The hippo sank back into the water, two eyes at surface level watching for his next move. This indeed was a serious problem.

'Don't worry.' Tom tried to sound more optimistic than he felt. 'It's not six o'clock yet and there's a bit of light left. Someone's bound to drive past here soon and we can get them to pull us out.'

Anita was not so sure. They could see a few other vehicles out on the plains but they were quite a way off. They tried to catch their attention by waving shirts and sounding the horn. This seemed to antagonise the hippo even more and one by one the vehicles disappeared up the hill towards the park exit. Samantha began to cry.

It was now getting dark and beginning to look as if they would have to try to dig themselves out, but every time they attempted to do so the ever-present hippo would heave itself threateningly out of the water and make its presence known. They were about three miles away from the park gates and Tom did not fancy walking through the bush with its supply of resident lions.

Another major setback was that they didn't have a spade. The only instrument to be found in the boot was a golf umbrella, not the most ideal digging tool. Tom had no choice but to use it. He started to dig into the mud under the front wheels to make tracks for Anita to reverse. In brief bursts, when the hippo was distracted,

Tom dug as though his life depended on it. By now it was dark and he had to work by the light of a torch, which Anita held for him. She also had to keep a sharp eye out for the hippo, shouting to Tom when it was about to launch another attack and often Tom had to hop back into the vehicle when the animal got too close. After about an hour's digging he had made enough progress to attempt to push the car out. Tom pushed and Anita put the vehicle into reverse and let out the clutch. The car moved slowly out of the hole and as the tyres found firmer ground they shot backwards. Both of them were covered in mud but very relieved to escape from their homemade bog. They waved a cheerful goodbye to the hippo and headed back to the park gates, which they discovered had been locked. The rangers on duty in the gatehouse, who were playing cards to while away the long night, were highly amused by the sight of two mud-covered, very stupid *mzungus* with a baby in the back of the car. They didn't seem too bothered that they were an hour late leaving the park and opened the gates laughing and making disparaging remarks about foolish visitors.

The Kora School was 'twinned' with an African school out in the bush, not far from a town called Machakos about fifty kilometres away. This school was always very short of resources and every so often The Kora would organise an event to raise money towards their running expenses. Pupils and parents would also be asked to donate any reading books they could and Fergus would do a 'clear-out' of the bookroom and, rather reluctantly, pass on any textbooks which were no longer being used. All these items were collected and delivered by Jim every six months or so. Tom wanted to see for himself what this 'twin' was like and so he arranged to travel with Jim and the Chairman down to Machakos to hand over the most recent consignment.

Peter drove the three of them in his silver Mercedes down the Mombasa road for about thirty kilometres. They then turned off along a small bumpy *murram* road, throwing up a vast cloud of red dust behind them as they went. Although they did not seem to be near any habitation that one could see, there were plenty of walkers along the side of the road. Mostly they carried baskets or boxes or small cases and they gazed uncomplainingly at the passing Mercedes. They also had to avoid a variety of goats, chickens and dogs. After about an hour's drive they came to a turning; a battered sign tied to a tree announced 'St John's Academy' and they drove through an open gate and down a track to the school.

It was obviously break time for all the two hundred pupils were out on the dusty field, kicking footballs around, playing 'it' or just sitting around in small groups under the sparse acacia trees that provided the only shelter from the now burning sun. They looked curiously at the smart car driving up to the front of the school building and then went back to their games.

The Headmaster, Mr Wanjiko, greeted his visitors

warmly and took them into his office - a small dark room equipped with a desk, three chairs and very little else. He was a younger man than Tom had expected, perhaps in his early thirties, neatly dressed in an open neck spotlessly clean white shirt and black trousers. He beamed at the three *mzungus*, his white teeth shining in the gloomy room - he had noted the promising contents in the back of the Mercedes. He apologised for the lack of light.

'We do not have electricity here. I have been promised that we will be able to have a connection soon, but I do not know when that will be.'

Between them they unloaded all the books and other items from the enormous boot and back seat of the car and stacked them in a corner in his office. As they were doing this, a bell was rung loudly outside. This did not seem to have an immediate effect but eventually the pupils began to make their way into their various classrooms.

'Would you like to have a look at the work my pupils are doing?' Mr Wanjiko seemed very keen to show his visitors around the school.

The other two hesitated, but Tom quickly said that he would be very interested to see what was going on.

Mr Wanjiko led them first to a classroom where about twenty-five twelve-year-olds were being taught maths. It was very quiet and it was also very dark. Tom went over to a desk near the window and peered over the shoulder of a boy. He was working out quite a complicated sum involving pounds, shillings and pence. Tom picked up the textbook he was using. It must have been at least thirty years old but was in quite good condition - textbooks were treasured here and treated accordingly.

Tom asked the boy what he was doing and he was able to explain very well. He patiently returned to his work as Tom went over to Mr Wanjiko.

'You will find more modern books for mathematics in the boxes we brought. That boy over there is a very capable student.'

'Yes, we think he is a bright boy.' Mr Wanjiko was clearly pleased that Tom had happened on a good pupil. 'Shall we move onto the next class?'

They spent the next half an hour visiting different classrooms. In one, the teacher asked Tom to explain to her class what school was like for the children in England. He told them about his last school in London and how children travelled to school - mostly by car. The pupils wanted to know whether the school had computers and if the boys were any good at football.

As they went back to Mr Wanjiko's office, Tom asked him how his children travelled to school. He looked at him as if that was a particularly stupid question.

'All the children and teachers walk to school. There are no buses which come here.'

'What about you? Where do you live? What time do you have to get up to get to school?'

'I leave my *shamba* at about half past five in the morning and arrive at school at half past eight in time for the pupils who must be here at nine.'

Mr Wanjiko must have been one of the fittest headmasters around – Tom worked out he probably walked about twenty-five kilometres a day. He felt very guilty driving, as he did, the few hundred metres to his school each day.

They returned to Nairobi pleased that they had been able to help in a small way but not envying the lifestyle of Mr Wanjiko and his colleagues one little bit.

Ben and Charlie, Anita's twins, were well settled in as boarders at their new school, Oundle, which they enjoyed. As soon as the school holidays arrived however, now that they were teenagers and old enough to travel on their own, they would fly out to Kenya to stay with Anita and Tom. They quickly made friends and their social life became hectic, with plenty of parties. They were invited to join the Duckworth family for a week at the coast – this meant an eight-hour drive down the notorious Mombasa Road and then up the coast to Watamu. Anita reluctantly agreed that they could go. The Duckworths had a holiday house close to the beach – a large untidy place, which could sleep lots of teenagers on the living room floor. Jeremy Duckworth was in his element introducing Ben and Charlie to the delights of the nearby Ocean Sports Club – also known as 'Open Shorts' – where you could play a variety of pub games, drink beer and, if you had the money, rent a boat to go deep-sea fishing. After a good evening there the first night, a large crowd of youngsters returned to the Duckworth's house and eventually crashed out on a selection of sleeping bags and mattresses on the living room floor.

Ben was woken in the middle of the night by a scratching sound. It was very dark but at the open window he could just make out a black moving shape. A fine piece of fishing line brushed against his arm and he realised that it was attached to a fishing rod poking through the bars at the open window. Someone was trying to steal valuables with a fishhook from outside the house. Ben called out and at once the fishing rod disappeared. The lights came on but, by the time everyone had run outside, the angling burglar had disappeared, along with several watches, a wallet and Ben's camera, which had been lying on the floor beside him. Quite easy pickings really – Ben had learnt by experience.

When they returned from the coast, the twins received a most unusual invitation. They had been invited to visit George Adamson, of 'Born Free' fame. They were so excited they could hardly contain themselves. They were to travel to his camp in the middle of the bush and George's doctor had offered to fly them there in his very small plane on one of his regular visits.

It was about an hour's flight from Nairobi. After they had landed, by the side of the landing strip, they saw a notice which advised passengers not to disembark until the camp vehicle arrived as there were lions in the immediate vicinity.

George had become a bit of a recluse preferring the company of lions to people, making this visit for the boys even more exceptional. He encouraged the animals to roam around outside the camp by regularly feeding them camel meat so they didn't have to indulge in too much hunting! A Land Rover duly appeared and five minutes later George was giving them a brief tour. His camp consisted of one large wooden hut with a table outside sheltered from the sun by a thatched roof together with a number of other smaller huts. The camp was surrounded on three sides by a rather flimsy wire fence. Outside the fence several lionesses roamed up and down eyeing the barbecue area. Despite the lack of a fence around one side of his camp, George told them not to concern themselves as the lions would not come into the camp. The visitors were obliged to be trusting. Ben and Charlie were particularly impressed by the camp's two-seater open-air lavatory – which consisted of a pair of enormous elephant's jawbones turned upside down on which you would sit – possibly chatting to your friend and admiring the view. The boys spent a couple of idyllic days, watching the abundant wildlife, seeing George feed his lions and chatting to the doctor.

Back again in Nairobi, Ben and Charlie started to get acquainted with their little half sister. They would chatter away to Samantha for hours. Samantha would watch them intently, gurgling occasionally. Anita was really in her element, showing the boys around the sights and shops in Nairobi. She was becoming increasingly confident at finding her way about and it was wonderful having Irene to help with Samantha. Irene was brilliant with her - she had infinite patience and would hold her for hours, rocking her to sleep, singing Swahili songs softly. Although Samantha took up lots of her time, it did not stop Irene from doing her normal washing and cleaning. She would take her *kikoi* and wrap Samantha carefully in its long folds, passing the end over one shoulder and around her ample bosom and then tying it together at her waist. The little baby's face would then peer contentedly over her shoulder as Irene washed the dishes, scrubbed the washing in the bath or swept the floor (Anita had no washing machine or vacuum cleaner). David, meanwhile, not wishing to miss out, would come up and tickle Samantha under the chin till she giggled. It was not surprising that the little girl would grow up preferring black faces to white ones.

As in England, children moving onto secondary schools

from The Kora normally took the Common Entrance examination at the age of thirteen. The exams were held at the beginning of June and The Common Entrance Board would dispatch by courier all the papers needed by the Kenyan schools to The Kora. From there the various packages would be distributed to the other Kenyan prep schools in plenty of time for the exams.

It was around this time that parents would have to decide which would be their first choice school for their child and it was often a very tricky one to make. It was one that faced Mr and Mrs Duckworth for their son Jeremy. He had befriended Ben and Charlie on their visits and was a very likeable and sociable boy. In the classroom, however, he was, at best, an average pupil and inclined to be rather lazy. He had the potential to do well in the future and his parents were undecided whether to send him to boarding school in England or to keep him in Kenya and send him to Highbury, the local British curriculum secondary school.

The Duckworths had lived in Kenya for years - Martin Duckworth ran a fairly successful safari company and was often away from home with his clients, camping in the bush. His wife Daniella was a very attractive woman who had, let's say, an active social life in Nairobi while her husband was away. Tom was discussing the pros and cons of schools with them.

'Highbury has very good academic record, their A level results are pretty good and they seem to get a good proportion of their pupils into top British universities. The admission tutors must look at applicants' A level grades and think that if they can get good grades from a school in the middle of Africa they have to be bright - so they offer places. It's probably much more difficult to get a place at a decent university from a school like Radley or Marlborough than from Highbury.'

'These boarding schools also cost about three times as much as schooling here,' mumbled Martin, avoiding his wife's accusing glance, 'but I guess we could afford to send Jeremy to the UK if it was the right thing.'

Daniella intervened. 'We have heard that pupils are using drugs quite freely at Highbury and also that drinking goes on at the weekends. Is there enough control there, do you think?'

Tom replied quite confidently. 'David Whetton is a hard man. He keeps a fairly tight hold on what goes on; but I don't think there is a secondary school anywhere in either Kenya or Britain where you won't find drugs and drinking. That, I'm afraid, is how things are. At least if your son is here you would have a better chance of keeping an eye on what he gets up to.'

They moved on to the question of whether Jeremy would pass Common Entrance.

Tom thought carefully before putting forward his opinion. 'I think he will be OK for all of the schools we have mentioned, provided he keeps working hard - which I think he is at the moment. However, he would need to get slightly higher marks for Highbury than for the boarding schools in the UK we have been talking about.'

Eventually it was decided that Highbury would be Jeremy's first choice school and that his papers would be sent there. Tom also promised to have a quiet word with David Whetton and point out what Jeremy would be able to contribute if offered a place.

In Kenya the importance of sport and the winning of

matches against other schools was a major issue and it was this that led to a rather unfortunate incident. The Kora's under eleven rugby team was due to play against St Anstell's. St Anstell's had an abrasive Scottish games master in charge by the name of Angus. You could say that he had been around a bit – he would certainly be the type of person you would want on your side in an argument in a pub. He was a hard man and his teams played to win.

The match was to be at home and Ross, who was running The Kora team, was waiting in the car park with his captain for their minibus to arrive. In due course the St Anstell's bus appeared and Angus climbed down from the driver's seat in high good humour, followed by his team of ten-year-old boys.

Ross was rather surprised to see one enormous boy emerging from the bus with their team who he assumed would be acting as a touch judge. He was at least six foot tall and solidly built. However it soon became apparent that he was a member of the team. Ross went and spoke to Angus.

'Angus, that boy over there - is he playing in your team?'

'Aye, he is. Do you have a problem with that?'

'Well, I must say he does look a good deal older than eleven. Boys must be under eleven on the first day of term to be eligible to play in under eleven teams.'

'Are you accusing me of cheating?' Angus's genial demeanour turned quickly to thunder.

'No,' said Ross hastily, 'I am just asking you to confirm that this boy is qualified to play in under eleven matches.'

'Right you are.' Angus's voice resonated across the

field. 'Boys! Get back in the bus - we are not playing a school which accuses us of cheating.' The bewildered St Anstell's boys trooped back into their minibus and were driven away by their irate coach. The match was obviously abandoned.

Who was actually in the right over this altercation was difficult to determine, but after Ross had reported what had happened, Tom rang up Damian McHuish, the Head of St Anstell's and tried to pour oil on troubled waters. It was not easy - Damian said that as far as he knew the boy was under age but he did admit that the documentation he had at school, which was a copy of the boy's Ugandan birth certificate, might not be too reliable. Damian said he'd send a copy of this document over and maybe they could agree to play the fixture later in the term when tempers had cooled down. That was how it had to stand for the time being. Ross remained convinced that this boy had to be far too old - but boys did mature early in Africa and maybe he wasn't much of a player anyway!

One of The Kora's more interesting parents was Mike Allen. Mike worked for the World Food Programme, a UN agency, which supplied food for various UN projects in third world countries. He was a rugged ex-army character and a qualified pilot often flying around East Africa organising the supply and distribution of food. One day he came into the office and suggested that Tom might like to join him on one of his trips. Mike knew that Tom was a keen photographer and asked him if he could bring his video camera in order to make an informal film about a large project in a district called Turkana in the north of Kenya. The film would be used for internal UN information purposes. The trip would mean a weekend plus a day or so away from school. Tom naturally jumped at the idea, but said that he would have to arrange things with Jonny and, of course, see what Anita thought about the plan.

Anita was not too happy for Tom to be away for a couple of nights but she knew he was very keen to go and very sensibly arranged for herself and Samantha to stay with friends in Muthaiga on the other side of Nairobi. She did not relish the thought of being in the house on her own. Tom arranged for Jonny to cover him for that particular weekend plus an extra day or so for the trip up north.

Mike had to obtain a special permit from the Ministry of the Interior to film in this region. The project they were to visit involved a scheme known as 'water harvesting' and Mike briefed Tom on what to expect. The local nomadic people were 'paid' in food for work constructing earthworks designed to catch the rainwater. Rain fell very rarely in Turkana. In that very arid part of the country, any rain which did fall quickly ran off into Lake Turkana - which was a soda lake so inevitably the water was lost. The idea was to build low earth dams or 'bunds' as they were called, to hold the rainwater long enough to plant sorghum, a fast growing cereal crop which would provide food for both the local population and their animals. The people were also building 'micro-catchments' - small earth walls a foot or so high and about five metres square. Again rainwater could be contained long enough for trees to be planted and survive. This project had been underway for a couple of years or so and supported up to twenty thousand people. It promised to be a fascinating trip and Tom could not wait for it to come around.

The social life of Nairobi was quite lively and Anita and Tom were invited to some pretty unusual supper parties. Sandy Martin was quite an unconventional mother. As well as looking after her two children, Sasha and Duncan, who were at The Kora, she was employed by an international wildlife organisation to carry out research into endangered species. She had just returned from Uganda where she had been hiding in the forest watching gorillas and recording their behaviour. She was an attractive woman, much admired by The Kora fathers, but she could be quite fiery and unpredictable. Her husband spent most of his time in Europe on business and was seldom present when his wife entertained. The much used question 'Are you married or do you live in Kenya?' might well have applied to Sandy! She liked to live life to the full.

Anita and Tom had been cordially invited to one of her suppers, along with the Duckworths, Martin and Daniella, who were always very good value at parties. Sandy's niece Melanie who had just started as a journalist with the Evening Standard in London had recently arrived from England. Melanie was tall, articulate and argumentative as well as being a very pretty girl. She was staying with her aunt for a few days before joining a group of young people who were planning to climb Mount Kilimanjaro - they were all being sponsored and hoped to raise lots of money for charity. Beaudry Kulei, an official from the Kenya Wildlife Authority and another Kora parent, was sitting opposite Tom and there were various other people he and Anita didn't know arranged around Sandy's long table.

Before supper Tom had managed to move around the assembled company in order to chat to the fragrant

Melanie. She hadn't been to Africa before and was keen to find out how people could exist out of contact with the 'civilised' world of London and England. Tom explained that they did manage though it was a bit difficult when the only way of communicating was by means of drums or forked sticks carried by natives. She had the grace to smile. As Tom settled into his chair, enjoying this conversation, he felt something hard behind his back. He turned to investigate and discovered a revolver, which had been hidden under the cushion. Tom casually held the weapon up.

'Anyone claim this?'

'Oh, thanks.' Martin Duckworth didn't bat an eyelid. 'I always carry that with me, you never know when you might need it.' He leant over to retrieve his pistol and carried on chatting up Sandy.

Beaudry Kulei turned out to be rather heavy going and a man of few words. Maybe he preferred animals to humans. Daniella Duckworth on the other hand couldn't stop talking and she brought everyone up to date with all the latest gossip. Tom looked across at Melanie. Perhaps she would come and talk to the pupils about being a journalist - the boys would certainly enjoy that.

There was a pause in the meal while Sandy busied herself in the kitchen. She came back into the room holding what looked to be a live white mouse. It **was** a very live white mouse.

'Frightfully sorry, everyone, but I've forgotten to feed Mugabe.'

Mugabe turned out to be a medium-sized orange-coloured snake asleep under a rock in his glass tank, which stood on the sideboard. Everyone turned to watch. Mugabe took very little notice as Sandy popped the unfortunate mouse into the tank. The mouse unwisely started to explore and moved too close to the snake. Mugabe moved his head slowly, his tongue flicking in and out. Suddenly he opened his mouth and struck. The mouse's head disappeared into Mugabe's bulging jaws, its tail thrashing about in vain and slowly Mugabe dislocated his jaws and swallowed his supper. Sandy's guests watched in horror as the last bit of tail disappeared into the snake's mouth. As they turned back towards the table Sandy brought in a tasty looking chicken casserole; oddly enough no one felt very hungry.

Once again it was time for the dreaded Common Entrance exam. For three days twenty-four thirteen-year-old boys and girls would be sitting the same exams as their peers in England. Tom went into the large classroom used for the exams to wish them luck - the sun was streaming through the windows as the children settled down for Maths 1. Across the road a troop of monkeys chattered cheerfully from the top of an acacia tree. Lucky them - they had no exams to worry about. Later that day Jim drove into Nairobi laden down with various brown packets. He was off to post the fruits of the candidates' first day's labours to their respective schools.

Mike and Tom flew to Turkana on a Friday afternoon. They took off from Wilson airport, on the edge of Nairobi, in Mike's small four-seater plane. The route took them up the Rift Valley, passing over first Lake Naivasha and then Lake Nakuru, glinting in the sunlight with a ring of pink flamingos around the edge. To the right the glistening white peak of Mount Kenya stood firm and proud.

Whilst Tom was taking in this glorious scenery Mike casually told him to take over flying the plane while he made some calculations on a clipboard he had balanced on his knee. 'Just aim for that mountain over there and keep us at the same height.'

Quite trusting, Tom thought, but said nothing and started to concentrate.

After another hour or so they flew over the perfectly circular crater of an extinct volcano filled with bright green algae rich water. They could see ahead of them the shimmering haze over Lake Turkana. Mike took over and they headed left towards Lodwar, their first landing point.

The only way to describe Lodwar is that it's a small town a very long way from anywhere else! The man in charge of the Turkana Project, a remarkable Norwegian called Aslak Bergland, used the town as his base. He also was a pilot and had his own small twin-engined plane, which was really the only practical way of getting about this vast area. Mike and Tom spent the night at his house on the edge of the town.

The next morning the three of them returned to the

airstrip and they took off again. They were to visit one area where bunds and micro-catchments were being built near a place called Kakuma. After half an hour Aslak indicated to Tom the ground below. On the bare brown earth he could see dark curved lines about a kilometre long. Nearby there were also areas covered with a patchwork of small squares.

Aslak quickly explained, 'The lines you see are the bunds we built last year - if you look carefully you can see some green. That is the beginning of the sorghum crop, which the Turkana people have planted. It should be ready for harvesting in a few weeks. Those squares you can see have had trees planted in them; you'll see when we land.'

They landed on a bumpy strip of ground and came to a stop just before some thorn bushes. Within a few minutes a crowd of about a dozen people appeared from what seemed like nowhere. Aslak introduced Mike and Tom to a grey-haired man wearing a torn old linen safari jacket - he turned out to be the project manager for this locality. The other men were wearing blankets over their shoulders and a few were carrying spears. They all set off into the bush to see what work the people had been doing.

They soon came upon a large group sitting in a circle on the ground listening intently to a man who was explaining something to them. As the visitors approached the man stopped talking and turned to welcome Aslak. Nearby under a tree there were shovels, picks and buckets in a pile - the implements the people had been using for moving the earth. The bund they had been working on was about a metre high and stretched away into the distance. It was constructed from earth and all of it had been moved by hand. Aslak had told Tom that the 'rate of pay' was one kilo of maize meal for each cubic metre of earth moved. This was incredibly hard work!

Then an amazing thing happened. The manager came over to Aslak and said that the people would like to sing. All the thirty or so workers, a few men but mostly women, went over to their pile of tools and picked up an implement. They put their shovels and picks over their shoulders and, under the direction of the manager who acted as a conductor, they all started to march around the site in a long snaking line, singing a rhythmic and joyful song. For these very poor people, who really had nothing, to sing such a moving song for their visitors was a humbling experience for these rich outsiders. Tom wondered if it would be acceptable to take photographs and gestured the question to Mike. Mike and Aslak talked briefly to the local manager who nodded his head in agreement. Tom filmed away busily.

There had been some rain recently and later that day they saw how the sorghum was beginning to grow. Tree seedlings had also been planted in the micro-catchments and would be valuable in the future. The benefits to be gained from trees were clear - they would provide shade, firewood and browsing for goats. They would act as windbreaks, halt erosion, dampen dust and attract rain. One type of acacia tree being planted had twigs which broke into tough fibres which were excellent for cleaning teeth - an unexpected benefit to the Turkana!

Would this project be successful? To some extent it already was - food had been distributed to those who needed it and the people had had to work for it thus retaining some pride. Some crops would soon be harvested and trees were starting to grow. It seemed to Mike and Tom as they returned to the relative civilisation of Nairobi that an amazing job was being done by Aslak and his team. Tom hoped that the video he managed to shoot would give an idea of what was being achieved.

Chapter Fifteen

Tom, Anita and Jonny Hutton were sitting under the shelter in Tom's garden enjoying a quiet drink after school. Two Tusker beers and a glass of white wine stood on the table.

Jonny seemed a bit worried. 'Tom, I think I ought to tell you that there may be a bit of a problem in the staff room. You know you were talking at the staff meeting about a new way of grouping the children for different subjects in the Junior School?'

'Yes, we discussed that at some length with you and Jane beforehand. Why do you ask?'

'Well, no one said much at the meeting and you may have taken that as a signal of general approval. That may not be the case. The fact is Jane has been lobbying behind your back against the idea with the junior teachers. And they are rather afraid of her, you know. She didn't disagree when the three of us talked about your ideas, but I think she is being rather disloyal – she should come to you and say what she feels rather than undermining your position.'

Tom stroked his chin. 'I see. Thank you for telling me. What do you think I should do?'

Anita, who had been listening intently to this conversation, bristled and thumped her glass down on the table angrily - she felt very protective of her husband - and moreover had never trusted Jane who, as Head of the Junior School, had resented Anita's presence.

As soon as Tom had arrived at The Kora, Jane had attempted to establish some sort of special relationship with him in order to guide him in the direction she wanted in respect of school policy. This would have meant extra meetings in the evenings and cosy chats. Tom was wary of this and, of course, he wanted time with Anita. He had therefore kept his distance, though he was careful to consult her at school and support her in the efficient way she ran her department.

Tom's mind went back to the time soon after they had arrived in Africa when the Chairman, Peter Mallinson, had warned him about Jane. He had been proved right.

Jonny leant forward. 'Listen, let me have a quiet word with her first. No decisions have yet been made and we can always have another meeting with just the three of us. I'll point out that she hasn't gone about this in the right way.'

Tom agreed to this and thanked Jonny again for his support. How careful one had to be when in charge of anything - 'always watch your back' was good advice. Jane was quite capable of leading a minor revolt, which would make running the school very difficult. Tom was sure that Peter Mallinson would back him up if necessary but if possible he would like to deal with this hiccup without bothering the Chairman.

The next day Jonny reported back to Tom. 'I think it's OK. Jane was not happy with my intervention but she has agreed to stop lobbying against you and we have arranged a meeting tomorrow morning with the three of us.'

Eventually a compromise was reached but Tom became very wary of Jane and a rather strained atmosphere prevailed for some time between them. Anita was quite upset by this episode and suggested that Tom should get rid of disloyal staff. Maybe he should, he thought. He did nothing however and things eventually calmed down. Such were the joys and delights of headmastering.

One quiet morning a surprise visitor appeared. Veronica tapped on the study door just after assembly and said there was a Mr Mwangi to see Tom. He would not say what it was about but was insistent and looked important. Tom asked her to show him in.

'Good morning, Mr Mwangi.'

Tom greeted a smartly suited middle-aged man with rather distinguished grey hair and thick horn-rimmed glasses as he came into the study.

'What can I do for you?'

'Are you the Headmaster, Mr Thorne?' Tom confirmed that he was.

'Excellent! I am Joseph Mwange and I am the Schools' Inspector for your district - Karen and Langata.' He handed Tom his card.

'Please sit down, would you like a cup of coffee?'

'No, thank you - I have work to do.' He smiled and explained that he had to make unannounced visits to schools in his district every so often and he would like to look around The Kora School now, please.

'You are very welcome. I would be delighted to show you round - just give me a moment to arrange cover for my lesson with the secretary.'

'You do some teaching yourself, Mr Thorne?' Mr Mwange raised his eyebrows. 'That is good. What subjects do you teach?'

Tom explained that he taught some maths and also games. He asked Veronica to find Jonny, explain what was happening and ask him to cover his lesson. Then they set off round the school on a tour of inspection.

'What would you like to see first?'

'I would like to go into each classroom - starting with your youngest children. What Standards do you teach here?'

Tom explained that the curriculum was English and that The Kora did not use the Kenyan Standards system as such - they worked towards the British Independent Schools' exams taken at eleven and thirteen years of age.

'Do you teach Swahili?'

'Yes, we do.' Tom could be honest in saying that, but did not mention that it was only a very small part of the weekly timetable.

They spent the next two hours going into every classroom. The Inspector examined in some detail the exercise and textbooks of every class. He asked each teacher what they were aiming to teach in that particular lesson and then he asked the children what they had been learning. He was very polite and gentle towards the children, extracting all sorts of comments about the school. During break time he looked at the kitchens, games fields and swimming pool. Eventually they returned to the office.

'I would like to see your staff list now. Are any of your teachers away sick today?'

Fortunately there was a full complement that day; usually someone was absent for one reason or another so Tom was lucky.

Mr Mwange looked at his watch.

'I have to make one more visit today, Mr Thorne, so I will have to leave you now. May I congratulate you on knowing where the classrooms are! You would be surprised to know that I have visited schools where the Headmaster is not at his school but away playing golf! Your students are well provided for and I will be able to make a favourable report to the Ministry.'

With that the Inspector went on his way. It left Tom thinking. Mr Mwange had, in one morning, managed to find out a good deal about the way the school operated on a normal school day. His mind went back to the last inspection he had had to endure at Shaftesbury. Tom wondered what Mr Mwange would have discovered if he had made surprise visits to British schools.

David Whetton rang up with the results of the Common Entrance. 'The good news first, Tom. Your girl Rose Best was very strong - particularly good in English. We've decided to award her the one scholarship we give. Twenty per cent off the fees - not a great deal I know but worth having.'

'Excellent, well done Rose.' Tom wondered what was coming next. 'What about our other candidates?'

'Well, I'm afraid I can't offer Ragi Patel a place. He was pretty weak all round especially in maths. I really think that he would do better in a less academic environment. I know he is a good games player but he really would struggle with us. All your other candidates were fine - even Jeremy Duckworth turned out to be better than you said!'

Tom's heart sank. He was not looking forward to breaking the news to poor Ragi or his parents. He knew that one of the other British schools in Nairobi would be pleased to have him but his parents were very ambitious and would not easily be placated. Tom decided to try and bend David's ear.

'Any chance of Ragi going onto your waiting list, David? He's a very enthusiastic character and will not let you down - and he would be useful on the sports field.'

David hummed and eventually agreed that he could say to Ragi's parents that he was on a reserve list but Tom knew David wouldn't take him.

Later that day Tom rang Mr and Mrs Patel and said how sorry he was that Ragi hadn't been offered a place at Highbury. Not surprisingly, they were upset and asked if they could come in for a meeting. An hour later they were seated in the office and Tom was trying to point out how he would do very well at Bell House, a pleasant, small and friendly school out on the road to Limuru. Tom knew he'd be welcome there. Mrs Patel was keen to wait on the off chance of Highbury having a last minute place but her husband was more down to earth and agreed to take Ragi to Bell House to have a look. They eventually departed after Tom had fixed an appointment for them the next day. He was then able to enjoy telling all the other CE candidates their good news.

Molly Brown, one of the Year One teachers, who had lived in Africa for years (she was also the school's snake expert!) should have known better. Working late after school one night she left her handbag in her empty classroom while she took a break for a cup of tea and a chat in the staff room with a couple of other teachers. She wasn't away for that long but when she returned her bag had disappeared. Plenty of cleaners and ground staff as well as teachers were around. Of course, there was some cash in her bag - a great temptation especially for those on the very low wage paid to most of the unskilled staff.

Molly went immediately to Jim Broom. Jim, being a direct type who called a spade a spade, told her she was a fool but also promised to do what he could to persuade the thief to return the stolen goods. He hurried round to the African staff quarters at the back of the school and sought out Gideon.

'Gideon. I want you to spread it around that Mrs Brown has mislaid her handbag and wonders if anyone has seen it. Mrs Brown has said she would give a reward to the person who finds it.'

The Major did not want to accuse anyone of stealing - much better if the bag was quietly returned. Gideon understood the Major perfectly and nodded his head sadly.

'Yes, *bwana.* I will speak to all the men. I will do what I can to make sure the bag is returned - but also there were some people delivering supplies for the kitchens who were here then - maybe one of them was responsible?'

'Perhaps.' The Major was doubtful. 'We will speak again tomorrow morning.'

'Yes, *bwana.*' Gideon went off to gather up the workers.

Not surprisingly Molly's handbag had not appeared by the following morning and so the Major assembled all those workers who were around the previous evening outside his office. There were about a dozen. They stood around in a semi-circle looking at the ground as the Major explained the situation.

'As you know, Mrs Brown's handbag, containing money and some other things which she particularly values, disappeared from her classroom last night. I do not think the people delivering food to the kitchen last night could have anything to do with this; the kitchens are a long way from Mrs Brown's classroom. I was hoping that the bag would have reappeared by this morning. It has not.' His tone was firm but quite kindly.

He paused and cast his eyes over the men in front of him. His gaze was not returned and there was an uncomfortable shuffling of feet.

The Major continued. 'If we do not find this bag it will be necessary for me to call in the police.' Again he paused. 'That would be most unfortunate - I think you would agree?'

There was an earnest nodding of heads. The police when 'making their enquiries' were inclined to be rather heavy-handed and witnesses or suspects were liable to emerge from 'questioning' with more bruises than they would like. No one wished the police to be involved.

'So maybe you could all go away and see if this bag can be found. I will see you all again this evening.'

The Major returned to his office and the men wandered off, mumbling to each other.

Surprise, surprise - after lunch Molly's bag, complete with all its contents was found under a cardboard box in the corner of her classroom. Well done, Jim!

It was four o'clock on a Friday afternoon and the St Luke's College minibus arrived with their rugby team who were due to play The Kora on Saturday morning. St Luke's was a thriving up-country boarding prep school close to the Ugandan border. Quite a few of their pupils came from Uganda - they tended to be a bright and talented lot. It was a four-hour drive down to Nairobi so they usually made a weekend of it and played a couple of fixtures. Ross had arranged accommodation for their team with members of his team for the night. The Kora teachers got on very well with their staff though there was a time in the past apparently when the then Kora Headmaster, Mr Forest, thought a certain master of theirs called Martin Bale used to cheat when he refereed. On one notable occasion The Kora team had travelled all the way up to St Luke's to play a match. As they had got out of the bus Mr Forest noticed Martin Bale had already changed into his games kit complete with a whistle in his hand. Mr Forest enquired whether Martin would be refereeing and when this was confirmed he said to his team 'Right, boys, get back in the bus, we're going back to Nairobi' and they set off on the four-hour journey home.

Martin had since retired and the two schools had repaired relations. The wife of the St Luke's Head, Mrs Beattie, who was a knowledgeable rugby coach, used to get carried away sometimes and her excesses on the touchline were an added source of amusement for the spectators. The Kora boys and their parents duly arrived and went off with their guests while Jonny, Ross and Tom looked after their games staff. Mr and Mrs Beattie, who arrived in a battered old Mercedes, went off to stay with friends in Nairobi. The games staff from the two schools spent an enjoyable evening at The Carnivore - a restaurant nearby which served a variety of barbecued meat including eland, crocodile, ostrich and impala.

Saturday morning arrived and without the weekly shop at Sainsbury's to tempt the supporters away, there were lots - well over a hundred - in attendance for this under fourteen game. An hour before kick-off the four-wheel drive vehicles started to arrange themselves around the edge of the field and bottles of Tusker and Whitecap were opened. Some of the older girls at The Kora came to watch - they would say they were there to support the school, but it was probably more likely they would be interested in watching Jeremy Duckworth or one of his mates. There was much banter between the two sets of parents as many knew each other well.

St Luke's had a powerful team with two strong running African centres. It was clear that The Kora boys would be defending most of the game. Tackle after tackle went in. Jeremy was outstanding and crash-tackled one of the St Luke's players into touch right next to Mrs Beattie. She clearly thought he was being rather rough and took her umbrella, which she was using to keep off the sun, and beat Jeremy over the head.

'Don't you tackle my boys like that!' she shouted much to the amusement of the many spectators crowding around.

'Sorry, Mrs Beattie.' Jeremy breathlessly rubbed his head and returned to the fray.

All good fun. The Kora lost 38 - 7.

Four of the Kenyan prep schools had invited Hugh Waters out to Kenya in order to present the prizes at their various end of term prize-giving events. The dates were carefully arranged to avoid clashes. In exchange the schools would organise a safari for Hugh and his wife, Diana. It did not take long for Hugh to agree! A few years earlier, Hugh had been the guest speaker at Shaftesbury Prep and so it would be the second time for Tom as host.

At The Kora it was the last day of the 'summer' term - hardly summer weather though - in fact it was extremely chilly with thick cloud overhead. Prize-giving was held outside on the field beneath the acacia trees. The children sat on rugs and the staff, wrapping their gowns around themselves to keep warm, sat on chairs facing them. Tom remembered the last time Hugh had been giving away prizes - on a swelteringly hot day in London a few years before. It was quite ironic that here they were again just south of the equator - and freezing! Behind the children stood rows of parents - listening intently to Hugh's speech. Hugh used the same lion and Christian joke - it was a different audience (apart from Tom) so it went down well.

Tom thought, I've seen it (or heard it) all before.

The following year, life at The Kora School went on much as before. Jim Broom continued to run a tight ship in the Bursar's office and was relieved when his *bete noir*, Veronica decided she would leave to join her brother who ran quite a successful travel agency in town. Tom managed to find a younger, more sensitive replacement. Jim immediately took a shine to her and the two of them started having coffee together in the morning breaks. Consequently, their two offices ran much more smoothly.

Ragi Patel, who had failed to pass Common Entrance to Highbury, went on to Bell House where he began to show a great talent for art; he also thrived on the cricket field and was selected for the Kenyan under 15 squad to tour India. Jeremy Duckworth went on to Highbury but found the work quite difficult; he also became very interested in girls and did little in the classroom. Eventually his parents decided enough was enough and sent him to a boys only boarding school in Dorset. Poor chap!

Development at The Kora School continued with the introduction of more up to date educational ideas imported from Tom's previous experience in London. The new art and music block was completed more or less on time; the view over the game park from the first floor art room was spectacular. Tom asked Mrs Olindo, wife of the Energy Minister and mother of James, to perform the opening ceremony which she did most graciously. No snakes were present.

Unfortunately, over the past year or so security had become quite a serious problem. There were too many car hijackings and robberies - in the old days people would be threatened with knives or pangas but guns were now much more easily obtained. One man was actually shot dead in the road outside Tom and Anita's house. They began to question as to whether this was the right place to bring up a young child. Samantha was growing up fast and loved playing in the garden on the swing Tom had attached to the branch of a large tree in the middle of the lawn. David would take her for rides in his decrepit, squeaky wheelbarrow around the garden. Soon it would be time for her to start nursery school. Tom and Anita discussed for hours what they should do. Tom felt that he had been able to move The Kora School forward and that it was a better and more up to date place than when he arrived. The children and almost all the staff were a delight to work with - but was it right with a young family to stay in Kenya? Several other families had moved back to a safer yet more boring life in England. It was a tough decision, but after much heart-searching, Tom and Anita eventually decided that they would leave Africa. They began to make arrangements for their return to England starting with Tom sending in numerous job applications. Peter Mallinson, having reluctantly accepted Tom's resignation, decided to appoint Jonny Hutton to take over as Head of The Kora School.

The goodbyes were emotional - especially with Irene and David who had become part of the family. They do say that if you have lived in Africa for four years or more you will always be drawn back. The wide-open spaces, the red dust, the people and the wild animals together create a heightened excitement not found elsewhere which will draw you in forever. Everything seems more alive and vibrant and at the same time spiced with an element of danger. It is a heady mixture. Tom and Anita would certainly never forget Africa and would always remember with affection the people and the smell of the place.

'Here's one you might be interested in.' Anita spoke from behind the pages of the Jobs Vacant section of the Times Educational Supplement. 'It's in Spain - plenty of sunshine there - it's for the Principal of a School on the Costa Blanca. They also say that some legal training would be useful. I wonder why. What's a Principal anyway?'

Tom looked up from marking some exercise books. 'Let's have a look. Hmm. The Costa Blanca International School, Altea. A Principal would probably be a bit like a Headmaster but would be more concerned with general policy and finance. Could be interesting.'

Since returning from Africa he had been looking, so far without success, for another interesting Headship. In the meantime he had taken on a temporary job at a small school, which specialised in providing the appropriate teaching for dyslexic children. Tom didn't really enjoy the job but he got on well with the eccentric American millionaire who owned the place. The well-heeled parents were amusing too - they included a Labour politician who had braved the wrath of her party's left wing in order to send her son to an independent school.

During the previous month or so Tom and Anita had been going through rather a low period. Having spent time abroad in what they had thought was a fascinating and exciting country, it was rather deflating to find that back in England no one was particularly interested to hear about their life in Africa - nor impressed either with the progress Tom's school had made under his guidance. Most people just said 'Ah, yes, Kenya - some friends of ours had a good holiday there last year' and then moved on to more relevant topics such as who they had met at their last dinner party.

'You've got some legal training – you qualified as a barrister.' Anita sounded enthusiastic. 'Why don't you send your CV in and we could find out more about this job?'

Tom agreed. There was nothing to lose so he composed a letter of application and sent it off together with a copy of his CV which included his former training as a lawyer.

That evening the phone rang. 'It's for you, Tom,' said Anita.

'Is that Tom Thorne?' A firm and confident female voice that Tom half recognised asked the question. 'It's Valerie Hudson here - you remember James, Simon and Harriet at Shaftesbury?' Tom certainly remembered Valerie and her three splendid children - Valerie had been a most effective though rather bossy Chairperson of the PA committee back in his first year as Head at Shaftesbury Prep.

'Of course I remember - how are you - and the children?'

The two of them caught up with the news from the Twickenham area - including the fact that the Chairman of the Board, Ted Whittaker, had retired and that Valerie, despite only recently having joined the Board, had taken over as Chairperson. There was a pause – 'why is she ringing me?' thought Tom.

'The fact is Tom that your successor Graham Lamb has not been a great success and he will be leaving us at the end of this term. The Board was wondering, now that you are back in the UK, whether you would be interested in taking on your old job again?'

Tom thought rapidly. People often said you should never go back, whether it was to return to an old job or to a place to live - maybe Spain would be more of a challenge - but on the other hand....

Valerie was still in full flow - '…and it would be a

popular move with the staff; and the Headmaster's house would be big enough for you all - there are four bedrooms, you know.'

'Yes,' replied Tom, remembering very clearly Anita's first visit to the Headmaster's house when they had both looked out of the spare bedroom window at the garden, 'I remember.....I remember it well. Valerie, thank you very much for your call. I'll need some time to think about your proposition and, of course, to discuss it with Anita.' Tom arranged to contact Valerie again in a few days.

A couple of days later the phone rang again. Anita answered. 'Tom, it's for you again! A Señor Martinez.' Tom took the receiver from her. 'Tom Thorne here,' he acknowledged.

'*Bueno*. Mr Thorne, my name is Alejandro Martinez. I am one of the owners of the Costa Blanca International School. We are most interested in your application, particularly since you have a legal qualification which we feel might be useful to us at the present time. Let me explain. The school is in the region subject to Valencian law. You may have heard about the problems which owners of property here are having with the Valencian land law?' Tom replied, 'Yes, I've read something about it. How does it affect the school?'

Senor Martinez explained. 'Our school owns two villas used by staff as well as the teaching premises together with some land used for sport. Under current Valencian law, developers can put forward a development plan which includes the appropriation of other people's land or buildings against their wishes with very minimal compensation. Not only do the owners lose some or even all of their property but they also have to pay the developer large sums of money which are supposed to go towards the cost of the provision of services for the new development such as roads, water and sewage systems and so on. This law has been declared contrary to European Union rules and has also been declared illegal by the Spanish Government in Madrid but the Valencian authorities pay no attention. The school is fighting a proposed development plan which would take one of our properties and a large slice of our games fields which would be incorporated into their new development. We are also being asked to pay a substantial sum towards the provision of new services none of which we want. It is a very big problem for us.' Senor Martinez paused while Tom digested this information. 'Our present Headmaster, Jonathan Armitage,' continued Senor Martinez, 'is extremely busy running the academic side of an expanding school and does not have the time or training to deal with legal problems. We are therefore looking for someone with an educational and legal background to oversee our school operation and to ensure its future, which is likely to involve some legal battles. It could be very nasty.'

Tom interjected, 'I know nothing of Spanish law, although part of my training did include International Law – maybe that would help. Can you tell me something about the school?' A long conversation followed, with Anita listening intently to one end of it. It was clear that a battle was looming in Valencia. Señor Martinez arranged to send Tom further information about the Costa Blanca International School as soon as possible.

'What do you think of all that?' Tom had explained as much as he could to Anita and they sat looking at each other wondering if this would turn out to be an exciting opportunity or the road to trouble. Anita replied, 'Well, let's see what he sends us. I don't mind going abroad again and I'm not sure it would be a good thing to go back to Twickenham again. Let's go forward!'

A couple of days later a fat package arrived bearing a Spanish postmark. Tom and Anita carefully went through all the contents. The Costa Blanca International School had been set up just five years earlier and had expanded rapidly. There was quite a demand since younger families were now moving down to Spain for a better quality of life from Northern Europe. The school catered for both Spanish and foreign children. The majority of the teaching was done in English and the students followed the British curriculum. The school appeared to have a promising future so long as the threatened 'land law' problems could be averted.

Señor Martinez phoned again and a meeting was arranged in a London hotel – Señor Martinez made a point of inviting Anita to attend as well. The three of them spent four hours discussing the school, what role a Principal might take and the owners' vision for the future. Finally Senor Martinez brought the meeting to a close. He shook Tom by the hand. 'Mr Thorne,' he said, 'I believe you are the man for the job. Will you take it?' Tom agreed to contact him again as soon as he had spoken privately with Anita.

'Well,' said Anita, 'we've coped with Kenya, why not Spain as well? Do they have any snakes in Spain?'

Tom laughed. 'Not many poisonous ones, I'm told. But they do have wild boars!'

Tom made two phone calls. The first to Valerie Hudson thanking her but politely declining her offer of his old job back and the second to Señor Martinez accepting the post of Principal of The Costa Blanca International School.

Printed in the United Kingdom
by Lightning Source UK Ltd.
127422UK00001B/52-54/A